PRAISE FOR HELE

"Ms. Myers never fails to give the reader a good, solid, entertaining story with fresh characterizations and dialogue that sparkles."

—*Rendezvous*

"Helen R. Myers makes your heart ache with emotion...."

—*Romantic Times*

"Ms. Myers really knows how to touch readers...with her emotionally charged writing."

—*Rendezvous*

"Helen R. Myers...will please her many fans."

—*Romantic Times*

Dear Reader,

Spring is in the air! It's the perfect time to pick wildflowers, frolic outdoors…and fall in love. And this March, Special Edition has an array of love stories that set the stage for romance!

Bestselling author Victoria Pade delivers an extra-special THAT SPECIAL WOMAN! title. The latest installment in her popular A RANCHING FAMILY series, *Cowboy's Love* is about a heroine who passionately reunites with the rugged rancher she left behind. Don't miss this warm and wonderful tale about love lost—and found again.

Romantic adventure is back in full force this month when the MONTANA MAVERICKS: RETURN TO WHITEHORN series continues with *Wife Most Wanted* by Joan Elliott Pickart—a spirited saga about a wanted woman who unwittingly falls for the town's sexiest lawman! And don't miss *Marriage by Necessity*, the second book in Christine Rimmer's engaging CONVENIENTLY YOURS miniseries.

Helen R. Myers brings us *Beloved Mercenary*, a poignant story about a gruff, brooding hero who finds new purpose when a precious little girl—and her beautiful mother—transform his life. And a jaded businessman gets much more than he bargained for when he conveniently marries his devoted assistant in *Texan's Bride* by Gail Link. Finally this month, to set an example for his shy teenage son, a confirmed loner enters into a "safe" relationship with a pretty stranger in *The Rancher Meets His Match* by Patricia McLinn.

I hope you enjoy this book, and each and every story to come!

Sincerely,

Tara Gavin
Senior Editor and Editorial Coordinator

Please address questions and book requests to:
Silhouette Reader Service
U.S.: 3010 Walden Ave., P.O. Box 1325, Buffalo, NY 14269
Canadian: P.O. Box 609, Fort Erie, Ont. L2A 5X3

HELEN R. MYERS

BELOVED MERCENARY

SPECIAL EDITION®

Published by Silhouette Books

America's Publisher of Contemporary Romance

For the Ladies Meece
Betty and Cindy

Stellar John Berry fans, angel builders
and, of course, lovers of happy endings.

 SILHOUETTE BOOKS

ISBN 0-373-24162-3

BELOVED MERCENARY

Copyright © 1998 by Helen R. Myers

Printed in U.S.A.

Books by Helen R. Myers

HELEN R. MYERS,

a collector of two- and four-legged strays, lives deep in the Piney Woods of East Texas. She cites cello music and bonsai gardening as favorite relaxation pastimes, and still edits in her sleep—an accident learned while writing her first book. An author of diverse themes and focus, she is a three-time RITA Award nominee, winning for *Navarrone* in 1993.

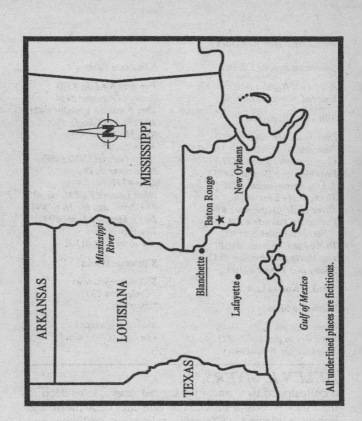

ARKANSAS

MISSISSIPPI

LOUISIANA

TEXAS

Mississippi River

Baton Rouge ★

Blanchette ●

Lafayette ●

New Orleans ●

Gulf of Mexico

All underlined places are fictitious.

N

Chapter One

For several minutes he'd been sitting in silence, studying the small wooden bridge arching over the beginnings of the stone stream he'd begun laying yesterday, inviting the garden's serenity to sweep away the morning's preoccupations. Then she emerged from the house behind his.

About to reach for another stone, he hesitated, finding that she affected his concentration the way the first butterflies of the season did. Bemused rather than annoyed, he withdrew his hand, and out of the corner of his eye watched her inch down the stairs and begin moseying around his neighbor's equally well tended, but aesthetically different yard. She must have spotted him early on, maybe while still inside; now she was cutting a cautious, serpentine path around the fig and peach trees, the vegetable garden and garage. The stockade fence meant to insure his privacy worked against him to hide her for a moment, and he almost missed hearing her footsteps on the concrete alleyway separating the two properties. But she was coming. He'd been hunted as often as he'd been the hunter; too often not to sense, even after being a civilian all this time, what was happening.

The instant he knew she was about to peer around the edge of the fence and through the square rungs of the iron gate, he felt the same quiet incredulity that still came when one of those fragile butterflies settled on his shoulder or hand; an inevitable dismay that innocence had once again ignored any survival instinct. Granted, he always recovered and enjoyed being singled out by visits from nature's creatures, but nothing much had changed regarding his aversion to any human invasion of his privacy. That was why he'd trained his neighbors quickly and well to avoid moments like this. Apparently, this intruder hadn't been warned.

It was her tow braid, tied with a Swiss blue ribbon, that first swung into view. Like a musician's metronome, it kept time with his steady heartbeat. Then a bit of head appeared. One third of her bangs yielded to gravity, separating from its regimental blond line, exposing a pale forehead. Finally an eye found him with the precision of a rifle scope. The iris matched the ribbon color to perfection—as it did her dress, except for the crisp white collar cut every bit as precisely as her bangs.

Trouble, he concluded, looking into that face as sweet and pure as the freshest of Louisiana mornings. He guessed her to be of preschool age, a kindergartner at the most—all the more reason to wonder what she was doing outside without adult supervision. This might seem to be a good neighborhood, serene with no history of criminal activity; however, he knew better than to trust appearances. Tragedy often occurred when one least expected it, even in idyllic places like Blanchette.

What gnawed at him the most, though, was that she'd come out of the Delmarco house. In the sixteen months he'd been working back here, he'd seen only one person over there, Dominic Delmarco, and the old guy lived alone. What's more, the kid's Anglo or even Scandinavian coloring and features bore no resemblance whatsoever to the burly Italian's.

And you're getting as imaginative as some of your nosiest neighbors.

He told himself that if he ignored her, she would go away. The approach had always worked before. She wasn't any of his business. Whether or not her parents were careless was their problem. In this day and age adults had to be careful, too; all you had to do was smile at a kid and you were looked upon as some pervert.

Resolved, he refocused on the stream bed. He'd been trying to visualize the path of one he'd seen years ago. It was his intention to create a smaller replica of it, with the water-washed stones piled in neat mounds on either side of the shallow ditch he'd hoed out over the past few weeks. The rocks were flat and bluish gray to denote deeper water; he chose two from the nearest pile. They were smooth and cool as he rubbed them between his fingers, willing the image to return. When it did, he set the rocks side by side overlapping the last row he'd set down yesterday, following the technique he'd noticed at a Shinto temple in Kyoto. Then he reached for two more, and another two after that. Only after he'd completed a full row did he sit back on his heels again to consider his progress thus far.

She was still there, peering at him in somber silence. Her reticence wasn't unusual. Children rarely spoke to him. What he found perplexing was that she hadn't run away as most did, reacting as though fleeing some malevolent shadow who might steal the very breath from their lungs. Not because of some hideous scar or other injury—in that respect, he was lucky; the worst of his scars were internal. But occasionally children picked up on what adults often missed. In his case it was that despite years of introspection and study, his soul remained dark, like a stain of blood on immaculate linen.

It was just his luck that this angel's antennae were all tangled in that blond braid.

Frowning, he reached for another pair of stones. Miniature

works of art they were; having existed far longer than him, they would last centuries after his ashes were offered to the wind and the sea as stipulated in his will. Such understated bits of matter, and yet they held within their strong little bodies a steadfast nobility and truth he couldn't begin to emulate. Being in their presence was inspiring as well as humbling, and he placed the oblong rocks with the others, feeling a renewed respect in the resilience of the universe.

At the same moment his visitor abandoned the protection of the fence altogether and stepped before the gate. Still silent, she gripped the rungs with both hands and pressed her cherub's face between them.

What a persistent bit of sunshine.

Without looking directly at her, he asked, "Do you think this looks like flowing water yet?"

After lengthy, somber consideration, she nodded.

"Have you ever seen anything like it before?"

She studied the layered stones, then the miniature mountains on either side, and finally him, before rocking her forehead against the iron bars.

He liked her for not being a prattler. And what serious eyes. No matter what her age, he had a hunch that he was looking at an old soul—a more common sight in locations where war had scarred both land and life.

"This is a stream of devotion. The rest—" he gestured at the surrounding garden "—represents meditation and magic. The problem is, my memory has failed me, and my intuition was never fine-tuned to Japanese gardens. I have no idea where the stream should be heading. Do you know?"

She met his steady look without temerity, which earned growing respect from him. After a slight hesitation, she viewed his progress thus far, and how his scraping of the earth had ended only yards from the lily pond almost invisible to her left. Slowly she pointed.

He had thought otherwise: to the gate, which faced due east.

Intrigued, he used the back of his hand to rub at his

bearded chin and considered the way the afternoon light embraced her. May was gentle in Blanchette, especially when one sat under a canopy of pine trees and dogwood. Sunlight filtered through the limbs of those at the southmost corner of his yard and touched her hair, illuminating silver, bronze and gold all at the same time.

"Maybe so," he murmured. "Maybe so." About to ask her where she'd strayed from, he heard quick footsteps on the concrete.

"Angel."

Focused on the child, he hadn't realized anyone else was around—a serious slip for him. But when a woman appeared at the gate, he forgave himself the lapse. Even if alert, she would have thrown him off balance.

"You shouldn't have wandered off," the woman said to the little girl.

Her soft voice held only concern and relief. For reasons he didn't want to analyze, that pulled a reassuring response from him; never mind that another more sarcastic inner voice reminded him that he owed none.

"She wasn't any trouble…or in any danger."

The woman met his gaze through the gate that was inches taller than her, and he tightened stomach muscles to deal with another irrefutable something. He told himself it was the relationship between woman and child; their hair was the same combination of precious metal colors, their skin identically flawless, and those grab-your-gut eyes… Lord in heaven. Add the air of vulnerability that hovered around them, and he half expected to hear harp music.

The relationship between woman and child was settled when she stooped to embrace the little girl. That tender enfolding told him more than any birth certificate could have.

"Thank you," she replied after a moment. "But we're new here." As she spoke, she stroked the girl's back soothingly. "If she'd wandered too far, she would have grown confused and panicked."

"I didn't realize there were any houses for sale in the area." He didn't like the idea that he'd missed noticing that.

"There aren't any that I know of, and who can blame people? It's really a lovely neighborhood. We've moved in with my father-in-law. Or rather, we're in the process of moving in. The majority of our things won't arrive until next week. I'm Brynn Delmarco. This is my daughter, Angela Lynn."

She looked barely capable of taking care of herself, let alone a child, and not simply because she seemed physically young. The body inside that slim black sheath confirmed she was all woman; it was her emotional condition he questioned. It was the black—black was too harsh, too draining for someone with her fine coloring. That left him putting two and two together and concluding that her choice of outfits was about more than fashion.

"I didn't realize Dominic had any family."

Before the woman could reply, the child wrenched free and ran off toward the house as though he'd pulled a gun on her.

"Angie!"

Between the anguish in the young woman's voice and the terror he'd seen in the girl's face, he knew he'd blundered, and badly. "I'm sorry. Obviously I said something I shouldn't have."

Although her expression reflected a prolonged anguish, the woman shook her head. "You couldn't have known. Her father...Dominic's son didn't have much opportunity to come down here after we were married. We lived in Chicago until... Tony was killed almost a year ago. He was a police officer."

Somewhere deep inside him a door slammed. He didn't want to hear another word. He had definite rules about lending his shoulder, especially to blondes who looked as though they'd stepped out from between the covers of a book of fairy tales; regardless of whether or not he felt compassion for whatever dirty trick life had played on her and her kid.

What she needed to understand was that any contact with him could only make matters worse.

His silence made her self-conscious and uncomfortable. He saw that as she glanced toward the Delmarco house in time to see the little girl disappear inside, and took a step away from the gate.

"I'm sorry for the interruption," she said. "But please don't worry that she'll be a nuisance in the future. She's an extremely well-behaved child."

Her manners were impeccable, but it was her inner pain that dragged the truth from him. "I meant what I said. She was no trouble. In fact, she never said a word."

The woman wrapped her arms around her waist. "No, she wouldn't. She hasn't said a word since witnessing her father's murder."

Brynn Hart Delmarco reentered her father-in-law's house only moments after her daughter did, but by the time she closed and locked the screened storm door behind herself, she saw through to the living room that her daughter was already on her grandfather's lap. She heard those terrible muted sobs—the only kind of sounds her baby made these days—and saw how Angie's small body was shaking from the force of them. A rattled but protective Dominic tried to console her.

"No, no, *piccolina*, why you cry? Did you fall? Brynn," he said upon spotting her. "*Per favore*, you help. I don't see anywhere that she could be hurt. What's happened?"

Brynn entered the pleasantly shadowed room and sat down before him on the burgundy brocade hassock, to reach over and stroke her daughter's thigh. "When she slipped outside, she noticed your neighbor. The one with the incredible garden."

"Kane!" A rush of Italian followed. "What did he do? If he said anything nasty to her, I'll—"

Such scorn vibrating in thundering baritone startled Angela, and she recoiled from him, throwing herself into

Brynn's arms. Brynn had her work cut out for her not to roll off the cushioned seat.

"Dominic, calm down! Nothing happened." She rocked Angie with the same urgency that she whispered at him. "There, there, angel, it's all right." To her father-in-law she added, "The poor man couldn't know he said something that reminded her of Tony. In any case, she'll have to get used to people mentioning him and asking questions." She kissed the top of her daughter's head. "He didn't know, love. And he was very sorry for upsetting you. Didn't he seem like a nice man otherwise?"

His black eyes wide with disbelief, Dominic sat back in the plush cushions of his easy chair and snorted. "Gideon Kane? Sorry for anything? *Lei si sbaglia!* You understand this? It means you couldn't be more wrong. I can think of plenty ways to describe that one, but 'nice' isn't one of them."

Brynn couldn't have been more surprised—or dismayed. Dominic was nothing if not passionate, but this amount of fervor was unusual, and unfortunate news under the circumstances. "You two don't get along?"

"There's getting along, and then there's getting along." Dominic portioned out blocks of space with his hands, then pointed with his thumb toward the kitchen and beyond. "But he's not a neighbor the way I, Dominic Antonio Delmarco, understand neighbors should be. Here, people wave to each other, they stop to share a few words. Something like the old country. Not like one big family, we don't overdo, *capiche?* But nice. Except for Mr. Big Shot over there. He goes out of his way to avoid us. Well, all of us but Lillian. Dean Littlejohn to him, because she's his boss! Touched in the head he is not."

As she watched his lively pantomime, Brynn thought of the middle-aged woman who lived to the right of her father-in-law. Lillian Littlejohn had arrived home only moments before they'd driven in from the Baton Rouge airport, and Dominic had insisted on introducing her and Angie right then and there, even though her little one had let it be known that a bathroom visit was required. Now Brynn was glad for the meeting, brief though it had been.

"Boss? Does he landscape her yard, too? From what I could see his is quite something."

Dominic's basset-hound face grew even longer. "You like all that primping and plucking? Me, I would be afraid to breathe in case I blow down one of those strange little trees he has all over the place."

"I think they're called bonsai, Pop," Brynn said, careful not to smile.

"I heard about them, and all I can say is that he should have taken all the money he spent on those twigs and bought one good-size tree. And you ask if he's a gardener—ha! He teaches at the college. We didn't pass it coming in because it's on the other side of town. You'll see tomorrow when I drive you around to show you what's what."

"I'd forgotten you have a college here. And so progressive with a woman at the helm." She wanted to tease him a bit to lighten his mood, even though she was curious and wanted to ask more questions, too. For instance, what did Gideon Kane teach? He hadn't looked like a gardener to her, either—but then, he also didn't seem the teacher type.

"Lillian is no ordinary woman. She could run this country, but always like a lady." Dominic's expression grew resentful. "And there are some who say Gideon Kane knows the lady well."

Brynn glanced down to see that Angie was almost asleep. Good, she thought, not wanting the child to hear too much of this. It was bad enough that she was indulging in idle gossip; however, after all but cloistering herself for months—except for visits to countless doctors on Angie's behalf—it was something of a relief to talk nonsense.

"Really, Dominic, she has to be closer to your age than his."

The corners of his wide mouth turned downward. "So?

She wouldn't be the first woman to try chasing a younger man. Apparently her first two husbands couldn't please her.''

"She's divorced?"

"And I'm not saying that Kane is that much younger than her.''

Brynn wasn't good at guessing ages, and what with the gate and her numbed nerves, she supposed her instincts were more off than usual, but surely Gideon Kane couldn't be more than forty-five or forty-seven. What's more, the head of Blanchette College didn't strike her as the kind of woman to "chase" anyone, especially not a man who seemed so…quiet and reserved. Was he even the kind to let himself be hounded, let alone caught?

No, this whole conversation sounded like jealousy. How intriguing.

"Maybe I should ask how you feel about Lillian Little-john, *Signor* Delmarco?''

His sparkling eyes, so full of life, as Tony's had been, avoided hers. "What are you talking?"

"You like her.''

"Of course I like her. She's my neighbor. I like all of my neighbors. I told you, this is a wonderful place.''

"I remember what you said. But I also have eyes and ears.''

For a moment he looked as if he might confide something, then he waved away the comment and pushed himself to his feet. "You're teasing me. Okay, now I tease you. This way.'' He kissed the tips of his fingers in that age-old signal of culinary ecstasy. "I'm making dinner. The best. I started the sauce yesterday.''

Brynn smiled. "That explains why the house smells like a *ristorante*.''

He cupped her chin, his callused, sun-bronzed hand con-firming his years in the merchant marines as well as his own enthusiasm for gardening. "My Tony taught you well. How long has it been since you and the *bambina* tasted homemade tortellini?''

"Not since you came up for our wedding and invaded my kitchen. But surely you're not going to go through all that trouble after driving almost an hour each way to pick us up at the airport?" What's more, a quick tour of the house had already convinced her that he must have spent every spare hour of the past month redecorating for them. He had to be exhausted. "Sandwiches or a salad would be fine, and I'd be glad to help."

Dominic lifted his palms and gazed upward. "She wants me to serve chicken food. Neither one of you looks as if you eat more than a bowl of soup a day, and I'm not talking minestrone," he added with mock scorn. "But I'm gonna fix that."

"I can see arguing with you in person is going to be as hopeless as on the phone." Brynn rose, shifting her daughter into the cradle of her arms. "But be warned, I intend to do my share—now and from here on out. First let me put this one upstairs for a bit. She was so excited about flying down here, she barely slept last night. Can you tell?"

Dominic leaned close, his animated face drawing into a playful pout for the stretching little girl. "Angel face! You didn't even nap a few minutes on that long trip?"

"Afraid not." Brynn kissed her daughter's hair as the child hid from her grandfather. "She was also too busy looking out at the clouds to see if she could spot her daddy." She exchanged a meaningful look with Tony's father. "A half-hour nap will put some color back in her cheeks."

"*Bene, bene.* And I'll go pour us a glass of Chianti. You need some color, too."

Brynn shook her head as she headed for the stairs, but she was grateful for his intent: to keep her mind preoccupied and off her heartache and worries. He knew she'd debated for a good while over accepting his invitation to move down here. True, she'd liked him the moment they'd met, but she really didn't know him beyond what stories Tony had shared, and those few visits Dominic had made up to Chicago. Was that enough for them to live compatibly under the same roof?

The house certainly was big enough, she mused, pausing at the top of the stairs to catch her breath. Angie hardly weighed more than an armful of Dominic's crusty homemade bread, but it was quite a climb to the four bedrooms on the second floor. When she'd first seen the place, she'd realized her husband had been right: Dominic had always intended that his family would eventually join him down here. Why else would anyone buy a house this size, not to mention establish such a big vegetable garden out back, just for himself? The dear man probably kept the entire neighborhood in fresh produce, and his favorite hobby must be trying out cleaning solvents.

Butter yellow hallway walls brightened her path to the far room on the right, which Dominic had prepared for Angie. He'd painted the corner bedroom a powder pink, and she couldn't help but smile as she again considered the rest. A white bedspread with frilly raspberry trim complemented a canopy bed, and feminine white-and-gold furniture helped finish what was a little girl's paradise. Even the lamp was a fantasy—an antebellum doll dressed in an umbrella skirt and carrying a matching lacy parasol that did double duty as the lampshade.

"Did Grampa read your mind about decorating this room, or what?" she whispered, laying the child on the bed. "I'll bet sleeping on this bed will feel like you're on top of the world's biggest ice cream sundae. Let's cover those bare legs with this fluffy throw, and you close your eyes again and listen to the birds singing outside your window, okay?"

Naturally, Angie didn't respond, but then that's not why Brynn kept to a normal routine even when it came to idle conversation. It was her hope, and the experts' one opinion that she believed, that as long as she persisted, Angie would continue to absorb and learn, regardless of her traumatized state. And one day, God willing, when she spoke again, it would be without being too disadvantaged compared to other children her age.

Brynn planned every hour of every day around that goal.

Planning and praying, that was her life. It was how she held on to her sanity.

The breeze ruffled the fine draperies that matched the bedspread, and sunlight beamed through the fine netting, casting a pattern of roses onto the confection-colored walls. It was the kind of room she'd intended to create for her child once Tony had earned his master's degree and they'd moved out of their apartment and into a house in the suburbs. They could have done it sooner. She'd inherited everything after her parents' death, so finances weren't the problem. But she'd seen how tired he was juggling his on-duty schedule and school; she hadn't had the heart to add a lengthier commute to complicate things.

She should have, though. Then he would be alive today.

She blinked back the inevitable tears that still came too easily, and glanced over at Angie, concerned that her child not see her upset. Fortunately, Angie was already drifting off again, a white teddy bear—another gift from Dominic—clutched close. It saddened her to note that this was the only time her daughter looked truly at peace.

"Things will get better," she whispered, as much for her child's reassurance as her own. "And one day you'll tell Grampa yourself what a lovely room he's made for you."

She tiptoed out to the hall, learning for future reference which floorboards creaked. Dominic had put his granddaughter in the room across from his, while putting her next door to Angie. Clearly, he meant what he'd said about intending to do his share of bedtime-story reading and sitting up when the little one came down with a bug or had a nightmare. It was a sweet gesture, and she did appreciate that Angie would have one of the best views of her grandfather's wonderful yard.

Feeling a bit too sentimental, she decided to detour to her own room and check her makeup. Dominic didn't need to see that she'd gotten all weepy again after he'd tried so hard to make things festive for them. A wry smile tugged at her lips as she entered the room and was reminded that his intention to spoil hadn't stopped with Angie.

Her room showed a great deal of thought and affection, as well. The textured walls were an eggshell white, and the carpet and bedspread were a rich blue close to the color of her eyes and Angie's. She loved the mix-and-match effect of the antique furniture, especially the high bed. When she'd first seen it, she had remarked that he would have her feeling like the heroine in "The Princess and the Pea."

Just above the dresser was a gold-and-white crucifix. Below it was a photograph of Dominic and his late wife, Angelina, along with a copy of a favorite picture of Brynn and Tony holding a days-old Angie.

She reached for a tissue from the box next to the double brass frame, thinking how lucky she was to have this thoughtful big bear of a man in her life. As considerate as he was emotionally, and physically strong, he represented the rock of stability she needed, having come to the bottom of the barrel of her own strength. Now, if only Angie continued to show signs of accepting him....

Ever since Tony's murder Angie had withdrawn from people, including friends—everyone who'd been in their life. As for strangers, they made her recoil in sheer terror. Things had gotten so bad, it was a trial just to get to Sunday mass. That's why when Angela had left the room minutes ago while she and Dominic were talking, she'd assumed her daughter had simply gone to find a secluded corner where she could sit and rest.

How odd that she had been drawn to Gideon Kane.

Brynn went to the window and parted the sheer draperies an inch or two. From this vantage point she could see the man continuing his work. It wasn't as hot as Dominic had warned it would soon get, but she'd felt her dress begin sticking to her during those few minutes outside. How did he stay so calm and cool? Well, his T-shirt was cotton, which breathed, of course, but in humidity like this those jeans had to feel like a girdle on a woman.

Maybe it was the bare feet, a detail she hadn't noticed before. What kind of man gardened in bare feet?

A true man of the earth.

There really was something…unique about him. Dramatic, but not theatrical like Dominic, who was all emotion and action. "Over the top like an opera," Tony used to say. Gideon Kane was like Lake Michigan on a winter's day—dark, uncertain, yet very present.

Not at all the kind of person who should have attracted her psychologically wounded daughter, and Dominic's opinion of him didn't help. Brynn nibbled at her lower lip.

As though he felt her studious gaze, he turned and looked up at the house, directly into her window. Brynn stepped back, embarrassed at being caught spying like the cranky old lady back in Chicago who would crack her door every time she or Tony stepped out of their apartment, but had never said one word in reply to their cheerful greetings.

No more of that, she told herself. Pressing her hand against her pounding heart, she headed back downstairs.

Whatever had drawn her daughter to Gideon Kane's gate, she would just try to be grateful that for once her baby had chosen the sunshine instead of shadows.

Gideon didn't move when the woman across the alley retreated from the upstairs window. Still feeling her, he waited until he sensed her complete withdrawal. Only then did he exhale and lower himself to the warm ground.

Almost every bone in his spine ached; so did most of the muscles across his shoulders. And one glance at the irregular pattern of the last several rows of stones he'd set told him that his concentration had been off for longer than he'd wanted to admit.

He didn't let the choice curse he was thinking pass his lips, but that he'd thought it at all told him something, too. Disgusted with himself, he took out all of the badly placed stones. It didn't slip by him that, once again, destruction went far faster than construction.

The day's not wasted, Tanka-san. A lesson is learned.

Breathing deeply, rhythmically, he concentrated on purging the tension inside his body, then concentrated on relaxing his outer core. He also allowed himself to dwell on what had triggered all this.

So Dominic Delmarco had a widowed daughter-in-law moving in. A beautiful widow…with a child as angelic as her name.

The only news that could be worse is if a sinkhole suddenly appeared in the middle of this garden.

He grimaced, having almost sworn again. The fact was, he sometimes missed doing it as badly as a three-pack-a-day smoker trying to survive on medicated chewing gum. Tension remained in him, subtler than it had been, but there…when it should be gone. He was skilled at meditation, and before he'd learned that, he'd been skilled at thinking absolutely nothing.

The woman and child had set something in motion. He could no more deny it than he could pretend he'd never crawled on his belly through jungles like the most cunning of predators, or turned burning deserts into even hotter pits of hell, thanks to his deadly skills.

Bad luck to lose a husband and father so young. The child had seen hell, too; the old ones would say she was half ghost. He'd met her kind before, and those like the woman. Her grief and loss remained an open wound he could feel too acutely. That was the problem. She reminded him of another woman from long ago, of all he'd been, as well as what he would never be; of everything he had struggled to put behind him. She and the child had known love and devotion, had been happy, and had lost that happiness because of some monster.

She hasn't said a word since witnessing her father's murder. Her words echoed in his mind.

Now they were here, "being time," to quote one of those sage Eastern lessons. He had no right to resent their presence, but everything human inside him wanted to.

Because of them, his deepest scars were tearing open. It was as if he was being mocked. He half expected to hear a snickering voice declare, "Sorry, pal, you just think you've been through it."

What if everything before had been rehearsal, and only now was he to begin paying?

The possible answer made him glad he didn't have a gun in the house.

Chapter Two

It took Brynn several days to accustom herself to her new surroundings. That left her little time to get to know the neighbors beyond the polite waves they exchanged when Angie was willing to venture outside for a bit of fresh air. It appeared that while her daughter had been all for the flight down from Chicago, she soon sank back into her withdrawn behavior and didn't like leaving the big house, even for the opportunity to explore their new community beyond what Dominic had shown them on Sunday after he'd attended church services. Brynn told herself not to expect too much too soon, something she repeated regularly to Dominic. And to be truthful, there were changes…she simply didn't think it helpful to share the most inexplicable with her father-in-law.

Dominic made a big production every morning when the three of them had breakfast together. It was a noisy, musical half hour, all designed around coercing Angie to eat, although their success tended to be mild in comparison to the energy expended. Afterward, he took off for Fresh and Fancy, the upscale supermarket where he worked part-time as a bagger. In the midafternoon when he was replaced by teens from the local high school or a college student, he would return home to give Angie piggyback rides through the house, or watch her favorite TV program with her. When Brynn convinced him it was her turn to prepare dinner, he would set Angie on his lap at the kitchen table and tell them both one of the innumerable stories from his seafaring days.

On one occasion Brynn drove him to work so she could use the car to explore the area on her own, thinking Angie would like that better, but she didn't. Thereafter, she accepted that Angie preferred to color drawings that she designed for her, or watch her hand-stitch outfits for the new teddy bear. Dominic always oohed and aahed over whatever Angie was willing to show him, and his enthusiastic responses seemed to win him points with her.

But nothing captivated her daughter like Gideon Kane and his garden.

Whenever they were outside, the child made a beeline for his gate. If he wasn't home, or not outside—it took her several days to determine his schedule—Angie stubbornly tried to stay and wait, and pouted when led back to the house. If Brynn set her down for a nap, she knew she would come back an hour later and find the child already sitting in her window seat waiting patiently for a glimpse of him. Doing that was also the last thing she did at night, and Brynn became a worried wreck for fear Dominic would catch on and be upset.

Just when she wondered how else she could preoccupy her daughter, the moving van arrived with the rest of their belongings. It was the second Tuesday since they'd arrived, and, following Dominic's advice, she had the workmen stack the few dozen boxes in the freestanding double garage out back. He'd also told her to leave the unpacking and sorting until the weekend, when he was free to help. "I hardly ever park the old car in there, anyway, so no problem," he said.

But even though some of the boxes were heavy, Brynn decided to start on her own. If Angie had more of her playthings, she reasoned, she might be less inclined to fixate on their neighbor. There was the weather to consider, too. Storms were forecast for Wednesday and Thursday. Just the other day, Marjorie Olsen, who along with her husband, Arne, lived on the south side of them, had shared her dread of the hail that often came with spring storms in the South. Brynn didn't want to risk Dominic's car getting damaged because of her.

On Wednesday morning, right after washing up the breakfast things, she changed from her cotton shift into jeans and one of Tony's denim shirts, and brushed her hair into a ponytail like her daughter's. A pleased Angie then signaled that she wanted to be the one to get the garage key from the rack by the wall phone, and Brynn lifted her, glad to see her apparent enthusiasm.

As the two of them headed for the garage, birds were already serenading the neighborhood and flittering from one place to another making their first rounds in search of seeds and insects. Dominic kept a feeder full of mixed seeds near the back steps, and after opening the old-fashioned swing doors on the garage, she brought out a chair and small table for Angie so she could watch.

"Now," Brynn said, setting out paper and crayons that they'd carried out in a tote, "you draw what you see, and we'll show Grampa when he gets home, okay?"

Angie nodded and bent studiously over her notebook.

Hopeful, Brynn turned to face the mountain of cardboard before her. Not for an instant did she expect this to be an easy job—not physically or emotionally. There were so many things in these boxes that would prompt poignant reminders of her life with Tony, and that was the third reason she wanted to tackle this on her own. Dominic didn't need to see her losing it any more than he already had.

At least there was less to deal with than when she'd first agreed to move. She'd either given away or sold all of their furnishings and appliances, as well as both cars. As for the smaller things, Tony's partner and his wife had been sweethearts, generously holding a yard sale for her at their place, which relieved her of the majority of things she neither needed nor wanted.

"Somehow that still leaves us with an awful lot," she murmured, her hands on her hips. So much for thinking she'd been practical.

She set to work, determined to make up for that by being efficient. What she failed to keep in mind was Blanchette's humidity, and her daughter's growing talent for vanishing in the blink of an eye. Before an hour had passed, she accepted that she had her work cut out for her—and then some.

Instead of drawing, Angie wandered—but thank goodness always in one direction. The third time she had to go after her, the child had made it all the way to Gideon Kane's gate. To add embarrassment to frustration, the man was home.

Breathless from all the exertion, she could only shake her head in apology. He said nothing, and she quickly carried her daughter back to the garage.

She managed to convince Angie to stay put until they broke for an early lunch. Afterward, Brynn tried to get Angie to settle down for a nap, but the minx was suddenly obstinate and insisted on following her outside again.

Round two picked up where round one had left off. No sooner did Brynn open a box than she heard her little darling scrambling. Fortunately, she caught her by the fig tree.

"What am I going to do with you?" she asked, torn between laughing in exasperation and groaning. "You know what the neighbors are going to think if I tie you to a chair?" With a teasing smile, she nodded to a large hook on the garage wall. "What if I hang you up there by your suspenders, missy, hmm?"

Of course, her daughter knew exactly what a soft touch she was and wasn't fooled for an instant. She must, however, have sensed Brynn's growing fatigue, because she did settle down on the lawn chair Brynn set out in the shade; and, finally, when Brynn next glanced over, she saw that Angie had fallen asleep.

Relieved, she went back to work. She placed the things she could use right away, in a box by the door, and the rest she repacked for later stacking against the south wall.

She'd sorted through three boxes when she saw that the one for the house was full. That was just as well, because she was thirsty, too. She figured they could both use something to drink and—

When she emerged from the garage, Brynn realized it had done more than grow a little cloudy. Lightning flashed not far beyond Gideon Kane's house. It was soon followed by an ominous roll of thunder.

Already awake, Angie bolted off the chair and ran over to bury her face against Brynn's leg.

"There, there, angel. Let's get this box inside. Then Mommy will come back and secure these doors, okay? Grab your notebook and shove those crayons into the tote. Angie? Angie!"

Something else had caught her daughter's attention and she took off again. All but dropping the box, and barely avoiding being smacked in the elbow by the swinging door, Brynn raced after her.

To her dismay she saw her neighbor's gray sedan pull in to his driveway. The neighborhood had been designed by two separate sets of builders, and while Dominic's older house, like the rest on their street, had a driveway in the front, Gideon Kane and his neighbors approached their homes from the rear. That she'd missed his leaving confounded her; that he was returning just as all heck was about to break loose had her doubly regretting her preoccupation.

"Don't you have any sense?"

He burst from his car, his tone and expression as fierce as the wind whipping at them. His uniform of T-shirt and well-worn jeans had been exchanged for newer jeans and a dress shirt without a tie. The gray sports jacket gripped in one hand was obviously the maximum he would allow for conformity.

She was beginning to notice he cared for ties about as much as he did formal suits or dress pants.

Before she could do more than snatch Angie around the waist, a particularly strong gust blasted past them. It caught one of the garage doors, slamming it shut with a thud almost as bad as the thunder. Then came a telling crash.

"Oh, my— The boxes!"

She began running. Before she was halfway across the lawn the skies opened to a deluge that pelted at them with a ferocity that had her stumbling.

Strong arms came around to steady her. Even as she tried to sputter her thanks, Gideon Kane all but carried her and Angie the rest of the way into the garage.

"Get away from these doors!" He all but pushed her inside, then spun around to drag the huge doors shut.

The confinement left the interior pitch-dark, and had Angie moaning in protest and burying her face against Brynn's shoulder.

"It's okay, sweetheart. It's just a rain shower. Mommy remembers a flashlight Grampa keeps at the shelf by the light switch. Mr. Kane?"

"What's wrong with flipping on the switch?" he asked, and did exactly that.

Nothing happened, which came as no surprise to her. "The bulb burned out and Dominic hasn't replaced it yet. Can you find the flashlight? It's at shoulder level to your right. Well, maybe my shoulder level." Seconds later a beam of light blinded her. "That's the one."

He redirected it to the ceiling, then inspected the structure in general. "Perfect. This whole area is under a tornado watch and we're in something the Hollywood boys build for easy demolition."

She felt a loyalist's need to defend Dominic's property. "It looks no less sturdy than the house."

He uttered a guttural sound. "Mrs. Delmarco, if a tornado decides to cut a path through our neighborhood today, not only will it wipe out my place, you'll be lucky to find anything recognizable in that mass of tongue depressors you call a house."

"Mr. Kane!" Brynn covered Angie's exposed ear with her hand. She wished she could have covered her own, although that wouldn't stop the images. If his house was brick and he had no confidence in its ability to survive such a forceful assault, what chance did the rest of them have?

"You're the one who decided to move down here. If you're planning on staying, you'd better get used to dealing with the weather as a force to be reckoned with."

Brynn watched him recheck the latch on the doors, and reluctantly admitted he was right. What's more, she couldn't keep expecting life to tiptoe around her just because she had a child with special needs.

Pressing a kiss on Angie's cheek, she turned to look for something with which to dry the girl—and promptly stumbled over something. Once again she was saved by their neighbor's quick reflexes.

"Easy." Strong but careful hands held her at the waist. "It's never a good idea to move around until you can see where you're going."

She'd already determined he had an orator's voice, low and rich. Coercive. But as his warm breath tickled her ear, it took on a new power, the ability to soothe as well as compel.

"You're right. Again. Would you aim that beam at my feet and let me see the damage? I'm afraid I've located the result of that crash we heard earlier."

He did, and what she saw had her fighting back a cry of despair. In her haste to go after Angie, she'd apparently been careless where she'd moved the last box she'd been opening. Subsequently, the wind had knocked it off its precarious perch, sending the contents to the unforgiving concrete floor.

She dropped to her knees. "Not those."

The crystal music box had been a gift from Tony—one of several he'd given her during their time together. Now the hand-blown glass hummingbirds that had graced the top lay shattered like frozen tears. Angie must have caught a peek, too, because she made a mewlike sound of a hurt kitten and came reaching for one of the birds.

"No, angel." Gideon Kane stayed her hand, then lifted it to his lips and kissed it. "Sharp glass will hurt pretty fingers."

Brynn couldn't believe it when her child not only didn't jerk away in horror, but actually reached up and patted Gideon Kane's cheek. The look of shock on his face told her that he hadn't expected that response, either.

"Mr. Kane," she murmured, "I think you're more surprised than I am."

"Only disappointed. I thought after what she'd been through that she had better survival instincts."

What a self-deprecating thing to say! "Somehow I think they're just fine," she replied gently.

He didn't respond, simply stared at her, long and hard. From what she could tell, his eyes were a dark gray, as full of mystery as that lake he'd made her think of when they first met. Everything about him—his rough features, the grim compression of his lips framed by that precisely trimmed beard and mustache that might otherwise be called exotic—suddenly transmitted an image of warning, even danger. A complete contradiction to his protective behavior.

Brynn was beginning to understand how Dominic could have come to his negative opinion of the man, and for the first time wished she'd encouraged him to expand on his reasons for disliking his neighbor.

"You see?"

"What?"

"How quickly doubt can set in." He shifted his focus back to the mess on the floor. "Assume nothing, Mrs. Delmarco."

No, she wouldn't. But neither would she forget his kindness. "The name's Brynn."

He righted the tipped box. "That sounds Welsh. Are you?"

"The family tree lists ancestors just about everywhere in

the British Isles except for Wales. My mother simply picked up the name from a character she'd liked in a book.'' She eyed him with new curiosity. ''How did you know its etymology?''

''To people without family and who aren't stampeding their way up a corporate ladder, twenty-four hours can be a long time. I spend my free hours filling my head with useless information.''

She found his indifferent air disingenuous. ''What do you teach at the college?'' When he shot her another of those laser-sharp looks, she felt as she hadn't since she was fifteen and had missed a curfew by twenty minutes. ''My father-in-law said you and Mrs. Littlejohn were both affiliated with the local school.''

''Your father-in-law is a clever man.''

''He doesn't like you very much.''

''I rest my case.'' He picked up what was left of one of the hummingbirds. ''This isn't salvageable.''

Brynn shifted her daughter so that she wouldn't have to see it. ''I shouldn't have put the box where I did, but my only thought was to get Angie.'' She bit at her lower lip. ''Why do you do that, shut down people without giving them a chance?''

He didn't reply. She would have let the matter drop, but the storm wasn't easing whatsoever, and she was beginning to believe what he'd said about the vulnerability of this building. If she hoped to hide her anxiety from Angie, she needed some other focus, even if it was one that annoyed him.

''I understand wanting to be left alone,'' she said gently. ''I've felt that way myself.''

He ignored that, too. Then, abruptly tossing the second broken figurine in with the rest, he asked, ''Why does she keep doing that? Coming over? Watching me?''

Brynn rubbed her cheek against her child's silky hair. ''Ask her. If she answers, we'll both know.''

''Well, it's not a good idea.''

"She seems to be getting something out of it."

He scowled into the box. "There may be a number of things broken in here."

"I'm afraid you're right, and that's oddly...fitting. The music boxes are all gifts from my husband. Were. Are."

Feeling a lump growing in her throat, Brynn cleared it and rocked Angie, hoping the child didn't begin reacting to her own fracturing emotions. "Dominic was right. I should have waited for him to get home before tackling this."

"Why didn't you?"

"I thought the reminders of—" The tightening of Angie's arms around her neck had her checking her words. "You don't teach on Wednesdays?"

"No." He rose. "The storm's going to sit over us for a while. I'll look for another flashlight and do something with all this to make sure you don't make things worse."

The crack of thunder right over her head was as bad as his biting words. Brynn winced and hugged Angie as fast as her daughter clutched her. At least they didn't have windows, although some of the blue-white flashes of lightning could be seen between cracks in the walls and the roof. Still, the place was secure enough...too secure to be locked in here with a stranger who worried her as much as he mesmerized her daughter?

Feeling a bit weak in the stomach, she sat on an old work stool and settled Angie on her lap. Gideon Kane continued to step over toppled boxes and around stacked ones. He was taller than she'd originally guessed and he moved with a male grace she found as impressive as the thorough track of the flashlight's beam throughout the garage. When man and light vanished for several seconds, leaving her and her child hostage to the roar of rain and the ground-shaking thunder, she sat like her daughter, rigid and eager for his return. Once he did, he brought with him a kerosene lantern and a metal fuel can.

Mercy, she mused. Part hero and part magician on top of everything else.

"You might remind your father-in-law that forgetting about stuff like this makes him as much a menace as an arsonist."

She accepted the censure in silence. No need to tell him that she was debating not letting Dominic know anything about this meeting at all.

Angie squirmed on her lap, and Brynn realized she was following his every move. Once he filled the lantern and managed to get it lit, she wriggled off Brynn's lap to inch closer.

Realizing the child's intent, Brynn tugged her back, pretending to need to adjust the suspenders on her pink overalls. "I, um, didn't realize you smoked," she said to their Good Samaritan.

"I don't."

"But you carry a throw-away lighter?"

He pocketed it in the shirt that was otherwise plastered to his torso, thanks to the rain. "I used to smoke. Haven't lost the habit of fidgeting with the lighter when I feel the craving to light up."

"How long has it been since you stopped?"

"Seven years, seven months and eleven days."

Brynn wasn't prepared for how the stern lines of his face changed when he indulged in a bit of self-deprecating humor. His usually tight lips softened and took on a sensual—

Dear heaven, what was she doing?

"Princesses and angels shouldn't crouch in dust. They should sit on thrones."

Brynn snapped to attention in time to see Gideon Kane lifting her daughter and settling her on a solid tier of boxes. That Angie had extended her arms to him amazed her as much as his scooping up a silver-and-white candle wreath that had also fallen out of a box and placing it on her head.

"There...that's more like it. Now I recognize you."

Angie came as close to grinning as she had in months.

"You're really very good with children," Brynn said, wholly confused about this push-pull tendency of his. "You mentioned not having any family, but what about distant relations? Any nieces or nephews?''

"None."

"I'm not trying to pry. I'm just impressed. And grateful."

He gestured to the boxes. "You'd make better use of your time telling me what you want where."

She tried, but had minimal success. The boxes were well labeled—that wasn't the problem—but, as she'd feared, too many reminded her of her former life as lover and wife to Tony Delmarco. It was impossible to hide that, even from someone who made it clear he didn't want to know the first thing about her.

After what seemed like an hour, but was probably only minutes, he stopped her as she stood before the next box massaging her throbbing temples.

"That's enough."

"Oh, no, I'd rather work than—"

"You're in luck. It's stopped raining."

Relieved, she tore her gaze away from the box labeled Wedding Photos, Mementos, grateful to be greeted with fresh air as Gideon Kane pushed open the tall garage doors. Brynn filled her lungs. Warm though it was, the air stung a throat raw from unshed tears.

"I'll shut off this lamp and go."

Brynn swept Angie into her arms and carried her outside. Storm clouds churned before them, but, glancing around, she saw that the sky behind the garage was a bright blue. Soon the sun would be out again, and the humidity would turn the area into a huge sauna. Too uncomfortable to continue working, even if she wanted to.

Her mother's tenacious lectures compelled her to face their neighbor with the gracious smile of a hostess. "Can I get you a glass of iced tea before you go?"

"No need."

"It's the least I can do."

"But not what you'd prefer."

Her smile wavered. "Mr. Kane, you have a strange way

of making a person feel stroked one moment and slapped the next.''

''Unless you're planning on enrolling in my class, and I hope you won't, you might as well drop the 'mister.' In fact—'' he used both hands to comb back the dark brown hair that was just this side too long for neatness and too short for a rubber band ''—I'm going to say something that I hope you won't take the wrong way.''

Brynn's gut instincts told her that Angie should be spared whatever he had to say. Easing her daughter to the ground, she murmured, ''Sweetheart, it's time we get cleaned up for Grampa. Why don't you wave goodbye to Mr. Kane, go inside and start washing your hands. I'll follow you in a minute.''

The child did more—she wrapped her thin arms around his leg and hugged. He stared as though she had eight legs and pincers. Fortunately, she remained too shy yet to look up at him. Holding fast to her crown, she trotted to the house.

''Exactly what do you teach, Mr. Kane?''

He looked a bit thrown off balance. ''History.''

''Good. Because if it was psychology or something of that ilk, I'd feel compelled to advise you to get into a new line of work.''

He didn't get angry. Actually, he looked ashamed.

''That's what I've been trying to tell you. Your daughter's precious, but I'm the wrong man for her to bond with.''

''I understand. I'm even at the point of agreeing with you, but I can't control her feelings.''

''Try. And while you're at it, stop looking at me as though I was a puzzle you'd like to unravel. Believe me, you don't.''

Right now the look in his eyes made her want to run into the house and lock the door. Luckily, he was the one to leave, saving her from giving in to the urge. The sound of a vehicle did have her turning, though; but it wasn't Dominic, as she'd feared. It was Lillian Littlejohn.

The expensive sports car disappeared behind the hedge separating her garage from Dominic's, but not before Brynn recovered enough to return the woman's wave. Had Lillian seen Gideon Kane? Was his spotting her the real reason he'd left? He did seem to have something else to say. Could Dominic be right about them being lovers? If so, whatever would her neighbor think seeing him over here?

Angie appeared at the storm door, something suspiciously like orange juice dripping from all over her.

"Oh, honey!" Brynn ran for the house to clean up the mess before Dominic arrived. But secretly, she didn't mind the excuse to avoid having to find out what Lillian thought. Not when she didn't know what to think herself.

As with weeds in a garden, questions once germinated in the mind were tricky things to control. For the next few days Brynn failed and, as a result, found excuses not to go outside. She told herself it was to placate the man who wanted her and her daughter to keep their distance. Ultimately, however, she had to admit she was also afraid of running into Lillian, and this time not getting away. She really didn't want to find out the truth about Lillian's relationship with Gideon—nor did she like the fact that she was curious about it.

The boxes in the garage were her one concern, though, but she resolved it by letting Dominic help as he'd wanted to all along. On Saturday they worked most of the day sorting through what was left, and Angie, seeming to sense that she shouldn't venture out of the yard when her grandfather was around, sat at her little table and either drew pictures or played with the dolls they'd unpacked.

Her behavior inside, however, drove Brynn to exhaustion.

Without fail, after crawling out of bed every morning, Angie shuffled to the window to peer outside, then again after brushing her teeth, and again after dressing. Observing all of this had Brynn's heart aching for the wistfulness she saw in the child's face, an expression to be repeated numerous times throughout the day. But Gideon Kane was holding to his end of the deal—he was keeping out of sight, as well.

By Sunday afternoon, however, Brynn had had enough.

Deciding the need for advice was more important than being embarrassed, she slipped outside when she spotted Lillian Littlejohn in her backyard.

The woman was working in the flower bed that circled a large birdbath. Dressed in khaki slacks and a gauzy orange-and-purple tunic top, she looked ready for a photo shoot for a pricey garden magazine. Brynn already knew she kept trim by playing everything from golf to tennis, and she thought the wedge-style hairdo chic as well as easy to manage for all that activity. Coming to a stop before her, she hoped she wouldn't blow this; Lillian had a canny but warm quality that reminded Brynn of her own mother. She would like to be friends with her.

"Please, Mrs. Littlejohn," she said after Lillian's bright greeting, "Dominic is sleeping in front of the TV, and Angie's upstairs napping, too. Will you help me with an increasingly complicated problem?"

The woman brushed her silver hair off her forehead with the back of her wrist, then began tugging off her gardening gloves. "Not unless you loosen up and call me Lillian. Would you like to sit under the umbrella?" She gestured to the romantic setting on the patio. "I was looking for an excuse to have a cool glass of wine."

"You're sure I'm not interrupting at a bad time? I know how busy you are. As it is, I don't see how you keep things as lovely as you do."

"Well, you've probably seen the lawn service people come around, and they help. But I'll let you in on a little secret—the flower beds are my therapy. Sit. I'll be right back."

Brynn used the time to take several deep breaths to calm the sudden flood of nerves invading her stomach. It really wasn't like her to succumb to the jitters. Growing up in an extremely social family, she'd been weaned on all kinds of parties and events. Talking with composure and confidence to strangers of any age was something that had been expected of her. Even after marrying Tony, when their social life had been far less active, she'd enjoyed drawing out people—different people than those of her parents' circle, but interesting ones nonetheless.

She didn't know what had happened to Brynn Hart Delmarco. These days she sometimes avoided mirrors for fear of not recognizing the person she'd become.

"So, Angie still naps after lunch. Lucky you," Lillian said as she emerged from the house carrying a tray with two long-stemmed glasses and the wine cooling in a crystal decanter. "But then, she's not even five yet, is she?"

"No, she only turned four in March. And sometimes it's already difficult to get her to lie down." Brynn swallowed. "She still has nightmares."

Lillian nodded as she set the tray on the glass-topped table and poured. From her compassionate expression Brynn concluded that Dominic had told her some of what had happened.

"Often?"

"Less than at first." Brynn had to swallow again to stop the emotion she heard creeping into her voice. "But this past week there's been an increase again."

"What changed this week?"

"Mr. Kane."

Lillian's eyebrows lifted. They were elegantly plucked and only a shade or two darker than her silver hair.

"Gideon gives her nightmares? Well, I know he intimidates the devil out of his students, but he wouldn't try to frighten a child. In fact, he does everything in his power to avoid them."

"I wasn't clear." Brynn clasped her hands tightly in the folds of her white shirtwaist dress. "Angela isn't afraid of him. On the contrary, she's...there's no other way to say it, I think she's developed a hero-size crush on him. I'm surprised you haven't seen her chasing toward his gate every chance she gets."

Lips lightly tinted coral pursed. "Dear, in case you haven't noticed, I try not to make your property a focal point. It encourages your father-in-law, and the indomitable Dominic needs no such help."

Brynn couldn't help but smile. "He's very fond of you."

Lillian shook her head as she reached for her glass, her smile wry. "Let's leave him for the day the rest of the world's problems are resolved, and get back to your Angie and Gideon. Is she projecting or something?"

"I don't know. Maybe." Brynn rubbed at her forehead, the past few weeks a blur thanks to her own broken sleep pattern. She could only imagine how things must seem to her child. "Heaven knows he doesn't resemble Tony, not physically, and certainly not in personality. But it's not just Gideon that draws her. It's the garden, too. There's something about him that gives her...what? That's the question. She seems more tranquil when she's hanging on to that blasted gate. Happy. Almost reassured when she sees him.

"But he doesn't want to be bothered!" Her anguish threatened to choke her as she remembered his last words. "Oh, he's wonderful to her. It's incredible to see his power when he turns on the charm. But then he turns to me and basically says, 'Don't do this to me.'"

Once she stopped, Lillian gently pushed Brynn's glass toward her. "Taste it. My second ex-husband owns a winery in Texas, of all places, and every year he sends me a case of his best vintage. His way of letting me know what I walked out on."

Brynn sipped. She knew what Lillian was doing and she was grateful. "It's quite fruity but mellow."

"Indeed. Mellow and Texas aren't two words you think of at the same time, are they? Poor Ian can't understand that I knew this is what he was passionate about. Not women. Not me."

Brynn took another sip and felt the wave of emotion that had threatened to overcome her recede. "Thank you. You're very good at handling people, aren't you?"

"My hunch is that we have that in common. Everyone is good at something, though." The woman glanced toward

Dominic's house and her left eyebrow twitched slightly. "Most of the time. Now about Gideon…" She leaned toward Brynn. "He is the most private man you're ever likely to meet."

"I recognize that. And while I've tried to respect his request for privacy, what's happened to Angie, her connection with him…it's unlike anything I've ever had to deal with."

"No doubt. I'm fascinated myself."

Brynn sat forward. "I'm glad, because that's why I'm here. Despite your relationship, I thought you could make him understand."

"Darling, you jest? No one *makes* Gideon anything." Suddenly the fine lines between Lillian's eyebrows deepened. "Wait a minute. What do you mean, 'relationship'?"

"Aren't you two lovers?"

Chapter Three

Lillian's expression went from flattered to annoyed. "Tell Dominic his affection for garlic is pickling his brain."

"But how did you know?" Brynn asked, more intrigued than embarrassed.

"We've been neighbors for three years. He's been trying to be—if I may be frank—more than neighborly for three point one years."

"Excuse me?"

"The man hit on me as I was house shopping."

"I knew it!" Brynn sat back, glad that not all her instincts had left her. "I'd sensed something between you two from the moment he introduced us."

"What's between us is that he's narrow-minded, stubborn, bossy, irascible...and he's accused me of having an affair with everyone except the man who keeps getting arrested for driving nude through downtown." Lillian sighed. "Unfortunately, he's also one of the most romantic, charismatic men I've ever met."

Brynn nodded slowly. "That certainly clears up any confusion I may have had about things."

The dry response wasn't lost on her neighbor. "I'm not making any sense to you. Well, I shouldn't be surprised, I'm not doing a good job of figuring us out myself, which is why I keep my distance. I'm afraid I might find conflict an aphrodisiac. You, on the other hand, don't like conflict, do you?"

Brynn shook her head. "Maybe because I was an only child, and my parents were older than most. Ours was an extremely civilized home."

"And a happy one," Lillian murmured. "It shows. Yet you married a passionate Italian police officer...?"

As she spoke, a pair of cardinals were showing their young where to find food. It was a poignant reminder of what could have, should have been for her and Tony.

Brynn sighed. "The heart responds, it doesn't plan. Of course, my parents were concerned when I first introduced him to them. My mother thought I should connect with one of the sons or nephews in her garden club or bridge group, my father one of the eligible men he met at the bank he'd co-founded."

"Dominic said you have no one left up north. Your parents have passed?"

"Yes, they were avid travelers. A month before the wedding they took a train trip through Canada, and there was an accident." It had been terrible then; they'd even postponed the wedding for six months. Now she could accept that it was perhaps better that her mother and father had gone together. Neither would have been whole without the other. She and Tony had had only a handful of years as a couple, but they had been enough for her to understand how for some, lives became intertwined, so much so that eventually it was all one purpose.

She sighed. "I'm sorry for what I said about you and Mr. Kane. I realize now that I was totally off base."

"Don't apologize. You've done wonders for my ego."

Nevertheless, Lillian tilted her head. "But more interesting is that you're a little relieved."

That had Brynn frowning. "Why do you say that?"

"Because of the way you looked when you spoke of him. And please don't take this as a warning, but let me just say that many people, particularly men, are threatened by the Gideons of the world—even Dominic, who had to be fairly tough to have spent all those years at sea. Still, he knows when and how to be a team player if necessary. Gideon on the other hand is a lone wolf, and a badly injured one at that. He had to reinvent his world entirely to find a way to exist in it. There's an inevitable romance to that that can be quite seductive to women."

Uncomfortable, Brynn focused on the glass as she reached for it. "You're misinterpreting things. I'm simply concerned for my daughter's sake."

"Correction noted."

Unfortunately, Brynn's curiosity had been piqued. "So, what happened to make him the way he is?"

"If I knew the complete story, which I don't, I wouldn't be free to tell you. But I only met him several years ago when we were both up north. I had the number-two spot at a small university and he was a student waging war on the curriculum."

The math didn't figure. "A student?"

Lillian's smile was mysterious and rueful. "He came late to teaching."

Although the evasive comment spawned more questions than she'd started with, Brynn didn't want her neighbor to get the wrong idea. "I meant what I said. I'm not one of those women you described. The only thing that interests me is his hold on my daughter, and whether it can be used for some measurable improvement in her condition."

"What do the doctors say about her?"

"They can't find anything physically wrong. I've taken her to a number of therapists, but that upset her so much, I promised not to do it again until she gave me some sign that she was ready.''

"And has she?''

"No. She seems content to keep things the way they are. She doesn't even draw pictures of anything from the past, let alone that awful experience, the way they told me she would. It's difficult for Dominic, who wants to tell her about when her father was a little boy. Most of those things are remembered from letters his wife had sent him, because he was away from home so much. Still, they're important for him to share them. But...it's as though she wants to believe her life began just months ago. Do you see?''

"She's justifying her silence. Babies don't talk.'' Lillian's exhale came out as a silent whistle. "Some survivor tactic. So you're saying if she ever starts talking again, it might be by experimenting with baby talk?''

"Heaven knows. However, you can guess how far that would set her behind in school. I dread the mere thought of her having to endure that. That's why I'm interested in understanding how and why Gideon seems to reach her in a way the rest of us can't.''

"What a responsibility.'' But confidence soon brightened Lillian's hazel eyes. "Well, this will probably seem like little to you, but you have nothing to fear about Angie seeking him out. Gideon is someone who would cut off his hand before using it against a child. Believe that.''

"Thank you. I'll try,'' Brynn said slowly. "At the same time, I realize I'm probably kidding myself that anything can be achieved. Even if Gideon didn't mind some contact with her, I have Dominic to consider. He wouldn't tolerate it.''

"Excuse me all to heck, but since when does dear Dominic take precedence over your daughter?''

Just then the sound of a door opening caught their attention, and Dominic stepped outside. Spotting them, he waved and hurried down the stairs. As he drew closer Brynn watched him thrust out his chest, watched his smile grow boyish.

"What a nice surprise—the two prettiest ladies in town at one table. But, Brynn, where's Angelina?"

"Still napping, I hope." Brynn pushed back her chair. "Maybe I should check on her."

"What's the rush? Let the child sleep." He drew back a chair. "I'll join you."

"Maybe you should," Lillian drawled. "You can explain yourself."

Brynn's heart plunged.

"I've been asking Brynn if Angie's had a chance to see Gideon's pond yet. He has a few of those flashy big goldfish—oh, I forget the name of them at the moment—but I think her daughter would find them a treat to watch. At any rate, she tells me she hasn't. That you wouldn't approve."

"Lillian." Brynn couldn't believe it.

"I would not." Dominic crossed his strong arms over his chest. "Brynn is a good girl, and our Angelina is an innocent. Kane is not the kind I want around either of them. Besides, he unlocks his gate for no one." He shot Lillian a reproachful look. "Or so we are led to believe."

Lillian sat back and touched her hand to her chest. "Whatever do you mean? Dominic Delmarco, are you suggesting that Gideon is my latest conquest?"

"Please. I'm not one to intrude in someone's personal business." He looked away. "Besides, it's a ridiculous idea."

"Do tell."

"He's too young for you. If you want to make a spectacle of yourself, go ahead. But a woman of your position should get rid of that toy you drive and act her age!"

Narrowing her eyes, Lillian smiled. "And what should I drive, a gas-guzzler like that motorized whale you plow around in?"

"At least it's American made."

Brynn rose. "Pop, how can you?"

"She started it."

He pointed like a stubborn six-year-old.

Having heard and seen enough, Brynn turned to Lillian. "Thank you for the wine, and…your assurances. We really have to go check on Angie." She took hold of her father-in-law's arm.

"I just sat down," he told her.

"I know, but I think I hear something over at the house." With a sigh, he rose. "*Mi scusi.* I'm needed."

Lillian sighed. "Another opportunity gone with the wind."

"I could come back."

"Actually, I have a date to prepare for."

That got him moving faster than Brynn's pressure on his arm. With a formal nod, he led the way to the house. For her part, Brynn could barely wait for the door to close behind them.

"How could you do that to me?" she asked, aghast.

He ran his hand over hair that remained as black as polished onyx. "Brynn, Lillian and I know each other a long time. Please don't interfere in what you don't understand."

"I understand that you embarrassed me."

"You didn't have to sit there."

"We were having a conversation. You're the one who intruded."

Dominic stabbed at the air with his index finger. "That reminds me…exactly what did she assure you of? I didn't like how that sounded."

Lillian had been right; Brynn had lived the thirty years of her life with few moments of serious conflict, always preferring to work out problems, always biding her time until a more emotional person calmed down. She needed only one finger on one hand to count the number of times she had actually lost her temper, the last coming after Tony's funeral when she'd learned that his murderers had not been apprehended, and probably never would be. There was no way that this silly if distasteful incident equaled something of that magnitude.

"I'm going upstairs to check on Angie," she said quietly.

Angie was rousing. After giving her a kiss, Brynn sat on the foot of the child's bed to watch her go through her little ritual. Of course, Gideon wasn't out there, and though she knew her daughter was disappointed, she let her sit there for a while. She needed the time herself to take in what Lillian had said.

No, she wasn't involved with him, yes, he was a strange character, but she trusted him. It wasn't much to go on, definitely nothing that would justify risking Dominic's anger. The way he'd reacted to Lillian's small provocation about seeing the fish—Brynn shook her head remembering. No, she couldn't tell him.

But she had to make peace with him regardless of how disappointed she'd been with his behavior. They were guests in his home, and he was Angie's last living relation. Every relationship went through some growing pains. And if people left every time they didn't like the simplest thing about someone and someplace, they'd run out of places to go.

Besides, who knew what another uprooting would do to Angie?

When they finally went downstairs, Brynn gave her daughter permission to watch TV and slipped outside to where Dominic was hard at work pulling weeds in his vegetable garden.

Although she didn't think his stubborn look was fair, she crouched down beside him to touch his arm. "I don't want this strain between us."

He pulled another handful of chickweed before sitting back on his heels.

"*Lo so, cara.* I know. Nor I." He handed her the basket with the radishes and red onions he'd picked. "It's all behind us, *sì?*"

About to agree, Brynn rose and looked straight at Gideon.

He stood on his back porch watching her through the iron gate. Wearing only his jeans, his hair and upper body wet as though he'd come straight from a shower, his hands on his lean hips...the effect was powerful. Sexual.

"Brynn!"

Embarrassed to have been caught staring, she excused herself and hurried back to the house. The entire way she was acutely aware of two pairs of eyes on her.

Dominic didn't say anything that evening, but it soon became evident that he wasn't about to let her out of his sight for long, either. When he had to be at work, he called two or three times a day, ostensibly to check on Angie or ask her if she needed him to bring anything from the market, but she knew he was really keeping tabs on her.

She began to feel like a teenager who'd been grounded. "Dominic, really. You have to stop checking up on me," she said one day when she'd had enough. "It's not fair to your employer to be spending so much time on the phone. Everything's fine here."

"I'm from the old country. As long as my son's wife and his child are under my roof, I'll watch over you. You stay indoors this afternoon, *si?* The big heat is coming."

It wasn't the temperature he was worried about, and it was several more days—days of living like someone in an incubation cubicle—before he relaxed somewhat. Relieved though she was, she also knew she couldn't endure much more of such old-fashioned and stifling behavior. That's what had her brooding on the back steps the following Thursday night. Dominic was supposed to be watching a children's video with Angie, but Brynn had peeked and seen him sleeping. What's more, Angie wasn't even pretending to watch, and the sight of her plaintive expression as she sat staring into space was all Brynn needed to convince her to take a risk.

She was hoping that maybe Lillian would return soon from wherever she was tonight. Certain that part of Dominic's behavior had to be because Lillian was giving him the cold shoulder again, she hoped to appeal to Lillian's good nature. A wave, a simple "Good morning" would put him in a better mood and make him stop acting like a nursemaid in some medieval play.

A movement out of the corner of her eye had her looking across the alley.

He was outside, too.

Dressed in black, he was a shadow moving about in the night. The only reason she'd seen him was that he'd turned and for an instant the lights from their place had lit his face.

That's what we've reduced him to.

Before she could stop herself, she was striding across the yard and alley. It was foolish, really; unlike him, she wore a pale lavender sundress, and if Dominic, the Olsens, anyone looked outside, they would see her without any difficulty. Adding to her dilemma was that once she came to the gate, she didn't know what she intended to say.

Then again, it might not matter. Suddenly he'd vanished.

"Mr. Kane?"

Several stone lanterns were scattered around the yard, and he'd lit the candles. Although they only faintly lit their immediate surroundings, it was well enough to disappoint her.

She leaned her forehead against the cool metal. "Gideon."

"You're out late."

Gasping, she stepped back. He'd come from the side, where the fence had protected him. That told her he'd seen her all along.

"Did you enjoy that?" she asked, wrapping her arms around her waist.

"I can think of more pleasant ways to pass the time." He glanced past her to Dominic's house. "Does your bodyguard know you're over here?"

"What do you think?"

"I think you'd be hard on any man's willpower, no matter how resolute he was about denying you something. Maybe he gave in to your gentle persuasion."

She wished she could ignore the tension that was an immediate presence between them, but his intense scrutiny made that impossible. "Dominic is with Angie." The words barely made it past her dry throat and drier lips.

"And you? What are you doing?"

"I..." She didn't know. Her brain ceased functioning because he, this, was frightening her. There were messages in his eyes—some spoke of pain and death...others of hunger.

"Go home, Brynn."

"I need to talk to you."

"I can't help you."

"You don't even know what I'm going to say."

"It doesn't matter."

"That's rude!"

"No, it's self-preservation."

"At the cost of a little girl's sanity?"

She had him. He might want and succeed in avoiding and rebuffing her, but he had a soft spot for her daughter. Brynn saw it in the slight flicker of his eyes, an even subtler spasm in his right cheek.

"You have no right."

She couldn't keep from shivering. Dear heaven, he made her sound as though she was asking him to point a loaded gun at his own head.

She stepped closer, close enough to feel his heat. "I don't know how to manipulate, and I thought the only man I would ever beg anything of was my husband, but I'll beg you if that's what it takes."

He closed his eyes for so long she thought he was trying to meditate her out of his sight; and all the while he stood there in those strange pajamalike clothes with his hands loose at his sides as though waiting for nothing more important than a Don't Walk sign to change.

Slowly he bowed his head. "All right, tell me."

"She misses you."

"She can't miss who she doesn't know."

"She misses what she'd been seeing, what she felt comforted by. You. This garden. But you've made a point—an understandable one, of course—to avoid her, to avoid even letting her see you."

"I told you why."

"No, you made a judgment that it was for the best. I disagree. She's reacting as though you've abandoned her. She can't handle that, and I want you to stop. Go back to your old routine."

"Then what?"

"I don't know. I don't know!" She pressed the heels of both hands against her aching temples. "You want my assurance that she won't haunt you like some voyeur in training—well, I can't do that. For all I know she might become an even greater annoyance."

"What a sales pitch."

"If there was time, I would try to explain properly, but you've seen how my father-in-law feels about either of us being anywhere near you."

"And yet here you are risking upsetting him again."

"Because during those days that Angie had contact with you, I saw a marked improvement in her. She stopped being the listless rag doll she's becoming again, and her appetite was better. She liked it when you talked to her, and she had even begun to occasionally accept being around others like at church or the library. She also didn't have those nightmares."

He frowned. "She's having them again? Never mind. I can see by the darker shadows under your eyes that she isn't sleeping. But surely you can't think—"

"I don't know what else to think." Brynn rubbed her arms, the warm night air doing nothing to ease her bone-deep chill. "We've dealt with a battalion of experts. I've read book after book. I've done everything but take her back to the scene of the crime as one psychotic—believe it or not—suggested.

"This is a child we're talking about. A child who has been scared to the core of her being, and whose heart for good measure was broken. Do you think I care that you didn't really hang the moon? Angie believes it, and for now I don't mind that she does."

"Proof that *you* need more therapy, too."

She ignored his comment.

"Didn't anything I said to you after that storm make an impact?"

"All of it. Then I spoke to Lillian."

"Did you?"

The response was calm, but not his eyes.

"She didn't divulge any deep, dark secret. She simply reassured me that I could trust you with my daughter."

"'With'? That suggests more than what you first suggested."

"No." She shook her head, absolutely not wanting that. "Achieving for her mere glimpses of you from her bedroom window while keeping her grandfather from catching on will probably finish giving me a nervous breakdown."

"You're planning duplicity? You?"

"I'm glad I'm able to provide you with a bit of amusement."

"Believe me, I'm not."

"Then answer me and I'll spare you from having to endure any more of my company." She gripped the bars again. "Will you?"

"I'll think about it."

"That means no."

"It means I'll think about it."

"Do I have to get on my knees?"

"What the hell for?"

"To beg. I told you I would."

"Never, ever to me. Do you understand?" He gripped the bars just above her hands. "Go home, Brynn. Let me beg *you.*"

"I can't. Not without an answer."

"Yes, all right? Yes!"

Relief left her weak. "Bless you." She brushed her fingers

over his knuckles before backing away from him. "Good night!"

Bless you.

Her words haunted Gideon throughout that night. That caress of her fingers against his nearly drove him mad. By the time he arrived at the college the next morning, he found himself grateful that it was Friday, and relieved that his lesson plan for the day's class allowed for almost total student direction. He had enough opinionated souls in that one to guarantee he wouldn't have to say a word except to kick them out at the end of the session.

Bless you.

By the time class was over, he wanted the words out of his head. He knew of only one woman who could do that, and he found her trying to escape to the parking lot herself.

"A word, Dean."

Barely polite and in no way a question, his words had Lillian stopping in her tracks and lifting her left eyebrow. "My. You don't look like your normal, cheerful self. What's wrong? Did one of your students try to use an industrial cleaner on a favorite bad guy's track record again?"

She was always teasing him about his dogged insistence on full disclosure in his classes, despite the fact that she agreed with him. He supposed it was her right to give him a little hell, since she'd laid her job on the line for him with the regents a few times. Only he wasn't feeling quite as appreciative today.

"We need to talk."

"I can see that. I'm free for lunch. Want to come to my house and start more rumors?"

"You've done me enough favors by talking to Brynn about me."

Lillian sobered and nodded to their cars. "Every place in town will be packed and noisy. The park empties in the heat of the day. You can buy me an ice cream."

He let her lead, knowing the place only from his infrequent

jogs there. Usually he preferred quieter locations, and he had no idea where this vendor she spoke of would be located.

The cart was by the dam. He bought her a vanilla double scoop, then led her along the bank.

"Still not the ice cream type, huh?" she drawled as he walked beside her, his thumbs hooked in his pockets.

"You know what I am, Lillian. More or less. Which is why I'm finding it difficult that you pulled what you did."

She adjusted the napkin around her sugar cone. "Brynn needs help."

"Then pass her over to one of your better shrink friends."

"I may. Later. Right now she needs instant relief and she thinks you're it." Lillian shot him a sidelong look. "When did you two talk?"

"Last night. She must have finally noticed that I've been taking care of the garden then. She snuck away from your Italian admirer."

"Don't call him that. These days he's thinking I'm more trouble than I'm worth."

"Keep up your meddling and I'll be agreeing with him."

Lillian made several ladylike licks at the melting ice cream. "All right, I'm properly chastised, so stop keeping me in suspense. What happened?"

"It's not what happened," he said, wondering if she could hear the lie as clearly as he did. "It's what will happen if Delmarco picks up on the little deception going on around him. Don't you think Brynn has been through enough?"

"Well, well. You do like her." Lillian looked pleased.

"I never said I didn't. But that isn't a relevant point."

"On the contrary, dear heart. In fact, I think it's so germane you're scared."

She'd hit the mark, all right. Stopping, Gideon stared at the ground. "She's too much, Lillian. I can't deal with it. I can't be what she wants."

"She needs you."

"And how will you defend yourself for encouraging her if she finds out the truth about me?"

Lillian responded with a full diaphragm groan. "The truth is that you are a wonderful man. The past, whatever it is, is just that. It has nothing to do with who you are today, who you've worked so bloody hard to become."

Then why did he continue to feel soiled and guilty? Why did his flesh where Brynn had touched him still burn as much as make him ache?

"You amaze me," Lillian said, watching him. "You're so good at dissecting issues and seeing the forest as well as the trees when it comes to your lectures, but all that common sense goes out the window when you're thinking about yourself. For me, for once, remember all the good you've done since coming here."

He snorted. "Some good. I put those kids in my classes through the wringer semester after semester—you think I don't hear what they call me?—and what's it all for? Next month some movie star or other quasi celebrity will get in front of a camera, make a half-baked ideological statement, and everything those kids learned in class will be gone like vapor. By the next day they'll be repeating the media's sound bite of the event as though it was the most brilliant utterance of the century. Not one of them will hold the idiot's feet to the fire and question why what's babbled about on Monday is contradicted the other six days of the week. Why? Because some other genius has captured the spotlight."

Crumbling the remnants of her cone, Lillian tossed the treat to the ducks that had been paddling alongside them. Clearly, she didn't suffer any of his frustrations.

She was both the bane of his existence and his personal hero—in those fleeting moments that he almost believed in such things. He certainly wouldn't have a job if it hadn't been for her. When they'd met he'd still been frighteningly rough around the edges, still bleeding internally. Suspicious. Angry.

He'd caught her eye when he'd not only stopped a nasty and unfair fight outside the administration building one evening, but also made the jerk provoking it wet his pants before running off. Lillian had witnessed all of it, had recognized he was not your average student; thereafter, she'd been like a terrier gripping a pants leg, impossible to shake loose, and insisting he accept her wisdom and support.

Newly divorced for the second time, and both amused and saddened by her failure in the marriage arena, she'd been a new commodity for him. At first he'd hung around to see if she was as sharp and interesting as he'd first thought; then to see what giving her word meant to her. He found out once he got his degree. Already down here, she'd phoned him that evening and asked him to join the faculty.

He hadn't regretted his decision. Until now.

"Feeling better?"

"I like you least when you mother me," he muttered. "That wasn't a tantrum. I was making a point."

"The one that teaching is a waste of time, or that you alone are no good, so we shouldn't look to you to effect change? I have only one question—how can you stand before dozens of young people every day and ask them to do what needs to be done if you aren't willing to do it yourself?"

He clenched his teeth so hard he wondered he didn't snap his jaw. "If you were a man, you'd be on the ground for that remark."

"I didn't call you a hypocrite…yet. I was showing you that if you turn your back—note, please, I'm aware this would be the first time—you *will* have earned the judgment you heap upon yourself. Dear, dear Gideon," she said, completely serious, "tell your demons to take a hike for a while. Help Brynn."

They walked in silence for several seconds.

"She reduced me to swearing. Twice," he said at last.

"Everyone has their Achilles' heel. Surely one of your Buddhist guides pointed that out to you?"

"The arrival of the latest Victoria's Secret catalog must have precluded that lesson."

Laughing softly, Lillian rubbed the sleeve of his sports

jacket. "Now I know you're going to be all right. That droll wit is coming back."

After she left him, Gideon stood for a few minutes longer gazing across the water and listening to the breeze in the oaks behind him. He wished he felt Lillian's confidence, but she had overlooked something vital.

Yes, he was dangerously attracted to Brynn Delmarco—and he wasn't so blind that he didn't see he stirred something in her. But she didn't want it any more than he did. The woman was still mourning her husband, for pity's sake.

If he could keep remembering that, he might survive this.

When he reached his own car, he saw that he had a flat tire. It was, he decided, an appropriate punctuation to the day. Lillian could play the optimist, but he would be better off recalling the saying that "the place where optimism most flourishes is the lunatic asylum."

"Please, *mia fiore*, you gotta eat for your grandpapa, *sì?*" Dominic leaned so far over his own plate, his ear almost dipped into the remaining pasta salad.

Brynn touched his bronzed forearm. "Don't. You tried. We both tried. When she's hungry, she'll eat."

"You've been saying that for days. Look at her. She barely has strength to sit in that chair."

The reason she was tipping and slumping was that, as usual, she hadn't slept well, and although Brynn had high hopes in that department, as well as for her appetite, she didn't dare encourage Angie. Not until she was sure.

"You really needn't have taken the day off," she told Dominic.

"How could I work when she's like this? Besides, I'm exhausted, too. You think I got any more sleep than you? I tell you, we need to take her to the doctor!"

Not surprisingly, Angie's eyes widened in fear. She began shaking her head violently, her braids whipping her face.

"Oh, Dominic." Brynn had told him more than once to be careful what he said in front of her. "No, sweet. Grampa didn't mean it. He's just upset that you didn't so much as taste this yummy salad. The peas and carrots are from his garden." Playfully, she scooped one pea onto Angie's spoon and coaxed it into the child's mouth. "That's my good girl."

"*Una piselli.*" Dominic rolled his eyes.

The child turned her head away from him, which worried Brynn, too. That was another trait becoming more routine. Dominic had to stop pushing or he was going to risk having his feelings badly hurt.

"I can't finish," he said, pushing his plate away. He rose. "I'm gonna lie down."

Brynn watched with concern. "You aren't coming down with something, are you, Pop?" His coloring did seem somewhat pale beneath that tan.

"I'm fine. You got your hands full there. I'm fine."

She heard the TV click on, then him settling on the couch. Oh, dear, she thought. He always settled in his easy chair after lunch—unless he was feeling particularly tired. It made sense, though; it was one thing for her to adjust around Angie's needs, and quite another for someone his age. At least Angie could relax for an hour or two before—

Angie gripped her wrist.

She turned to see her daughter looking more alert and happy than she had in days. As soon as she followed her gaze, she saw why.

He was out there. This morning she'd had her doubts when she'd seen him dressed for work, even though today was supposed to be his day off. But he was back, and he'd kept his word.

Brynn leaned closer to her daughter and whispered into her ear. "I talked to him last night. He's been very busy, that's why you haven't seen him, but he said to tell you hello. If you'll hurry and eat, we can go upstairs and I'll let you sit in your window seat for a while before it's nap time."

Angie kept her eyes on Gideon, but opened her mouth like a little bird.

Smiling, Brynn reached for the spoon.

Chapter Four

Dominic may not have understood the abrupt reversal in Angie's behavior, but it had Brynn smiling more and more. Over the next ten days Gideon held to his former routine, and that made her daughter content. Granted, after a month in Blanchette, she still wasn't speaking, but her appetite had improved to where she began regaining some of her lost weight, and the nightmares eased. Considering where they'd been heading, Brynn thought it excellent news.

Having learned from her initial attempts to hide Angie's fascination with Gideon from Dominic, one morning after he went off to work, she sat the child down to explain it to her.

"Grampa loves you very much, and he only wants to make sure you're happy and safe. Sometimes he and Mr. Kane haven't been as friendly as Grampa is with some of the other neighbors, and this is one of those times, so we have to be considerate about not making Grampa feel that you like Mr. Kane more than you do him."

Angie accepted that with a somber nod, and soon, just as

she'd become more content, her grandfather relaxed and was almost like his old self again.

As for Gideon, she could have hugged him for the little extras she hadn't asked for. Once when she let Angie go to his gate for a minute while she was shaking out throw rugs, he came up to the child and gave her a lovely violet-and-orange iris as delicate as a butterfly wing. On another day he presented her with an exquisite paper fan with dozens of cherry blossoms painted on it.

Although she usually felt it wiser to keep her distance, Brynn had to go over and thank him, too.

"It's absolutely lovely. I know she'll treasure it. But you know you didn't have to."

"Isn't that the best reason for gifts?" He shifted his gaze to Angie, who had begun to pretend it was a butterfly moving from one of her grandfather's bushes to another. "Besides, it's my first. I wanted to know what it's like."

Brynn was sure she'd misunderstood. "Not the first gift you've ever given? What did you do, live most of your life in a cave?"

She'd meant it as a joke; however, when he didn't respond, did in fact simply stare back at her with those mysterious eyes, she was at a loss as to what to think. "I'm sorry," she murmured.

"It doesn't matter."

But as he walked away she knew it did.

His words troubled her the rest of the day, and it was her preoccupation that had her slipping up by failing to make sure Angie put away the fan before Dominic saw it.

She was in the bathroom draining the water from the tub after Angie's bath when she heard the sharp report of her name from down the hall. Something about the anger in his voice told her that he knew.

Dominic stood at the foot of Angie's bed. Her daughter hid under the sheet.

"This is your doing?" he demanded, pointing.

She couldn't see the fan. Angie had it tucked deeper under the bedding, but Brynn could identify its shape.

She supposed she could lie, fabricate some story, which he wouldn't believe due to the fear in Angie's eyes and the guilt that had to be in hers. Besides, she was tired of having to pretend that the man deserving the credit for Angie's improved state of mind didn't exist.

"Let's go downstairs. I'll explain."

"There is nothing to explain. You think I have no mind? You're encouraging her. The question is, for how long?"

No way would she answer that one. Hoping that Angie would forgive her for minimalizing her gift, she said instead, "It's a small thing, Dominic, a paper fan. What's the harm?"

"The man shuns everyone else, but gives a child a present? It's not normal. He's hiding something, I tell you." A faster rush of Italian spilled out of him, then he added, "For all we know he's a—"

"Dominic, don't! That's awful!"

"He's no good, I tell you, and if you don't do something to stop this, I will!"

The old guy was ticked. As Gideon walked down the imported seasoning aisle of Fresh and Fancy, he pretended not to be aware of the pair of eyes boring holes into his back. It was a challenge, though, to look for the familiar box of sea salt knowing someone behind him wanted his hide. Leave it to the grocers to choose this week to rearrange everything. He had no respect for the marketing geniuses who constantly conspired new ways to encourage impulse buying. And the world wondered why mass random shootings were becoming more and more common.

"Baggers needed up front. We need baggers."

The announcement over the intercom had him exhaling with relief. As expected, it had Dominic Delmarco uttering a gruff oath and shuffling from his post at the end of the aisle to answer the page. An inevitable scene had been avoided—for the moment.

Gideon found the salt and added it to his basket. The need to get back to his haven was now a pulse all its own inside him. He had never grown used to crowds, and the store was filling fast with people rushing in to grab a few things for dinner.

He located the other few things on his mental list, and wheeled his wagon to the front. An additional express cashier was opening up, and the young woman signaled him into her line.

Always the considerate customer, he bagged his purchases himself, paid cash and convinced the boy who rushed over to help him that he could manage them himself.

The heat was oppressive as he strode across the parking lot. It rose in steamy waves that had him pitying the children tugged by harried mothers and wearing next to nothing on their feet. Upon reaching his car, he quickly unlocked the trunk and began lowering the bags inside, then felt the air change, heard the rush of an assault.

He spun around just as metal struck his knees and shins.

"Son of a— Damn it, Delmarco!"

"Damn yourself!"

Pain blinded him. He grabbed the wagon to keep the old nut from getting in another blow, only to find himself in a wrestling match. The crazy fool had to be mad to pull a stunt like this. "Do you realize what you're risking? Knock it off!"

"You won't win!" Dominic shouted back. "Do you hear?"

Gideon didn't care about winning; all he wanted right now was to get out of there without attracting any more attention than they already were. "Look, whatever you're imagining is wrong. Besides, it's hotter than Hades out here, and you don't look—"

"I know what you're doing. Every time my back is turned, sneaking around trying to put a spell on my Angelina and Brynn. Bad enough that you have Lillian brainwashed, but I'll kill you before you do that to my family! I'll—"

He gasped and bent low over the cart's handlebar. Gideon had to push down on his side to keep it from flying over onto the man, and at the same time maneuver around the thing to save Dominic from hitting the ground too hard.

They both went down onto the baking asphalt.

Someone screamed. Brakes squealed.

Hearing footsteps behind him as he lifted Dominic's head and shoulders off the searing ground, he yelled over his shoulder, "Call 911!"

Heat burned through his jeans as he wrestled off his jacket to get it under as much of the man as possible. Remembering the blanket in the trunk, he twisted around to pull it out in order to offer the same protection to the rest of Dominic's body.

"Come on, Delmarco," he growled to the deathly still man. "Tell me this is only heat prostration. Don't you die on me."

Not wanting to think of how Brynn would take the news, he worked fast to loosen the man's tie and open the top button of his white dress shirt.

"Does he need CPR?"

"What happened?"

The people collecting around them provided some shade; that was the only reason Gideon didn't tell them to get lost. But they were limiting the air circulation.

"Back off, folks. We need air! Anyone with medical experience here?"

A woman crouched across from him, announcing she was a nursing student. She checked his pulse and breathing, and reached for the bottled water she'd just purchased. Then, using a handkerchief someone in the crowd thrust at her, she wet it and began cooling down Dominic.

"I'm hoping this is heat and not his heart," she said. "Either way, he needs stabilizing, and fast."

There was a collective sigh when the ambulance arrived. They were only blocks away from the hospital, which was across the street from the college. As they loaded Dominic into the ambulance, Gideon gave one of the medics what information he could about him.

Six weeks ago, that would have ended his involvement there. Now there was no question about him following.

Once in his car, though, he realized a problem and momentarily regretted not being one of the millions with a car phone. But just as quickly he dismissed the thought. What did a man like him need with something like that? Besides, this wasn't something you handled over the phone.

Not wanting her to hear the news from some stranger, he drove over to the Delmarco home himself. Besides, she had no car, he reasoned, no quicker way to get to Dominic.

Heaven help him, though, if she blamed him for this.

He was the last person she expected to see at the front door; he saw that immediately. Her expression went from stunned to concerned…and then he knew she was guessing the worst.

"Oh, God. What?"

"You have to come with me. Dominic collapsed at the market and he's been taken to the hospital."

She immediately went into a survivor's mode; he'd seen it too often not to recognize the signs. Nodding, she looked around as though making a mental list of what needed doing first. The kitchen towel was dropped, barely landing on a chair; a hand absentmindedly touching her denim workshirt—her husband's again like that day in the garage, considering how it nearly covered her jeans to her knees. She didn't often wear pants, and he couldn't help but remember the first time he'd seen her in them…and how he'd ached to see her without them.

"Angie. I can't take her. She panics at the word *hospital*."

Gideon brutally reined in his wandering thoughts. "Is there a neighbor…?"

"You. But I need—I'd be grateful if you could take me to the hospital."

"It goes without saying."

"I'll call Mrs. Olsen. She has a sweet grandmotherly disposition that Angie seems most comfortable with."

Marjorie immediately hurried over, still wiping her hands dry on her apron. But one look at Gideon and her smile froze. "Are you sure you wouldn't like Arne to go with you, dear? He's just watching some fishing show."

"Thank you, but Mr. Kane will be with me. If you'll simply stay with Angie until I get back. I've explained to her that I have to take care of something important."

She didn't tell the woman that Gideon had gone upstairs with her to assure the child. Or that Angie had been surprisingly calm once she'd received hugs from them both. Gideon wished he could say the same for himself.

"She'll want a snack. Two cookies and a half cup of milk about fill her."

"Not enough to keep a bird alive. Want me to make her a waffle or—"

"She's a light eater, Marjorie. Besides, I expect to be back by dinner. And please. Remember, she doesn't answer if you ask her anything."

"Don't you worry, dear. We'll be fine. You just bring home Dominic safe and sound."

Gideon could see that leaving her daughter was difficult for Brynn. To give her time to regain her composure, he remained silent when they first got into the car and he backed out of the driveway.

"I should be thinking of Dominic. I am...I am..." As she recited the phrase again and again, she pressed her hands to her face, only to glance back as they turned the corner and lost sight of the house. "This is so hard."

He had the strongest urge to reach across the seat and close his hand over hers. Considering that he'd never been a toucher, the revelation jarred him plenty.

"If it's any consolation, I heard the medics say that they thought he's only suffering from the heat."

She shifted to study his profile. "They did? What happened? How did you come to be involved?"

"I was at the market. He...you might as well know, he spotted me and was determined to make a point."

Brynn closed her eyes. "Oh, Dominic." She covered her face with her hands. "It's my fault."

"Don't be silly."

"He saw the fan. I should have hidden it, but... I can't believe this."

"I'm the one who should have known better."

"No, I made him so angry last night. I'm proving to be a huge disappointment to him."

"If he thinks that, he's a bigger fool than I already thought."

"Did he make a scene?"

"He waited until we were outside. Brynn, don't do this."

"Didn't he realize he could get fired? He loves being at the market. I think he would do it for nothing if necessary."

"I can always deny anything happened, and that he was just asking to help me with my bags when the heat overcame him."

Brynn stared. "You would do that?"

"Don't try turning me into some kind of hero. This way we both win, because I can live without dealing with cops, lawyers and a court appearance."

"Of course, generosity has nothing to do with it."

"You're seeing what you want to see," he said, keeping his tone terse.

Brynn didn't answer. She simply folded her hands in her lap and waited for the hospital to come into view.

Gideon parked near the emergency entrance and had to take full-length strides to catch up with her as she dashed for the glass doors. Even before they reached the admissions desk, she announced Dominic's name to the attendant there. Unfortunately, it came out all backward.

"Dominic Delmarco," Gideon said on her behalf. "An EMS admission from the market about twenty minutes ago." He took hold of her arm, afraid she was going to drop. At this stage his conscience couldn't deal with two Delmarcos in the hospital.

"You're family? They're working on him now," the nurse said as Brynn nodded. "Have a seat. Someone will come out to brief you on his condition as soon as possible."

The waiting room was packed with too many others experiencing the same tension and fatigue that Brynn was dealing with—and too many rambunctious children. He ignored the receptionist's advice and led Brynn down the hall near the examination rooms.

"No chairs," he said, "but then I doubt you want to sit."

"No. I'm too upset to do that."

"Then we'll walk the fear out of you, or else put you to work helping to hold up these walls. Whatever it takes."

"There you go again, trying to prove how bad you are."

He couldn't believe she could find humor, dry though it was, at a time like this. She looked ready to break, her eyes overbright and already red rimmed from lack of sleep and maybe tears, too, her ponytail coming undone and her lips almost bleeding from being bitten. It all reflected a fragility, coupled with an ongoing inner purity of purpose.

When she shivered and wrapped her arms around herself, he frowned. "Cold?"

"Who wouldn't be? The air-conditioning is always set so blasted low at these places."

The temperature didn't bother him as much as the medicinal and human smells emanating throughout the building, but he did wish he'd put his jacket back on. But after it was no longer useful as a pillow for Dominic, he'd tossed it into the back seat of his car. He glanced around. "Want a cup of coffee? I saw a couple of machines on the other end of the hall."

"The last thing my nerves need is the added kick of caffeine. I'll be fine."

She didn't look it; and unwilling to stand there and do nothing but watch her fray around the edges, he ignored all the alarms going off inside him and drew her against him.

"Don't panic," he whispered in her ear as she stiffened. "In another minute your teeth'll be chattering and you'll have interns and nurses running around wondering what all the racket is about."

"It's not that bad."

"Right. That's why your nose is pink and the rest of you is blue." He tormented himself further by almost letting his lips brush against her ear. It was a pretty ear, like a seashell, only finer. As with the rest of her, it carried the smell of her bath soap, stirring thoughts of things most Southern like cream-drenched peaches, and made his stomach pull with hunger. "Talk to me. Take your mind off worrying."

She uttered a brief choked sound. "You don't want to know."

"Try me."

"I'm trying to forget I'm not...fully dressed."

"Ah. Well, if I can't, why should you? Just close your eyes and pretend I'm somebody else."

"You have a strange sense of humor."

"That's already an improvement. My students would tell you that I don't have one at all."

"I heard."

"Lillian strikes again," he drawled, glad to sense her beginning to relax despite her protest. He wanted that, though also dreaded it, concerned that his body would betray how long it had been since he'd been this close to a woman, let alone a woman wearing no more beneath her shirt than he was.

"She was only trying to help."

"And those good intentions are part of the reason we're standing here. She should have known that Dominic would react badly. No, don't hold it against him," he said, as she began to protest. "A man has a right to protect what he cherishes."

The words grew thick on his tongue, and he knew he was in danger of losing himself in her sweetness, becoming intoxicated from it. Slowly he drew her scent deep into his lungs while memorizing the curl of her sable lashes, the fine line of her nose, the soft bow of her lips. Skin too perfect for hands as callused as his had him wondering how it would feel to brush his mouth against it. Against her. To trace his tongue in a similar exploration to learn her tastes.

His thoughts spawned an ache wholly foreign to him. It had nothing to do with loneliness. He had enough interests to keep himself busy around the clock and then some. No, this ache was about a hunger as sexual as it was spiritual. Complicated. Devastating.

"Brynn, Gideon, thank heaven!" Lillian rushed in through the sliding doors, bringing with her a waft of hot, humid air. "Have you heard anything yet?"

"Nothing." At the sound of their neighbor's voice, Brynn had all but jumped away from him, her face flooding with color. "How on earth did you find out?"

"I had to stop at the market. It's the only thing they're talking about." Barely two inches taller than Brynn, she enfolded her into her arms as though protecting a child. "Did he really attack you with a shopping cart?" she added over Brynn's shoulder.

Gideon shot her a look to communicate that the question would have been best left unasked. "He stumbled. It looked worse than it was."

"Oh, Gideon." Brynn spun around, her expression one of new despair. "You needn't make excuses for him."

"Well, I know what I'm going to say to that big lummox when they release him," Lillian declared. "He has no right to put you through this."

"Maybe the less said the better." Once he got her attention, he gave her a meaningful look. "He's almost as jealous about you as he is Brynn and her daughter."

Before Lillian could answer, a tired-looking internist arrived. "Mrs. Delmarco?" His gaze slid from Lillian to Brynn and back again.

Lillian pointed to Brynn. "This is Mr. Delmarco's daughter-in-law, Doctor."

"Please," Brynn said, clasping her hands again. "How is he?"

Gideon stepped behind her just in case. He placed his hands lightly at her waist.

"He's resting comfortably. I'd like to keep him under observation for tonight—to get his fluid level up and keep an eye on his blood pressure. His heart looks good, though, no abnormalities in his EKG. Nevertheless, I'd be more comfortable taking certain precautions."

"Thank you for that, Doctor." Brynn swallowed hard, as though she wasn't sure whether or not to believe a word of what he said. "May I see him?"

"I wish you would. He isn't being exactly gracious about the overnight stay."

"I'll do what I can." She gripped Lillian's hand. "You can help."

"Me? Do you *want* him to have a heart attack?"

"Gideon's right about how Dominic feels about you. It'll make his day that you're here." She took two steps, stopped and glanced over her shoulder at Gideon. "I know it's a great deal to ask, but will you wait for me?"

"Go. I'll be here."

He'd made this whole experience bearable for her. With his words warming her, Brynn nodded and led Lillian to Dominic.

She peered inside her father-in-law's cubicle. As she feared, he was terrorizing the man and woman working briskly around him. It looked as though they were preparing to move him upstairs to a room.

"Where's my shirt?" he snapped.

"Lie back Mr. Delmarco."

"I want my things. I want to go. *Presto!*"

"I have a hunch what that presto business means, and, believe me, we want you gone, too," the male aide replied. "But the doctors have this thing about patients walking out instead of getting wheeled out in a bag, y'know what I'm saying?''

Brynn shook her head. "Pop, give these good people a break."

He spotted her and brightened, clearly thinking he now had an ally. "Brynn! Come talk sense to these two. They want to commit me."

She met the droll look of the woman attending him.

"Now, there's an idea," the nurse said.

Brynn gave her an apologetic smile as she exited the cubicle. "I'll see what I can do. Pop," she began again as soon as both hospital people had left to give them privacy, "you were out in the heat, you got excited. It only makes sense to—"

"How did you know about that?"

With a sound of frustration, Lillian entered, brushing past her. "Everyone knows about it, Rocky."

His expression went from disconcerted to delighted. "Lillian. You come to see me?"

"No, I have a hot date with the resident proctologist. What do you think I'm doing? Better yet, tell me what you're doing!"

Brynn watched in amazement as he fell back against the pillows and gestured weakly. "Who can say? These young doctors, they know nothing."

Lillian exchanged looks with Brynn before rounding the foot of the bed. "Well, you should be ashamed of yourself, wasting their time and scaring us half to death!"

"What did I do? I was working, thinking soon I go home to my family…"

"Do you believe this?" Lillian said aside to her. "He belongs on a soap opera."

"Pop, didn't you hear what she said when she first came in? We know. Everything."

He scowled. "This town. All spies and gossips."

"Fortunately, Mr. Kane won't be pressing charges."

"Of course he won't. Press charges for what?"

"Listen to me." Brynn moved to the opposite side of the bed from Lillian and leaned over to kiss his whisker-rough cheek. "You could have been in a good deal of trouble, both legally and healthwise. While you're resting, think about that, please. Angie and I want you home and well."

"And stop giving these poor people around here a hard time!"

Lillian's interjection had him beaming at Brynn. "You hear? She pretends she doesn't care about Dominic."

"Maybe he hit his head and suffered minor brain damage," Lillian offered. She sat on the edge of the bed. "Earth to Delmarco. If you want to make points with me, try behaving yourself. You can start by getting over whatever it is you have against Gideon Kane. You sound like an irrational teenager, for crying out loud."

"So you say. You who've run from it all your life know nothing about tradition and honor in family. You think I'm gonna give him a chance to steal from me what's left of my Tony? Bad enough he's brainwashed you."

That had Lillian throwing back her head and groaning to the ceiling. "Brainwashed? How?"

"I told you before. This is not a good man. He's too— too—"

"Private? Since when is that a crime?"

Dominic shook his head. "I understand privacy. This is different. He's hiding something."

"More like trying to forget something. Something like a few tough years in the military, serving his country like thousands of other brave men who didn't get a parade like you did when you returned from your war."

"You think so, eh? Well, Arne Olsen's grandson is in the service and he knows how to find out things about people with his computer. You know what? There was no record of a Gideon Kane in the military as both you and he said. Ever!"

"Pop!" Brynn was aghast. "You tried to pry into Mr. Kane's background?"

"People have a right to know who their neighbors are."

"And just because this nosy twerp wasn't able to dig up the right information—probably because of his own ineptness as a hacker—you assume the worst? You know, old friend, there once was a man called Columbus who was told by some other Italian geniuses that he would fall off the edge of the planet if he sailed too far out to sea."

For a moment Dominic looked properly embarrassed. "I'm only telling you the truth as it was told to me."

"You're repeating hearsay and gossip. Thank goodness I didn't waste my money on flowers," Lillian added with disgust. "No sense bringing anything for a man who won't use the sense God gave him."

Some of the devilish light returned to Dominic's dark eyes. "You were going to bring me flowers?"

Lillian appeared to find it easy keeping a straight face. "I considered it briefly. And believe me, it won't happen again if you persist in this nonsensical line of thinking. I'll also forget that I was all but ready to come read to you if your stay was going to be lengthy."

"You mean like the newspaper and books?"

"Certainly not *Sonnets from the Portuguese*," she said with a sniff.

Brynn had to admire her. Lillian hadn't been any more pleased with this revelation than she'd been, but had recovered more quickly and seemed to know how to respond. She also must have seen Brynn's dismay, because a minute or two later she encouraged her to go home for Angie's sake, assuring her that she would stay and keep an eye on Dominic.

The slow grin that spread across his face at the prospect convinced Brynn. Promising to check on him later, she kissed Dominic on the cheek and left him to their neighbor.

Although she felt relieved about her father-in-law's physical status, it was difficult to return to Gideon with any confidence. As a result, she wasn't surprised when as soon as he spotted her, Gideon took a quick step toward her.

"What's wrong?"

"He's fine," she assured him. "But you know Dominic. He's not happy if he isn't railing about one thing or another."

"Now try telling me the truth."

He wasn't going to give her any opportunity to come to terms with what she had heard. She glanced around, took in the rush of staff scurrying around them, the curious glances of people who had been here when they'd come in, and gestured to the sliding glass doors.

"Can we get out of here?"

His hand was only a light pressure at the small of her back as they made their way across the sizzling parking lot, but she knew if she gave the slightest hint of unsteadiness, those powerful arms would be around her before she knew what was happening.

How did she tell him what she'd just learned?

His attentiveness proved almost as dizzying as the heat and her fatigue. It sensitized every nerve, so that by the time he helped her into his car and she tried to secure the seat belt, her fingers refused to manage and a fine sheet of perspiration broke out all over her.

"Let me do that," he said, taking over.

"It's so hot."

"I'll get the air conditioner going in a second."

He circled the car and climbed in beside her. Only moments afterward, he keyed the engine and cool air blasted her from the vents. She let herself lean back against the headrest and closed her eyes.

"Maybe I should take you back inside and have a doctor look at you."

Knowing he was fully capable of doing that, she summoned what was left of her energy and straightened in her seat. "Really, I'm fine. I'll be better yet when I get back to Angie."

"You're not going to try to come back today, are you? Did Lillian offer to stay with him until he falls asleep?"

"That seems to be the plan. If she lasts," she added, doubting the probability. "Gideon, there's something I have to tell you."

"He's sicker than they thought," Gideon guessed.

"No. It's about what Dominic and the Olsens did behind your back." She made herself meet his steady gaze. "They apparently knew you'd been in the military."

"It's no great secret."

"No? They had the Olsens' grandson search for you in military archives via his computer. It seems that because he was unsuccessful, you're a fraud and liar."

After a long silence he said, "I thought it might be something like that."

"That's it? How can you sound so calm about it?"

"Who said I was?"

No, on second thought she could see the white line around his mouth from the way he was compressing his lips. "I'm so sorry. I can't believe they condoned it, let alone encouraged him to do it."

"Forget about it. At least it made them keep their distance, which is what I wanted all along."

"But at what expense? Suppose their rumors spread to the college? I'm guessing they didn't, because Lillian was as surprised and offended as I was, but—"

"Brynn. Drop it. It doesn't matter."

It did to her. If he never forgave any of them, she wouldn't blame him.

Belatedly she saw he'd turned off the main road toward their house, and she realized she should have spoken up sooner. "Wait! I have to get the car."

"You're in no shape for that. I'll do it."

"That should be a neat trick. You can drive two cars at once?"

"I'll drop off mine, change into jogging clothes and run over to the market. It's only a mile and a half."

"It's also nearly ninety degrees."

"I average four miles a day and didn't do near that this morning. Believe me, I could use the workout."

Thanks to his neighbors turning his life upside down. Brynn shook her head and dug in to the pocket of her jeans. "I took Dominic's keys as I left the hospital. Please. Turn around and take me to the market. You've done enough for this family."

He did stop, but only to face her. "Let's get something straight. I didn't do anything for Dominic. I did it for you. For you and your daughter—and you know it." His grip was crushing on the steering wheel. "Maybe things are getting far more complicated than either of us wants, but that doesn't change what is. You needed help. I gave you my word."

And once given, he didn't go back on it. She'd known him a scant six weeks, but that was a point she would bet anything on. She might not know for sure who Gideon Kane was—but he was no fraud or liar. In a way, that was even more frightening.

"Turn around," she said softly. "You can always follow me home."

"That goes without saying."

Minutes later he pulled up beside Dominic's car. Brynn released her seat belt. "It seems I'm fated to constantly thank you."

"I prefer hearing that than an apology from you."

"One of those stands in reserve if you ever change your mind. You've endured enough, thanks to Delmarcos."

She shot him a faint smile. He didn't return it.

"Don't be sorry. Worry."

"About what?"

"You know, Brynn. You know."

Chapter Five

Dominic was released from the hospital on Wednesday with a new attitude—he decided he liked being a patient. The hardy performance he put on for his boss at the market notwithstanding, he was glad to accept the rest of the week off, as the man suggested. Brynn had mixed feelings about that, but at least the effects his constant presence and demands had on the household helped her keep her mind off what Gideon had said. Somewhat. So did watching the calendar race toward June 20.

The anniversary date still didn't seem to be causing her father-in-law as much distress Friday afternoon when he decided he wanted to sit in the shade of the driveway. Once settled there, he realized he'd forgotten the new issue of his newsmagazine, and, of course, he needed his reading glasses. Ten minutes later he called her for a glass of ice water. Several minutes after that, as she and Angie were heading back inside after lingering to pick fresh tomatoes for their dinner salad, he called for a towel to blot the perspiration from his face.

"Why don't you just come in out of the heat, Dominic?" Between running up and down the back stairs for him, and having the upstairs yet to clean, laundry to finish putting away, and of course Angie to work with, she was beat.

"Okay. No rush. I can wait until you come out to bring me more water."

Convinced he wouldn't be outside at all except for hoping to catch Lillian when she came home, Brynn let him wait for that towel and refill. But some fifteen or so minutes later when she heard a crash, she dropped the last pair of Angie's shorts she was folding in the wash room and raced outside. Guilt filled her with dread. What if he really was more ill than anyone thought? What if—?

Before she made it down the stairs, she heard the raised voices. As she came around the corner she saw Dominic, his reading glasses askew, bending to pick up his overturned chair.

"You're a crazy woman! Is that a way to treat an unwell man?"

"There's nothing wrong with you that a solid two-by-four wouldn't fix," Lillian snapped back as she bent to pick up her colorful straw clutch purse.

Brynn couldn't believe it. "What's going on here?"

"I was sitting here at peace," Dominic began, pantomiming as usual, "thinking how lucky I am. Then she comes. I think to say hello. After all, we are friends, as well as neighbors, *si?* Next thing I know, down is up, up is down."

Since she knew better than to buy his wounded expression, Brynn focused on Lillian. "What really happened?"

"He pinched me."

"Excuse me?"

"You know, the male Italian thing that they still warn female tourists about if you're going overseas."

Brynn gaped at her father-in-law. "You didn't!"

"Why you look at me like that? It's innocent fun. A gesture when you...how you say *ammirare?* Admire! For this she beats me with that thing." He pointed at the purse back under Lillian's arm. "And knocks me over."

Lillian scoffed. "I wasn't close. You were reaching to catch it and lost your balance."

"Me, a man just from the hospital."

"Who, it turns out, was nowhere near dying!"

"I'd have to be a corpse to get any warmth from you. My priest stayed with me longer than you did!"

"Did you confess what you did to Gideon? Never mind. I've heard all the excuses I want to hear."

It was a game with them, Brynn realized, seeing the sparkle in their eyes. They were actually enjoying this. But not her. She was insulted, especially by Dominic.

"Stop it!"

When she got their attention, she clenched her hands at her sides to control their shaking. "Do you even remember what tomorrow is?" she asked Dominic. "Maybe this is your way of coping, but to use me in the process, knowing how difficult this time is for me? Shame, Dominic," she whispered. "Shame."

She ran up the steps, too upset to say goodbye to Lillian. Once inside, she stayed in motion until she blinked away the angry tears burning in her eyes, first by washing her hands, then by taking out the casserole that she'd had warming in the oven. Spooning a portion for Angie into a bowl, she set it on a tray along with a glass of milk and carried it upstairs to her daughter's room, locking the door behind her.

At Angie's curious look from her post at the window, Brynn set down her meal to the side of where she was drawing.

"Careful, it's still a bit too hot to eat."

She, too, was careful, careful to withdraw quickly from the window. Only after the scene outside did she become aware that Gideon had been out there, too, and she didn't want to look over there for fear of what she might see on his face. This was not a time to be thinking of him.

"Mommy's not feeling too well, sweetheart," she said, upon noticing Angie's concerned gaze. "I'm just a bit tired, and I thought it would be fun for you to picnic up here while I lie down, okay?"

Angie rose and immediately urged her onto the bed, drawing the throw over her, as Brynn had done for her numerous times. The sweet gesture had her tearing up again, and she closed her eyes to keep from upsetting her.

She must have fallen asleep faster than she'd thought; it was dark when she opened her eyes again. The sound of Dominic's footsteps in the hall must have roused her.

He didn't knock, didn't try the knob, but he did stand there for some time. She was grateful for his restraint, because Angie was now curled against her, asleep, and she didn't want her disturbed.

Besides, she didn't have anything to say to the man.

Brynn slept only in snatches after that, and by five she let herself out of the house. Taking Dominic's car bothered her. She hadn't asked his permission, and thought it hypocritical to want to shun his company yet use his only means of transportation. Of course, she planned to have it back by the time he awoke. Nevertheless, the infraction mattered. Just not enough.

It was going to be a beautiful Saturday. The sun barely more than a glow on the horizon, Gideon was getting in his running before the rest of the town awoke and the thoroughfares became a traffic hazard for everyone. He'd passed one or two other early birds, but for the most part, the roads and pathways were his. Exactly the way he liked it.

As he approached the park, he thought about the last time he'd been here with Lillian. Thanks in part to her, he might have to do five miles or better to burn up all the negative energy that was bugging him today. That's why he'd altered his route and come out this way.

He circled from the left, the north, and took the trail that followed the creek until it emptied into the pond. A few of the tamer ducks that lived there year-round roused to complain at the early intrusion—especially when they saw that he had nothing to offer in the way of food; however, even that was an agreeable sound. It definitely beat the thuds, grunts and metallic clatter that he would have to face in a gym.

Farther down, by the pond's edge, was another early riser. No jogger, though. In fact, her attire had him slowing, almost stopping. He mentally listed every reason it shouldn't be her, but with each reluctant step he grew more certain that it was.

Don't even think it. No way. Run.

He forced himself to pick up his pace again and wished Lillian a job offer too good to refuse in Antarctica. Her phone call last night had told him more than he already knew about why Brynn was out here.

"I've been an idiot."

"Why call me?"

"Because it affects Brynn."

"I'll say it again, why call me?"

"All right, don't speak. Just listen...."

He still insisted it was none of his business—never mind that what Lillian had had to say had succeeded in keeping him up the few hours he normally slept. He was too involved with Brynn Delmarco as it was. Besides, the summer semester had started. Shorter but more intense, the classes required him to keep his wits about him.

That argument kept him going, and he passed her without letting himself look. She was crying softly, but not quietly enough. He resented her for that, tried to shut down his hearing.

Before he cut across the parking lot to head toward his usual route, he heard a shout...a woman's scream.... Then came the ugly sounds of a collision.

He ran, fire building quickly in his throat. He didn't pace

himself, he barely breathed; he was in an all-out race to get to her.

She'd apparently intended to head for home shortly after he'd passed her, and hadn't seen the guy on the bike. They'd met head-on. Now man, woman and bike were a tangle on the asphalt trail.

"Jeez, lady. Are you okay?"

"P-please. Get this off me."

The guy had good intentions, but as tangled in the bike and hurting as she was, he only caused more pain and slowed the process. By the time Gideon reached them, he saw nothing else to do but lift the man totally with his left arm, and toss the bike aside with his right.

"What the hell's wrong with you, man? Can't you tell that's choice?"

Gideon spared the bucktoothed youth a brief, heated glance. "Be glad I don't feed it to you with a nonfat dressing."

For all the kid lacked in height and weight, he made up in feistiness. "She stepped into my path!"

"You were going straight ahead. The sky was lighter behind her. You should have seen." Gideon pushed him toward the metal wreckage. "Get out of here."

Not surprisingly, the youth started swearing, but Gideon ignored him. Crouching before Brynn, he did a quick examination.

Her filmy broom skirt was up well over her thighs, exposing scrapes from the trail, friction burns from the tires and scratches from the frame of the bike. She also had abrasions on both arms, and her pretty hands were a dirty, bleeding mess. And her deepening sobs were every bit as terrible.

Gideon glanced around, hoping she'd driven and hadn't walked. Spotting Dominic's hearse-size sedan, he slipped his arms around and beneath her.

"Let's get you out of here."

"It's a-all right. I'm all r-right."

She tried to resist and hide her face at the same time. That made it easier to pick her up.

"Don't make a scene, Brynn," he said as she stiffened. "The likelihood of you making it to your car without causing another collision is about equal to me running for mayor. Relax and tell me that tank isn't locked."

She wasn't able to speak at the moment and merely shook her head.

Small gifts. He got the passenger side open and eased her onto the leather seat. While she immediately tried to curl into a ball, he stopped her and grabbed a handful of tissues from the box between the seats. Dividing his bounty, he placed half between her hands to soak up that mess, and used the rest to dab and wipe the dirt from her legs. Her lovely, sleek legs, sadly trembling as much as her hands were.

At his touch, she attempted to push down her skirt. "It's o-okay."

"No, it isn't. But at least you won't need stitches." He took hold of her wrists. "You're getting blood on yourself. Let me."

Poor hands. He could barely stand seeing such beauty destroyed. That it was her...

"You shouldn't have been out here," he muttered, not much happier with the violence seething inside him. "If I'd had a clue you'd do this—"

"How could you?"

"Lillian called me last night. She told me what today is."

She averted her gaze. "She shouldn't have."

"Agreed."

"I just needed to be by myself for a while."

"And what if that guy had been a mugger or rapist? What if I hadn't come along?"

She tried to turn sideways, to cover her face with the one clean part of her—her wrists, but they didn't provide enough coverage and she opted for the backs of her hands. The poignant movements, as well as her renewed sobs, were almost too much to witness.

"A year," she whispered. "A year."

He couldn't fathom a loss such as the one she'd suffered; it was an abstract to him. And yet despite that emotional crippling, her pain had the power to slice at him with razor-sharp strokes.

"I came thinking I could throw his ring into the water," she continued. "To let him go. I can't keep doing this—being his widow, hating his killers, waiting for justice I know won't come. It's too draining, and Angie needs me strong. Stronger. O-or she won't get better."

She began wiping at her eyes. As always, Gideon was impressed at how ruthlessly those who were truly maternal pulled themselves together in order to keep functioning.

He waited until her breathing had evened somewhat. "You didn't throw it, did you?"

When she showed him the ornate band still on her left hand, he felt an odd relief. "Keep it for Angie. Some day she can have it remolded into something else. I think she would find that special...and helpful."

She stared at the ring as though the design had suddenly altered. "I hadn't thought of that. What a mistake I would have made."

"But you didn't. What's more, it's not your fault for not being able to think clearly these days." He carried a good part of the blame for that. Under the circumstances, his behavior and comments on Tuesday must have been particularly unwelcome. So must his presence now.

He glanced around, wishing it was later. "I'd give you the time and privacy you need, but you know I can't leave you like this. Anyone could come by and take advantage. Why don't you let me drive you home?"

"I can't let them see me like this." She fumbled for clean tissues. "And I'm still too upset with Dominic. How could he act as though he didn't remember? As if it was just another day? It was difficult when I lost my parents, but I had Tony to cushion the pain. This time... The first year is an out-of-body experience, and when that day comes around, it's so hard. So very hard.''

As her voice cracked again, he could no longer hold back; shifting onto the edge of the seat with her, he drew her into his arms.

"Oh, no, please—"

"It's okay. I am capable of controlling my hands, if not my mouth.''

She hesitated in that way that was becoming familiar to him, before slowly relaxing. The only problem was that when she said something, it was muffled by his T-shirt.

"What was that?''

She shifted slightly. "I was muttering at myself for being a royal pain. I'm not like this, and I'm so tired of being weak.''

"Where do you see weak? You've lost your parents, your husband, your child's been traumatized, you've relocated, moving into the house of a near stranger.''

She made a negative sound, and he understood. She didn't want to hear anything complimentary. Survivors rarely did. He was also careful not to do more than hold her, but that was mostly for his own sanity's sake. He did, however, know she needed something else.

"Why don't you go ahead and talk about how it happened. Have you? Ever?''

"Some. I had to explain to Dominic, to friends, Angie's doctor.''

"Facts. What about feelings?''

"You and I shouldn't talk about feelings, Gideon.''

She had that right. But she needed to, and he'd stayed long enough in that lonely temple so long ago to retain some of those lessons about human responsibility.

"There are few fixed rules. Besides, you're right about needing to help yourself if you want to help Angie. So who was Tony, Brynn? What can you tell your daughter that will replace those images of horror in her mind?''

She swallowed several times before finding her voice. ''He

was confident and courageous—at least, that's the image he projected. In his personal life he was tender, thoughtful and so squeaky clean his closest friends teased him all the time. You know, the ex-altar boy, Eagle Scout, a wonderful son. Dominic had to be away from home a good deal when Tony was growing up, but Angelina never had to ask twice if she needed him to help in the interim. Oh, he was a kid, too. Flirted with every girl he met, but one call from his mother and nothing else mattered.''

"Did you know her?''

"No. She passed away during his freshman year in college.''

"And when did you two meet?''

"After he was already on the police force and had been on the streets enough to have a few commendations in his file. Being a cop was all he'd ever wanted, but he was ambitious in a good way. He was working on his master's degree, planning to move up into administration. It would have happened. He was one of those rare people who understood both sides of the job and could have mediated effective change.

"I worked in the college's administration offices.'' She smiled against his shoulder. "It seemed my role in life to keep him from taking on too much at one time.''

"I'll bet it was love at first sight for him.''

Honesty pulled the words out of him, an inexplicable sense of knowing. He didn't mean to embarrass Brynn, but he had no choice except to let go when she eased away from him.

"Sorry.''

She glanced away, her soft laugh self-conscious. "How do you do that, Gideon? Are you psychic or something? Is that your big secret?''

"Listeners always have the edge, and everything about you gives off the aura of a woman who'd been cherished.''

Her sigh was shaky. "I was.''

"Your Tony was a wise man...and a fortunate one. '

"How fortunate is a dead man?''

Her grief was a palpable thing. If left to steep, it would become toxic to her and everyone she came in contact with. He knew from experience, and didn't want that dark journey for her, could in fact lead her to the beginning of peace. It would cost her, though.

"So how did it go down?" he asked without warning.

She winced. "No more."

"You're not finished."

"I told you. He was murdered."

"And Angie saw it. Were there witnesses?"

"My daughter. If there were others, no one else came forward. A street gang's power is frightening."

"Tell me what you know."

She made a tormented, impatient sound. "What good would it do? He's gone!"

"And you still live with too much pain," he said with equal fervor. "Get it out. Tell me. Was it in daylight? In a store?"

"On the street! They'd gone to buy me flowers." She exhaled, the sound weary. "I'd so wanted to get out of the city, to buy a house with a huge yard. Tony tried to make up for the delay by bringing me flowers every Friday after he picked up Angie, who'd started day care.

"I don't know why they came after him. It was a good neighborhood with no reputation for gang-related crimes. I don't even know how he had time to get Angie into the car, or how she survived. I don't know. I don't know!"

This time Gideon didn't hesitate reaching for her. It was all he could offer. Too much to ask of himself, but what he needed to do.

This time he stroked her hair. It was loose this morning, as golden as the coming dawn would be. Its softness was a balm to his own emptiness...as was the smooth, warm forehead she stroked against his cheek.

"It's hard to live with questions," he said, looking far into the past. "But it can also be a kindness."

"Except in this case. Angie carries the answers alone. The least I can do is help her bear the weight."

"That's guilt talking. You weren't there, and you've convinced yourself that things might have been different if you had been. And you know what? You're right. You and your daughter would both be dead, because you're not the kind of woman to leave anyone to face danger alone." He closed his eyes, the picture frighteningly clear. "All wishful thinking does is make you crazy. I know. And even now there are times when I'm not sure I made it back from the darkness."

He felt her gaze, but didn't allow himself to open his eyes. She was too close to risk it.

"Who are you, Gideon?"

"When I figure it out, I'll let you know."

"Your eyes are always so sad."

"That comes from having made too many mistakes and being just smart enough to know it."

"But you're so reasonable, so…gentle."

"You know this, do you?"

"I know what I feel. What I sense."

God, she was destroying him, severing his willpower, thread by thread. He would only have to lean forward a few inches, less, to find out if she tasted as sweet as she smelled; and he wanted that knowledge badly enough not to let it matter what day this was.

The stench of his own self-loathing had him lunging out of the car. "I need a shower, and you need those cuts and scratches taken care of. I'm taking you home."

Brynn didn't protest this time, but he felt her gaze as he made his way around the front of the car. Her quiet study affected him, so that when he slid behind the steering wheel, his palms were damp. Him. The forty-five-year-old veteran tough guy with enough Zen philosophy in his head to put his students into a coma for months. It was almost funny if it didn't worry him so damned much.

"I didn't mean to make you angry."

He keyed the ignition and the car roared to life like an annoyed old lion. "You didn't."

"You don't like questions. I shouldn't have pried."

"There's only curiosity or Alzheimer's. Anything in between is self-absorption."

"I'll have to remember that one." There was the return of a smile in her voice. "Will you at least tell me why you're not home full-time, now that school's out for the summer?"

"Because Lillian always brainwashes or bullies me into teaching the summer semester."

"Do you mind, really?"

"It depends on the class."

"What made you want to be a teacher?"

"The guaranteed anonymity."

Her lips twitched. "All right. I'll stop."

He let her think his answer was a joke and quickly covered the short distance from the park to her street. As he pulled in to the driveway, his thoughts turned to concern about Dominic. A part of him hoped the old fool didn't hear them; the other part hoped the guy flew out with his fists up, so he could prepare him for dentures.

Dominic did emerge as he shut off the engine, but not with the charging-bear attitude Gideon knew him capable of. Although scowling, the man ignored him, rounding the front of the car to peer at Brynn, who was slower to get out.

"*Madre...* Brynn! What happened?"

"It looks worse than it is. Just a silly encounter with a bike."

"What can I do? Let me help you."

"Really, I'm only a bit stiff."

"You can barely walk. I'll carry you."

She shot him a look that had him taking a step back.

"Ah, *la figlia,* you are still thinking about yesterday. Forgive me. I was, as you say, insensitive. It's because I think—" he touched a finger to his temple "—tears cannot help. What's in the heart must be silent."

"I'm sorry, but I don't agree."

He nodded vigorously. "Right after breakfast I go to confession and tell Father Dolan to be extra strict with me."

"Tell him about your squabbling with Lillian, too."

The gentle rebuke had him ducking his head like a kid caught trying to make points with his first girlfriend. "Brynn, *mia,* I confess all that at one time, Dolan keeps me on my knees all day."

"At least the neighborhood would be quiet for a change." Lillian appeared from around the front of her house, sophisticated in an emerald-and-black bolero-style suit. When she saw Brynn she gasped. "Darling, bless your heart!"

"Don't get too close." Brynn warned her off with her palms as Lillian rushed over. "You look too pretty to mess up."

"Never mind me, dear, tell me about you. Did you fall?"

"Sort of. I, um, needed some fresh air, so I went to the park and didn't look where I was going. Fortunately, Gideon was jogging at the time and helped me home."

He found three pairs of eyes settling on him, covering the emotional spectrum of open dislike to warm approval and very little in between. Since Brynn's hands were injured, he offered the keys to Dominic.

"For what you did for my Brynn," the Italian said stiffly, "I thank you. I still don't like you, but I thank you."

"Pop."

"Oh, for…" Lillian sighed in exasperation. "It would cost you so much to say something nice for once?"

Dominic lifted his massive shoulders. "I just did. But I was honest about it."

"Let it go, Lillian," Gideon said. He didn't want to see this turning into a repeat of yesterday.

"Hey," Dominic snapped. "She's talking to me!" Then he turned to his neighbor and pointed. "And who are you to intervene? You who do not keep your word."

"Neither do you."

"I am like this ground. Solid."

"Try dense."

An exhausted Brynn shook her head and started limping for the front door. Gideon followed, more than willing to let the other two go at each other if it meant giving Brynn some peace.

"Are you going to be all right?"

"If you'll give me a hand up these stairs, I will be."

Maybe it was that his anger with Dominic got the best of him; maybe he simply needed to touch her one last time. In any case, Gideon swept her into his arms and up the six stairs to the storm door. Shifting, to keep her from reaching for the handle herself, he opened it and carried her inside.

She remained silent until he eyed the stairs.

"Don't even think it." Although she spoke softly, her will remained strong. "Unless you intend that I go to the hospital next."

"You weigh nothing."

"I meant when Dominic sees you in here. You think he's angry *now*. Though I may have myself admitted just to get some rest. Put me down, Gideon," she all but whispered.

He did, aware of how the air between them had suddenly gone electric again. "All right?"

"I will be, thank you. For everything."

"Then if you don't mind, I'll slip out the back way."

"That might be wiser."

He nodded, but didn't budge. It shouldn't have been possible, but tears had made the blue of her eyes clearer, deeper, and he felt like a high diver going down, down into territory no man had ventured before.

"I—I think I hear Angie rousing upstairs."

He forced himself to break the contact. "I'm going. Take care of yourself."

He didn't say goodbye because he knew it wasn't, and he didn't let himself look back. As he descended the stairs, he listened for Dominic's and Lillian's voices, but the birds had control of the air again. However, once he had started toward his house, he heard "Psst!"

He spotted her at the back door of her house. What she

was doing there he didn't know, but she was signaling him to come over.

"Aren't you supposed to be somewhere?" he asked almost at the patio.

"I'm too upset to be nice to a bunch of politicians. Come in and have a Bloody Mary with me."

"It's not even seven o'clock, Lillian."

"For pity's sake. You only sleep thirty minutes every other week or so, since when did time mean anything to you? Okay," she droned, "I'll throw in an omelet."

"You should at least let me go home and shower."

"Then you'll think of an excuse not to come back, I know you at least that well. Come on, Gideon, do an old broad a favor and let me ogle a sparsely dressed male for a change. I'll let you clean up while I'm mixing our drinks."

She was in a mood, and he supposed he should find out why. Certain he would regret it, though, Gideon followed her inside.

Chapter Six

Just like the classy gray-brick-and-white accents on the outside, the inside of Lillian's house welcomed with an air of low-key formality. Today, though, Gideon didn't plan to go beyond her stainless-and-ivory kitchen. He slid onto a rattan-and-leather stool and stroked one of the white and pink daylilies arranged before him.

"Why isn't Anthony Quinn Junior getting this invitation to Mary and Mush?"

Lillian pursed her lips as she slipped off her jacket and reached for the apron hanging inside the pantry. "Go ahead, get that rapier tongue primed. I deserve it."

"And more." He rested his elbow on the counter, his chin in his hand. "What are you doing, boss? You sounded like an aspiring fishwife out there, and then it's me you bring home for brunch? That's not the way to an old sea dog's heart."

"Why do you think I'm making these?"

With impressive precision she filled a tall cylinder, not

unlike her crystal vase, with ice, a large can of vegetable juice, hot sauce and vodka. Gideon lifted his eyebrows at the amount of vodka. Stirring briskly, she poured the concoction into two old-fashioned glasses.

"I'm sorry for coming out there and starting that nonsense again," she drawled, handing him one of the drinks. "Especially today of all days."

"Why did you?"

"Ask me the chemical ingredients in hair spritz, that would be easier."

He watched her down a third of her drink, thinking that he'd never seen her quite so on edge. She had a knack for fitting in and making you feel comfortable, which was why both men and women liked her, why funding for special projects came in with slightly less hassle than at other schools, why she was wanted at everyone's business event or social gathering. He didn't know the secret to them getting along so well, except perhaps for moments like this when she could be the real Lillian Winklebeck Brumley Littlejohn—and he could almost forget the real him.

"Evasion is my game," he said, preferring to stir rather than taste.

"Well, it's not as though you don't know. It's the same old story, okay? The man drives me nuts."

"Not that I feel remotely like defending him, but you're not doing a bad job on him, either. Which is the only reason I'm listening to this. You mess with his head, Brynn pays."

"You don't think I've figured that out?"

"Then for all of our sakes, have the affair and be done with it."

"This is the advice from the monk of Louisiana?" When he remained silent she made a face. "If I must spell it out, I made a commitment and got cold feet, which is the real reason Dominic is annoyed with me. It only happened because he was in that damned hospital bed and made me feel sorry for him."

"Did he? Before or after he confessed to snooping into my past?"

She winced. "Don't remind me, will you please." Clutching her glass, she paced the length of the kitchen. "It wouldn't work out, anyway. What do I have in common with a male chauvinist ex-sailor, who thinks there hasn't been any decent music since Guy Lombardo died? If I took him with me to a social event, he would be as likely to pinch a woman's bottom as he would to invite a man to arm wrestle."

"Considering some of the sleepers you've told me about, that might be a refreshing change of pace." But Gideon saw something in Lillian's eyes that he hadn't seen before. "You're afraid. This may be the one, but he doesn't fill the rest of the criteria."

Her guilty look told him that she agreed. "You want to know the kicker to all of this? I come from insurance, I married into oil, then booze...but he has the best name of all of them."

Gideon had heard enough. As disappointed in her as he was in Brynn's father-in-law, he headed for the door. "When you find out what that means to you, you'll have the answer to your dilemma."

Brynn cleaned up and changed before going to Angie's room. Not surprisingly, she found the child at the window, her head resting on one arm as she waved sleepily with the other hand. Joining her, Brynn fully expected to see Gideon waving back—but not letting himself into his yard still dressed in his jogging clothes.

Spotting her, he paused.

Aside from her curiosity about where he'd been that he hadn't changed yet, it struck her that she was no less aware of his maleness from a distance than she'd been when in his arms. Bad timing or not, he reminded her of all she'd missed this past year—the touching, sharing, loving...and her body responded with an ache of longing and hunger that had her almost groaning out loud.

She turned away from the window and sank onto Angie's bed, not at all happy with the weakness that had nothing to do with missing a meal. Upon rising from her seat and seeing her injuries, Angie wrapped her tiny arms around Brynn's waist.

"Oh, baby."

This is what she needed to focus on.

She needed to get a life for herself and her sweet child. Well, more of one. Maybe it was the day, but the truth had never been more obvious. Although they were making some progress—and she still didn't want to force her child into dealing with head doctors—Angie needed to be assimilated back into the mainstream. She needed to be with children her own age again.

She just wished that didn't make her feel as though she was abandoning the man who'd helped her bring this precious bundle into this world.

No light filled the room, no hologram-type image of Tony appeared to reassure her that this was the right thing to do. How much easier it was for people in the movies.

With a sigh, she hugged Angie once more. "Well, kiddo, what do you say we get you all gussied up and go find something good to eat?"

Less than twenty minutes later she and Angie entered the kitchen to find Dominic at the stove. She had already figured out by the smells and noises that he'd started breakfast. His movements and mutterings, however, made him look and sound as though he was trying to destroy evidence at the scene of a crime.

"Child on deck," Brynn murmured, wanting to at least protect her daughter's ears.

Dominic glanced over his shoulder, but avoided her gaze, focusing instead on his granddaughter.

"Hey, there she is. Your grampa makes pancakes with fresh strawberries today. Sit. Have some milk first."

"Don't get carried away," Brynn reminded him. "You know she still doesn't eat that much."

His gaze lifted as far as her hands and his frown deepened. "You put something on those?"

They were polite words—but a little short on warmth. "A little cream. They're fine."

"You limp."

"So, I won't roller blade for a few days. It's nothing serious."

He tossed the knife he'd been slicing strawberries with into the sink. "If you had stayed home, you wouldn't be hurt."

"I wanted some space and time to think. If you're upset that I took the car—"

"You want the car, you take it. But I can worry, no?"

It was a perfect opening. She almost imagined an invisible nudge at her back. "Well, it's interesting that you should say that. I've been thinking that it might be time to take the next step in getting settled here." Seeing the look he shot her, she continued quickly. "With Angie starting kindergarten next year, she's going to be behind if I don't start getting her back in contact with kids and learning."

"She learns now. You read to her, do lessons."

"That's different."

"What are you saying?"

Dominic paused, masher in hand. No "sissy" electric appliances for him, he'd told her before. He was convinced things tasted better when done the "real" way. Even the coffee was made in a nearly antique pot on the stove.

"Preschool. I'm going to enroll her."

"How can you? She can't speak."

"She doesn't speak. That doesn't mean she won't. And she can hear." Feeling better now that she'd started, she continued. "Having new playmates will make things easier, I think. Help her to forget."

"She will never forget her father!"

Brynn wondered what she could say that wouldn't sound

wrong to this man today. "Dominic, please. Of course I didn't mean Tony, and outbursts like that don't help any of us."

"You're right, you're right." He quickly kissed her on the forehead, as he often did. "Forgive me. It's the day, and seeing you that way... I'm all right now."

"Good, because I'm not done. I'm going to shop for a car next week, and then I'm going to look for a job."

He slapped the countertop with the flat of his hand. "This is because of what happened outside, *sì?* It's not my fault. The woman is like an angry hen—she pecks and pecks. Nothing I do or say is right."

Brynn drew a calming breath. "Dominic, I'll admit I'm disappointed that you and Lillian can't seem to communicate without ending up in an argument, but it's not one issue alone that's convinced me it's time for change."

"But how much change do you want? You moved here."

"And that's a wonderful beginning, but that's not all there is to my life. Look, didn't you need more when you retired, and didn't you take the job at the market as a result? Well, it's the same for me. For both of us," she added, gesturing to include Angie, who was more interested in turning her milk glass into a helicopter with the help of the silverware.

As Brynn stepped over to save her from creating a mess, someone knocked at the back door. A moment later Lillian stepped inside.

"Am I intruding?"

"Yes," Dominic snapped.

"No!" Brynn shot him a warning look. "Lillian, come in. I thought you had an appointment?"

The woman's expression was wry as she stepped inside. "I changed my mind." She handed over a bouquet of day-lilies. "These are a peace offering. To both of you," she added, sliding a glance to Dominic.

Since he made no reply, Brynn took control of the conversation. "How thoughtful. These are gorgeous. Won't they brighten the room, Angie? Lillian, why don't you sit down while I put them in water. Can I get you a cup of coffee?''

"No, thank you, dear. I'm beyond that point. And the truth is that I really don't want to intrude on your family time, especially today. I just wanted to say something to Dominic, but apparently my timing leaves something to be desired. Again.''

"You can say that again," Dominic said to no one in particular.

"We are not going to do this." Brynn took the spatula from him and thrust the bouquet into his arms. "It takes a big person to admit she made a mistake and to say she's sorry. Be angry with me later, listen now.''

He looked from her to the flowers and, drawing in a deep breath, reached for a large pitcher from a top cabinet. "The flowers are nice.''

"Thank you." Lillian appeared equally awkward. "Um, how are you feeling, Brynn?''

"Twice as embarrassed as I am achy." She scooped two of the smaller pancakes onto a platter and added whipped cream and strawberries before placing it before her daughter.

"Oh, well…we all get preoccupied and do things we later regret." Lillian cast Dominic another glance before leaning toward the child. "Why don't I help you cut that, sweetie, okay? Dear me—" She backed off at the sight of Angie's lower lip trembling. "Maybe Grampa can do it better.''

He was at Angie's side immediately, tsking and cooing and helping her cope with her knife and fork. "You're Miss Independent, that's all, eh? We all know someone like that.''

Brynn winced and held her breath, trying not to glance over her shoulder.

"It's not always the best strategy…for an adult," Lillian said.

Dominic hesitated. "But sometimes an understandable one.''

Exhaling, Brynn smiled into the new batch of browning pancakes.

"Then," Lillian said slowly, "do you suppose if a person asked a person to maybe have dinner, a dinner promised before but put off for...independent reasons...a person could ask?"

How did intelligent people get themselves into such a silly mess? Brynn could barely keep her silence. She wanted to help, to tell both of them to stop wasting time. Life was precious. Why weren't they enjoying it and each other while they could?

"A person could ask." The warmth had returned to Dominic's rumbling bass voice. Then he pointed his thumb at his chest. "But I'm buying."

They had their date on the following Saturday evening. Brynn had never seen anyone with such a case of nerves as Dominic. Days before, he tried on every tie he owned and ended up driving into town to buy another, adding a new pair of shoes on impulse.

"You ever notice Lillian's shoes?" he asked Brynn when he'd shown her his purchases. "She buys only the best. I don't want her ashamed of me."

On D-Day, a full half hour before he was due at her door, he stood before the full-length mirror on the inside door of the coat closet looking miserable with the results.

"I look like I'm from *il circo*. The circus."

He wore the navy blue suit he'd worn last week to church. She and Angie had accompanied him, because a special mass had been held for Tony. The new tie, in a rich maroon, set off the lightest of pink silk shirts—Brynn's input.

"How can you say that?" Brynn circled him and straightened the tie. "You look quite the distinguished gentleman, doesn't he, angel?"

Angie watched from her seat at the bottom of the stairs, moving her lips in what they were accepting these days as a polite smile.

"The tie...it's not too bright?"

"It adds the exact right amount of dash. I think it brings out the devil in your eyes."

"That's indigestion from lunch. I could use a beer."

"Is that a good idea? You'll probably have wine soon."

He mumbled that she was right and fretted some more. "She's a *prominent lady in town*, Brynn. Suppose I embarrass her?"

How amazing, she thought; anxiety about dating never stopped, regardless of one's age. "She's your neighbor and a woman who wants to be a good friend. Try to remember that and forget the rest."

When he finally escorted Lillian to his car and drove off, Brynn watched them from the front door, holding Angie in her arms. "Let's hope," she said, kissing her daughter's cheek before setting her on her feet again, "that this isn't the world's shortest date. And now, love of my life, what's your pleasure? A puzzle? Maybe a quick drive to the park to feed the ducks?"

Angie immediately ran to the kitchen and pointed out the door. It didn't take a mind reader to know what she wanted.

"Sweetie, if you were a robot, I'd check you for a faulty computer chip."

She glanced outside. The sun hadn't yet set, and as usual from this spot, they could catch long glimpses of Gideon as he moved around in his yard.

It wouldn't be right to intrude. He'd been wonderful all week waving to Angie, saying a few words to her when she clung to his gate. But Brynn knew he would prefer not to be the object of Angie's continued fixation; what's more, it was getting harder and harder for her to look at him without acknowledging the attraction that neither of them wanted but couldn't seem to stop.

She remembered something else that might work. "I have an idea. Do you know the Lapierres' mommy dog had her puppies the other day? Maybe we can get a peek before it gets dark."

Angie accepted that with a fair amount of grace, and after

locking up, Brynn led her down the oak-lined street. A few older children passed them on bikes and skateboards, reminding her again that there didn't seem to be anyone nearby who was Angie's age to play with—had she been willing to make friends. For the most part, though, people were staying indoors where the air-conditioning protected them from the late-June heat and humidity.

Arriving at their destination, she found her hopes had been too high; the Lapierres weren't home. Brynn supposed they wouldn't have minded if she'd opened the gate to spend a few minutes with the mixed-breed dog Molly, and to peek at her new family. The Lapierres were a friendly couple with teenage boys and went to the same church her family did. But she didn't know how Molly would take the intrusion.

Once she explained to Angie, her daughter bolted straight for the alley.

"Angie, not so fast. Watch for a car backing out!"

There was no question as to where the little imp was heading. By the time Brynn got to his gate herself, Gideon was there crouching before her daughter and reaching through the bars to brush a strand of hair from her forehead. Brynn couldn't tell what got to her more, the tenderness with which he looked at her child, or the electric charge that jolted her heart when he lifted his gaze to her.

"A bit steamy for jogging."

Still breathless, she tried for a chuckle that ended up more of a gasp. "Tell me about it. I was trying to make this one sleepy enough to go to bed by walking her down to see some new puppies, but the Lapierres are out." And if she'd known she would have to chase after her daughter, she would have worn something other than this coral pink dress. Despite its scooped neck and long gauzy skirt, the waffled thermal bodice and three-quarter sleeves clung to the rest of her heated skin.

"I see Lillian and your father-in-law are off."

The few times they'd been close enough to talk, they'd

filled the increasingly difficult silences by discussing the odds of the dinner date actually taking place at all.

"Can you believe it? To be honest, I half expected to see Dominic's car in the driveway just now."

"Maybe it will help both of them to be out of their comfort zone."

"It can't hurt. But if that pugilistic attitude is their idea of romance, they can have it."

"I couldn't agree with you more."

Inevitably, Brynn sensed the innuendo in the remark and she refocused on his garden. "Every time I look in here, there's something new. Oh, your Mandevillea is blooming." It was barely visible from where she stood, and from what he'd told her before, an accent piece to the pond that she also couldn't see.

After a slight hesitation, Gideon rose and began unlocking the gate.

"What are you doing?"

"Come take a closer look."

He knew the decision was a mistake—probably a huge one—but what could he do when she sounded as excited as her child looked? In a way, what he did was art, and even the most arrogant artists needed an occasional audience.

Although he swung the gate wide, she didn't budge, and because she didn't, her child hesitated.

"Gideon, are you sure?"

"I wouldn't have opened it otherwise." He didn't do anything he didn't want anymore. Letting her get used to the idea, he offered his hand to her daughter. "Welcome, princess. Would you like a tour of my oasis?"

Giving her mother a beatific look, Angie put her hand in his. The trusting gesture triggered a spasm of sweet pain he was careful not to disclose.

"Come see this." He led the way to a great stone that was concave in the center. "This is a *tsukubai*, for ceremonial washing." Although he spoke to Angie, he was acutely aware that Brynn had followed them. "Someone in Japan put it on a boat and sailed it all across the ocean so I could have it. Do you know where Japan is?"

Angie pointed toward Florida.

He smiled. "Well, you could take that route. But eventually you'd have to hang a sharp left." With a nod of his head he indicated the orange-and-lavender sky behind him. "See where the sun has gone? That's a slightly shorter route."

"Don't be too good at this, please," Brynn murmured. "Unless you want to start taping bedtime stories."

He watched her stroll on her own, stopping frequently to get a closer look at the compositions he'd made of plants, stone and sand, wondered if she understood that the almost understated design was typical of Eastern gardens; how the shape of the land, the feel of the earth, the very atmosphere had all been crucial in making his decisions of what to place where. No, he reminded himself. It took masters decades, a lifetime to comprehend the centuries of history and mythology that went into forming styles...and how that process, like evolution, was constantly unfolding its wisdom, offering new challenges. But she could and was appreciating the esoterics on an emotional level, and that meant enough to him.

"This is an *ishi-doro*. Lantern," he continued, interpreting for Angie's entertainment.

The stone lamp he stopped at was nearly as tall as the child and styled in the traditional shape of a pagoda. Within was a large white candle that he lit with the lighter in his pocket. The glow added to the radiance of the waning day.

A tiered, slatted stand against the southern side of the fence displayed his collection of bonsai, and he led his guests there next. The specimens took turns adding emphasis and drama to various parts of the garden, especially the blooming varieties like the quince Brynn paused by that he managed to coax into bloom more often than in the early spring.

"They're almost too delicate to be real," she said. There

was reverence in the way she reached out to touch a pink blossom, only to pull back. "And so mysterious."

"No more mystery than there is with mathematics. It's all about knowledge. In the case of bonsai, that knowledge is simply an extension of your basic horticultural principles multiplied by an increased investment of time. A great deal of time," he added dryly.

"It shows. So how old are these?"

"Nothing here is under ten years old. It takes that long before a plant starts coming into its own. Most are much older." He pointed to a two-foot-tall cluster of Ezo spruce that reminded him of the gnarled cypress found in the Louisiana bayou. "This one is twenty-five—in a way less time-consuming because it's to the point where it only needs repotting every three years or so."

"How often did it get repotted in the beginning?"

"Every year. Then around the age of fifteen, every two years, and so on."

"You can't possibly remember all that...can you?"

"No, I keep a journal. Also to keep track of the trimming, pinching, propagation and feeding."

Pleased that she seemed genuinely interested, he briefly explained the concept of thinning root systems and training branches to minimize the size of the plant, while maximizing the aging effect.

Brynn lifted Angie to point out unique features on several specimens. Finally she shook her head. "I've seen impressive photographs in magazines and attended a party once where all the centerpieces were bonsai, but I had no idea of the investment of time and labor involved."

"Most people don't, which is why there are so many bonsai murderers out there." He enjoyed the twitch of her lips. "For instance, those centerpieces you mentioned—the longer they remained indoors, the more they would have to have been misted. Central heating and air-conditioning tends to be too brutal on bonsai. I once read where a celebrated Japanese singer had a nervous breakdown after rushing home several times a day to mist and water his collection."

Brynn searched his face as though to check if he was teasing her again, then shook her head. "Incredible." Then she moved on, only to stop before a juniper close to the back deck that looked like the grandfather of all trees.

"One hundred and seventy," he said, guessing her question.

She took a step back.

He stretched out his arm as a guard because the path was narrow. "What?"

"I feel as though I should...pray or something."

He nodded. "You've grasped the underlying purpose for places like this. Maybe even for the art itself. Eastern cultures believe that we're all connected, and if we're all connected, then we all have a consciousness. Every stone, every branch, everywhere you place your foot or rest your back."

Angie looked down at the flat slab she stood on, an enchanted expression on her face. For her part, Brynn appeared dismayed.

"Then clue me in as to where we're supposed to step without crushing anything?"

"The earth doesn't mind you walking on it, only that you appreciate being allowed to."

"That's a great deal to be aware of," she replied quietly.

"I said the same thing once to my—to someone. Except that I didn't voice it as politely as you did. Even grasping a fraction of what it means to be universally conscious takes true masters like Tanka the major part of their lives, while the concept itself is as simple as picturing a blossom opening to receive the sun's warmth and light." He nodded at Angie. "She knows. It's only later when we get hardened and materialistic that we go deaf and blind."

Abruptly he turned away. It had been a mistake to mention Tanka; new questions brightened Brynn's lovely eyes, and he found himself too tempted to keep feeding answers to her.

"I have no skills at being a host." He gestured to the

simple bench on the porch. "Would you care to sit? Angie can play with the *tsukubai* if she likes."

He wondered if the words came out as coarse and halting as they sounded to him, but Brynn didn't seem to notice. Her attention was on the bamboo cup with the long handle lying across the stone.

"That doesn't look like a toy, and we've obviously kept you from your work long enough."

"I'm done for the day. I'd just been cleaning and wrapping my tools."

She considered the leather case lying open on the deck, which he'd gestured to. "Everything is so meticulous. Don't tell me there's a ceremony or law of some kind for handling them, too?"

"The law of ouch," he drawled, allowing his gaze to linger on her profile. "Some bonsai artists spend a thousand dollars for what a hack would substitute with a three-dollar clipper."

"Ouch indeed." Brynn caught Angie as she stepped toward the implements. "Are those...?"

"Not quite as valuable as the crown jewels...and more than a pizza."

"Angel, that does it for us. This isn't a playground." Brynn stooped to lift the child into her arms.

He knew he should let her go, knew he'd allowed himself the luxury of her company for too long as it was, but heaven forgive him, he wasn't ready to say good-night.

"I didn't say that to scare you off. Brynn. Sit," he said when she appeared intent on ignoring that. "I know I make you uncomfortable with my staring, but you must know you're safe with me in that respect?"

The amber of sundown had given way to the melancholy shadows of dusk; nevertheless, her expression was clearly visible and told him that she was as worried as she was confused and tempted.

"Are you sure, Gideon? And how am I not safe?"

Before he could answer, Angie settled the decision for

them. Once her mother's hold of her eased, she trotted happily to the lantern and squatted to watch the candle's flame dance in the mildest of breezes.

"Mutiny again," Brynn murmured. Slowly she sat.

No less aware, he lowered himself beside her. "Maybe we need to talk this out."

"I think I'd rather have my wisdom teeth extracted without anesthesia. As luck would have it, though, they're already out."

"Do I make you that uncomfortable?"

"I don't know what you make me, Gideon. That's the problem. You suck me in and spit me out, and I'm left spinning, without a clue as to how to act the next time I see you."

"Is that the real reason why you bought the new car?" he asked, nodding to the jade green coupe they could barely see beyond the fence. "And intend to put Angie in day care?" At her stunned reaction, he shrugged. "Dominic isn't happy about the school and complained to Lillian, who satisfies a subtle sadistic streak in herself by feeding me bits of information about you."

Brynn closed her eyes. "You see? You're doing it again, speaking in riddles, saying something entirely different with a glance…"

A dog barked somewhere, and the birds that had been chirping in the Delmarcos' yard as they enjoyed their last feeding of the day grew silent one by one. Crickets and tree frogs took up the responsibility of providing the music of the night.

"Things can't go on as they are," she said slowly.

"No. But is day care the answer?"

"It's not fair for me to ask you to be responsible for Angie's happiness. You're right about this being an oasis. She needed it when we first got here, and you can see she still does. But…"

"She needs more. So do you."

"I love Dominic dearly—however, not blindly. If I give

him the rein, he'll tie me so tightly to him and his house, I'll suffocate, or lose myself, whatever comes first.'' She exhaled, the sound a mirthless laugh. ''I would think you'd be relieved to be rid of me. Us.''

''Do you know what it's like to come home every day and know someone cares that you do? I never have. Not before you and your child moved in over there,'' he said, nodding to her home. ''Relieved? No, I'm not relieved. But I do know you two are a gift I can't keep any more than Dominic can.''

Chapter Seven

Brynn didn't know what to say. She'd never heard him sound so fatalistic and yet anguished.

"Have you always been alone, Gideon?"

"Basically."

She waited for more. It didn't come. "That's it?"

"Knowing about me can't help you, Brynn."

"You were the one to suggest we talk things out."

"Only because of what's happening between us. I don't want to upset your life any more than I already have. Otherwise I may have to consider putting my house up for sale."

That had her staring at him. "Gideon, no! After all that you've done here?"

"Do you think I want to? But I don't relish feeling as though I'm being gutted every time I look into your eyes, either. I don't know what's the greater torment, seeing your attraction or watching your guilt because you think being a normal human being is somehow making you unfaithful to your late husband."

She was that transparent? "Forgive me." She closed her eyes, wishing she'd never agreed to move down here.

"For what? Being everything a man could dream of? Brynn, if I wasn't who I was, I wouldn't let Tony's memory stand in my way, or Dominic's dislike. I'd even use your child to get at you if necessary."

He spoke those last words with such a cold confidence, she almost shivered. "There you go again, insinuating things as though you're trying to make me believe you're some kind of monster."

"Close."

"You're frightening me. I don't like it."

"It can't be helped."

She could see he believed that, and thought of the worst thing he could confess to her. "Are you...were you in prison, Gideon?"

Not a muscle in his face moved. "You don't put men like me in prison. If you can catch us, you kill us."

"My God." That left her with a short list of choices to contemplate, something she didn't want to do, either. And what would Dominic say if he heard this, knew that he'd been right about his mysterious neighbor?

"Now are you beginning to understand? I'm not fit to be within a mile of you, but I'm here anyway because I'm too selfish and too hungry for even this morsel of your time to deny myself."

Her heart pounded so fiercely, she thought it might burst against her sternum. "Maybe I'm the one who should move."

"You won't do that to Dominic. His beliefs might be archaic, his personality unrefined, but his heart is in the right place and it's filled with you and Angie. No," he said on a sigh. "You're doing the only thing you can do, but I want you to fully understand why. Aside from Angie needing to learn to trust again, to believe that she can be safe away from you...you have to look to your own needs."

He was throwing so much at her, she could barely think.

"How like you to know me better than I know myself. But Dominic is no more happy about me looking for work than he is with the prospect of Angie going to day care."

"Dominic finds comfort in clinging to simpler times. He doesn't understand what happens if you show a woman the sky and then tell her she can't fly. What kind of work will you look for?"

"I hate to disappoint you, but nothing that requires soaring. At this stage, I'm not about to turn myself into super-woman striving to balance a career at the cost of my child's emotional nourishment or stability. Just something part-time."

"Want me to talk to Lillian and see if she knows of anything?"

"Lillian the Subtle Sadist? Wouldn't she love that?"

"You have a point."

"There is something that you can do for me." She waited for him to meet her gaze. "Don't stop being my friend."

He didn't look altogether happy with that. "You have a strange perception of friendship."

"Whether you want to admit it or not, you have been one."

"Surely you still have ties to people in Chicago?"

"Of course. But that's so far away, and whether you mean it to or not, distance changes things." When he remained silent, she added, "You're friends with Lillian."

"There's just one small difference. I've never wanted to make love to Lillian."

Although her entire body tingled in reaction to those roughly tender words, Brynn struggled to remain focused. "I'm not going to let you get away with not answering me."

"You want this, after what I told you about me?"

"You intimated...and, yes, you did a good job of disturbing me. But whoever, whatever you were, you're not that now."

"You think I've redeemed myself?"

"We all change."

"I'd have to have more lives than a cat to do that. I was bad, Brynn. I was a nightmare. Believe it."

"What I believe is the goodness in the man who's twice come to my rescue and has touched my daughter in a way no one else has been able to in over a year," Brynn replied, growing surprisingly calm.

Angie returned, yawning.

"It is bedtime, isn't it?" She lifted her daughter, loving how the child wrapped her little arms around her neck, and pressed a kiss on her cheek. Over her daughter's shoulder she met Gideon's troubled but yearning gaze. On impulse, she rose on tiptoe and brushed a kiss along his jawline. "Good night, Gideon. Please don't brood too much."

Brynn herself had little time to worry over the next few days as she began visiting day care centers. Her schedule full of appointments, she was glad she'd decided not to job hunt at the same time, but rather wait until Angie was settled somewhere and seemed to be adjusting. However, after scratching off three centers from her list on Monday, and two on Tuesday, she began to worry that she might never get as far as reading the classified ads. All things considered, Blanchette was a small town, and she was running out of options. On the other hand, she wasn't about to force Angie to go to a school where she would be unhappy.

On Tuesday evening after dinner, the two of them sat at the kitchen table. "I can see only one other option," she told her daughter. "I think we're going to have to drive all the way across town and try Good Beginnings."

Through her inquiries she'd learned that the facility had the best reputation of all the day care centers in the community, but its location had stopped her from making it among her early choices. After all, she didn't know where she would end up working, and hadn't wanted to initiate a stress factor from the onset if it could be avoided.

"You don't have to do anything," Dominic said from the counter. Tonight was his turn to do the dishes, and he was putting them away. "You could stay at home with her until she's fully ready to be with children again."

He said variations of the same thing every night, but Brynn refused to let it get to her. Besides, she'd never expected this to be easy. Before Tony's death, Angie had shown no signs of taking after the never-met-a-stranger Delmarco men. Her trauma had deepened that reserve.

"Pop, you know yourself that there are very few perfect situations in life," she told him. "And I think this is the right time for moving on to the next step. Speaking of time, did you make those reservations for the Fourth at Claude's? You said those window seats looking out on the pond will get booked fast."

"Ei! Subito." He dropped the towel to run for the phone book in the living room. "Immediately, I do it."

Smiling, Brynn shared a conspiratorial wink with her daughter.

When Dominic had announced that his dinner date with Lillian had gone so well that he'd convinced her to try a second outing, he'd suggested arranging for a picnic and taking Angie with them to enjoy the fireworks scheduled at the park. But Brynn had reminded him that the crowds, not to mention being so close to the gunshotlike sounds of some of the rockets, would be too much for her, so he'd agreed something else was called for. Angie hadn't seemed to care about not going, but once upstairs, when Brynn had quietly told her that they might get Gideon to let them watch the show from his porch, the child had reacted as though she was being given her life's dream.

That was still a few days away, though, and there were a few things to be seen to before then.

On Wednesday morning Brynn dressed her daughter in a pretty blue-and-white-plaid dress with sunflowers on the bib collar and drove to Good Beginnings. She liked the looks of the place immediately, from its sunny yellow-and-green exterior to the schedule she went over with Vanessa Gordon, the administrative head of the school. More important, when they were given a tour, Brynn liked the large, bright room and homey atmosphere of the group Angie would join. Although conservative in her acceptance, Angie seemed to, as well.

"Then we'll see you tomorrow, Angie," Mrs. Gordon said, leaning down to smile at the child.

Brynn felt like celebrating. After buckling Angie into her seat in the car, she gave her a playful, noisy kiss.

"You know what this calls for? A new outfit!"

Finding the right one took another half hour, and they were coming out of the clothing shop in the shopping center down the street from the school when Brynn saw Lillian emerging from a French-style café a few stores down. She was with several people, and Brynn wouldn't have thought of intruding, but then Lillian spotted her.

"Well, hello!" Lillian said something to her group and hurried over. "What are you doing here?"

Though too shy to make eye contact, when Lillian crouched to smile at Angie, the child held up her bag.

"We've been doing that infamous girl thing—shopping," Brynn said on her behalf. "Angie starts at Good Beginnings tomorrow and our wardrobe is long on dresses and short on pant and top sets."

"Always a lady like your mama." Lillian nodded approvingly at the child before returning her gaze to Brynn. "So you're ready to go to work. Has anyone snatched you up yet?"

"You and your sense of humor. I may be forced to ask the ice-cream vendor at the park if he'd consider job sharing. You know I'm only interested in starting with part-time work."

Lillian put her arm around her shoulders. "Dear heart, am I glad I ran into you."

"You had to do it, didn't you?"

Gideon frowned at Lillian's smug smile. Their paths had crossed when he was heading for home and she was returning from a business luncheon. She hadn't wasted any time in telling him about running into Brynn and hiring her on the spot for the office.

"I thought you were fully staffed at the office?"

"Past tense. Usually, the kids applying for those summer positions that always open up are reliable, but one just tore up a number of ligaments during a hike, and another had a family crisis back East that is forcing her to relocate to a school near home."

"But Angie hasn't been placed in a day care school yet."

Lillian's eyes began twinkling. "As of today she has. I just ran into them not ten minutes ago. I thought you'd be pleased. You two seem to be getting along better and better all the time."

"Knock it off." Gideon was in no mood for her droll sense of humor.

"Oh, all right. I suppose it's only fair, since you are being a prince not to tease me about Dominic."

"Because it's none of my business."

"So there you are, then. Who I hire for the office is mine."

Gideon narrowed his eyes. "What this campus needs is a good, old-fashioned riot. It's clear you have too much time on your hands."

"Speaking of rabble-rousing, I heard you had another lively class yesterday defending a certain former president."

"I didn't defend him. I merely pointed out that if one subscribes to the theory of ethics being taught at certain law schools these days—which you know better than to ask if I condone—he was no worse than any of the others, except that he got caught."

"Gideon, Gideon. You would have made one sexy dictator for some emerging small republic," Lillian mused.

"If that means you're suddenly worried about my unfiltered approach to feeding history to these barely tested minds, stop wheedling me into teaching the summer session every year."

"My, my, we're more sensitive than usual." When he didn't respond, Lillian sobered. "Is there something new going on between you and Brynn that I don't know about?"

He clenched his teeth. "Stay out of it, Lillian."

"Then I refuse to apologize that you're going to have to look at that lovely creature more than you already do. Heaven knows she's overqualified for the job, and I fully intend to use her expertise with computers to work some snags out of ours, but I'm not taking too much advantage. She does get to schedule her own hours."

"All that for minimum wage. You're a veritable saint."

Nonplussed, Lillian shook her head. "You know very well she doesn't need or give a fig about money. She needs a life."

"And what about me? Or don't my needs matter?"

"More than you can imagine, my dear. But we disagree on what's good for you, for the simple reason that I don't happen to loathe you as much as you do yourself." She began walking away and abruptly stopped. "Oh. By the way...in case you were planning on inviting me to watch the fireworks with you on your porch again, I'm afraid I've already made other plans. Dominic is taking me to Claude's. And in case you're determined to be obtuse, yes, that was a hint."

Gideon was over his anger by Saturday evening when Angie appeared at the gate. But if he hadn't been, he couldn't have remained in a bad mood once he saw how adorable she looked wearing a sailor's cap and a red-and-white sundress.

Despite Lillian's blatant hint, he hadn't extended an invitation, deciding to leave things to Brynn, and it was just late enough for him to have convinced himself that they weren't coming. Prepared for disappointment, he instead found himself watching the child wave hello with her small American flag, and point back at her mother.

This time his heart shot to his throat and stayed there.

"Am I being presumptuous?" She held up the pail of ice

cream and a box of cones as she drew near. In the twilight her eyes shimmered like a blue lagoon, identical to the tropical colors of her sarong-style dress.

Somehow he managed to make his fingers unlock the gate. "This is a surprise."

"A nice one, I hope. I did bring a bribe—fresh peach. That's why I'm later than planned. It didn't want to freeze."

A tug on his khaki pants gave him no opportunity to reply. He glanced down to see Angie holding up a scroll he hadn't noticed before. Crouching, he accepted it, not sure what to say.

"For me?" He held the scroll between his hands and ran the tip of his finger over the yellow tie that he recognized had formerly been one of the little girl's favorite hair ribbons. "Another first. No one's ever given me something like this before. Thank you."

Angie hid her smile behind her flag.

"Shall I open it?"

She nodded.

"It's her first project at day care," Brynn offered.

Glancing up, he saw her concern. She was letting him know the magnitude of responsibility that had been bestowed upon him.

"Then I'm doubly honored."

The drawing was of his garden. He was charmed by the point of view—the lantern as tall as a person and giving off enough light to illuminate Baton Rouge and maybe New Orleans, the bonsai plants ant-size with pancake-thin tops...

"You recognize yourself, of course," Brynn drawled.

The stick figure would have been anyone, except for the pains taken to recreate the beard, the T-shirt—black, as he wore tonight—and khaki pants.

"Angie, this has to be framed. I'll put it on my desk. It'll be the first thing I see when I go into my office to check my schedule every day, and the last thing before I turn in."

Angie patted his cheek and pointed to the basin.

"You want to wash up. By all means. Be careful not to get that pretty dress wet."

As she hopped like a frog from round step to round step, he rose and faced Brynn. "I'm glad you came."

"Are you? I almost chickened out."

He understood. Their contact had been brief during the week, minimal enough to make one believe the intimate conversation last weekend hadn't happened.

"So how is it going with...?" He tilted his head toward Angie.

She looked relieved for the change of subject. "Well, I won't deny that a part of me hoped she might miraculously jump into the car reciting Dr. Seuss when I picked her up that first day, but otherwise, I think it's going as expected. She keeps to herself, and they call me to ask about what certain hand signals mean." She added more brightly, "At least she isn't refusing to go back. Yet."

"And you? How are you adjusting to everything?

"It's hardly brain surgery, but I earn my salary."

"Less to keep you busy than you'd hoped?"

"I'm afraid that may be the case. Oh, there's a few weeks of work there, but once that other girl gets back on her feet..." She ran her teeth over her lower lip. "Surely Lillian wouldn't have hired me because of Dominic, would she?"

"Not Dominic, no."

She formed her mouth into a silent O. After a few seconds she indicated the ice cream.

"This needs to be eaten, or I can take it back home to our freezer."

She was embarrassed, and maybe a bit angry herself. Gideon didn't blame her; he'd already put in his hours of steaming. But he didn't want to be alone tonight.

"I've never had homemade peach ice cream before," he told her.

Her smile returned, and she turned her attention back to her daughter. It seemed Angie had finished washing her hands and was now patting the koi in the pond.

Brynn chuckled. "Great. You don't have to worry about your fish catching any kiddie crud. Angie! Come fill your cone before the fireworks start."

It was so easy after that, they could have been reading their parts in a script, instead of having to make things up as they went along. Not that anything said sounded artificial or forced. That amazed him as much as the incongruity of this evening happening at all.

He would have called it magic...if he believed in such things.

He was finishing his second cone when the show began. Because he had no tall trees in his yard, and the Delmarcos' house was spaced so that they were between two ancient oaks, he did, indeed, have a perfect viewing spot for the bulk of the fireworks display. By then Brynn had also explained why she hadn't let Angie go with her grandfather and Lillian tonight, and so early on, after a particularly loud explosion, Gideon lifted the little girl onto his lap and covered her ears whenever he anticipated a stunner. He could tell by her occasional stiffness that a good deal of noise bled through, and that had him quickly adding his own commentary.

"Ah, there's a red one like your dress. Look at that curl! It's the color of your hair."

All three of them sighed at the starbursts, and groaned when an expected dazzler turned out to be a dud. In another life they could have been man, wife and child—except that the complete comfortableness he sensed between them wasn't as it would be with an intimate couple who shared a child; the tension was greater because he and Brynn hadn't learned the secrets of each other's bodies. It also explained why she hung on his every word, but eased out of the way if his knee accidentally rubbed her thigh.

It was heaven, and he didn't want the rockets to stop filling the sky. But even before it was over, Brynn touched his arm.

"Look."

Angie was asleep, slumped against his chest, her limbs limp.

"You were very good with her," Brynn whispered.

"Yeah, I bored her to sleep."

"She's had a full day, as well as week, and it's way past her bedtime. You'd better ease her over to me. I'll take her home."

Brynn thought he stared at her as if she'd suggested he drop Angie in the lily pond. "What's wrong?"

"You can't carry her all that way and up two flights of stairs."

"Yes, I can."

"And manage the door, too? I don't think so."

He rose, and so did she.

"Gideon, Dominic and Lillian will be home soon."

"Even if they leave right after the show, they'll be stuck in traffic for a half hour. It will be all right. Besides, we don't want to jostle her too much and wake her."

Brynn gave in, and, collecting Angie's hat and flag, she opened the gate for him as well as the storm door at her place. The stove light provided ample illumination to guide them to the hall, where she turned on a table lamp to keep from having to switch on the stronger hallway bulbs.

Barely a minute later Gideon eased Angie onto her bed. As he stepped back he looked enchanted by her peacefulness and innocence.

"She smells so clean."

Murmuring her agreement, Brynn set Angie's things on the dresser and only took off the child's shoes and socks before drawing the throw over her. From the window seat she took the bear, whispering to Gideon that that's where Angie had put him so he could watch them, and tucked him into the nest between Angie's arm and body.

Stepping back to where Gideon stood, she added, "Sometimes she still has that wonderful baby smell. There's nothing like it. You think they're so sweet you could kiss them to pieces."

Signaling him that they should go, she switched on the ballerina night light and followed Gideon into the darker hall.

It was the oddest thing. A few steps out of the room and the strap on her right sandal broke. With a gasp of dismay at the thought of ruining almost-new shoes, she stopped. Gideon must have thought she had hurt herself and was losing her balance, and he quickly caught her by her upper arms to steady her.

"Are you all right?"

Both startled and amused, she laughed softly. "Yes, but—"

"What's so funny?"

"You're very gallant, but I'm really not being a klutz. My shoe broke."

He stayed close, anyway, as she slipped off both sandals and inspected the damage.

"Well, buy for fashion and repent in dollars," she mused.

"I'm just grateful you weren't carrying Angie when this happened."

At the thought of what could have occurred, she touched his chest. "You're so right! Oh, Gideon."

"Shh." The hands that had been on her arms moved to frame her face. "I should never have said anything. Now that lovely smile is gone."

She wanted to smile for him again, but she could feel the atmosphere changing, the very air growing thicker, until simply breathing became a chore. Because his thumbs were stroking the line of her jaw, caressing her cheeks. Because of the messages in his mysterious eyes. He was making her feel things she hadn't let herself feel in a long time. She might as well be standing in a tide pool with the sea rising over every inch of her body; her awareness and sensitivity to him were that saturating. When she didn't turn away from the thumb tracing her lower lip, she knew some vital part of her mind had short-circuited.

"You're so warm," he whispered, inching closer. "You glow with it. I feel like an iceberg inside compared to you."

Brynn closed her eyes, afraid he would see too much in them. "We shouldn't be standing here like this."

"No. My God," he rasped, "it's been so long, I'm shaking."

She could feel it. Her own nerves were none too steady, but his...

"Gideon. Why? You don't want this."

"No." He brushed his lips across her forehead, her cheekbones, each corner of her mouth. "But that doesn't keep me from believing I'll die if I don't touch you. Really touch you—" his breath merged with hers "—once."

"And after that..."

"Never again."

"Never."

With that oath, his mouth owned hers. That was the only word for something so immediate and complete. In the space of time it took her to part her lips to him, she knew it.

Joined, their desire carried its own taste and temperature, and they drank as though consumed by fever and starving, craving the flavors as much as the heat. Joined, his hands grew no less unsteady, but they moved with deft skill as they skimmed over her face and hair. It was as though a storm was coming and a high wind was warning, "Hurry! Hurry!"

Swept away, Brynn let the sandals slip from her fingers, and she slid her arms around Gideon's neck and into his hair. She eagerly answered the bold strokes of his tongue, went willingly as he eased her against the wall to press himself closer to her.

Her name was a whispered prayer when he broke the kiss to suck air into his lungs. "Forgive me," he added as he exhaled shakily.

"It's all right."

"No. No, it's not. But necessary—"

He initiated another, almost desperate kiss that again ended so abruptly she thought her breath was being sucked from her lungs.

"To glimpse what would have been, just a taste."

He was such a private man, those fragmented confessions stole her heart. Behind her closed lids, her eyes burned. Her own lonely, lonely months had taken their toll on her, too. She was brimming with what he needed, overflowing with unexpressed love, and burning from sexual heat contained for too long. She knew what he yearned for, and she wasn't strong enough to deny herself what this compelling man offered in return.

As he pressed himself into the cradle of her thighs, she locked her hands in a tight grip on his T-shirt. He couldn't keep his hands still, but it was his hair—disheveled from her touch and his eagerness—that caressed her face. She went in search of its silky touch, and the mouth so adept at making love to hers.

Whispering something in a language she didn't know, he gripped her hips and rocked his lower body so forcefully against hers, she could feel the blood pumping through his fierce arousal.

And suddenly there was more than their strained breaths and murmurs. But the sharp cry echoing through the hall wasn't hers. Or his.

"Bastard! You *dare...?*"

Chapter Eight

Dominic! The sight of her father-in-law coming up the last of the stairs and down the hallway, his hands fisted at his sides, was one that Brynn knew she wouldn't easily forget. As Gideon stepped away, then protectively in front of her, she tried to think of something to do or say to avoid a scene.

Touching Gideon's arm, she quickly stepped around him to cut off her father-in-law.

"Please don't yell. Angie just fell asleep."

"So you think that allows you to turn my house into a—a—?"

Gideon was immediately beside her. "Stop right there."

Afraid they would turn this into a fistfight, Brynn grabbed Dominic's arm to turn him around. "Let's go downstairs. You don't want to do this up here. Angie's had a long week. She needs her rest."

"That didn't stop you from acting the tramp." He continued in a spurt of Italian that came out too fast to follow.

"So help me," Gideon growled, moving toward the older

man, "If you don't shut it down now, you'll be back in Emergency. Because that's the only way they'll be able to get your teeth out of your stomach."

Aside from her shame, Brynn was horrified by the violence emanating from Gideon and didn't know whether to cover her ears from the ugliness of both men's words, or her mouth to keep from sobbing. Then she heard a sound behind her and knew it was Angie.

"See what you're doing!" she whispered desperately to them. "Gideon, go home."

"I'm not leaving you to deal with this on your own when it's all my fault."

"I'll be fine. Please. It'll be much better if you go."

"You heard her, get out!" Dominic added, his chest thrust out.

Gideon still hesitated. She could see he was torn, but when another strangled moan came from the bedroom, he grimaced and nodded.

"If you need anything—"

"I know." Wanting to put her arms around him, to kiss away that terrible look from his face, she hurried into Angie's room.

It was some time before her daughter settled down again. Before she left the room, she looked out the window. Gideon hadn't gone into his house yet. He stood on his deck, a silhouette in the darkness, so still he could have been one of the straight support beams. She couldn't see his face, but she felt his gaze. Touching the glass, she willed him to hear her thoughts, prayed he wouldn't regret too much.

Once in the hall, she found the house silent, but Dominic wasn't in his room. Wishing she could retreat to her room, she went downstairs and found him sitting at the table, covering his head with his arms. The subtle light from the stove did little to ease the tension in the scene.

"Do you need aspirin or anything?"

He sat up, but didn't meet her inquiring look. The evasion, like his verbal condemnation earlier, made her feel less than clean, and extremely guilty. Logic told her she was being silly, that she'd done nothing wrong; but the feeling lingered nonetheless.

"What I need is a miracle to take the picture of what I saw out of my mind."

No, he was not going to be fair or open-minded about this. She saw no other way to respond but with total honesty.

"What did you see, Dominic, but two people kissing?"

"And had I been a minute later, what else would I see? You, my Tony's wife."

"His widow!" As much as she hated to point that out, he had to be reminded.

Dominic's slow nod could have been an indictment that she'd wished his son in his grave. "This is still my house," he said, thumping the table with his fist.

"I'm aware of that. Do you think either of us planned—" She took a moment to compose herself before she said anything that would make matters worse. It was long enough to make her consider something. "You were very quiet moving through the house."

He scowled. "What difference does that— No quieter than usual."

"Yes, more so." She nodded slowly, certain she saw a flicker of guilt in his eyes. "I think you were expecting something from the moment you entered the house. That's why I didn't hear you, and I have to tell you that I'm offended by that."

"You have no right to resent anything."

"Don't I?" Feeling herself begin to shake from the overdose of adrenaline rushing through her system, she crossed her arms beneath her breasts. "I owe you three things, Dominic. My respect, seeing that Angie grows up to love and respect you, and to do my share helping out around here. Everything else is my business, and as much as I would hate to hurt your feelings, I will not live my life as a result of choices you make for me. I was trying to make that point when I went back to work. I thought you were beginning to understand.''

"I only understand that you are chasing that dark soul.''

Gideon was a dark soul, but it wasn't fair to make that sound as though he was evil. They knew virtually nothing about his history, except that he had obviously been through a great deal in his life, and that much of it still haunted him. Having survived an ordeal or two himself, Dominic should have been less judgmental, if not compassionate. But of course he was in no mood to see anything other than his own black-and-white version of things.

"I'm sorry you're determined to make this into something ugly, and I know you think I owe you an apology, but I don't. I did nothing wrong. If you feel otherwise, let me know in the morning, and I'll—well, I suppose I'll make the necessary arrangements.''

Dominic's expression went from grim to stunned. "What are you saying, *la figlia?* All I'm doing is protecting my Tony's wife and baby, and you start with ultimatums.''

That he could still call her his daughter was a good sign, but Brynn could also feel the stranglehold of his image of her. "Pop," she said sadly, "Tony is gone. I hate that. If I could do anything to change it, I would, you know I would. But he's gone!" She gestured helplessly. "And I can't stop the clock, either. Life goes on, whether we're ready for it to or not. Look at you. You lost Angelina. Now you're dating Lillian.''

A closed look came over his face and he rose. "Do not mention that woman's name to me again.''

Without another word, he went upstairs.

He was gone the next morning when she came downstairs with Angie. Guessing he'd decided to go on to church without them, and aware that Angie wouldn't be up to sitting through the long service, she decided to give her a treat. Not hungry herself, she let Angie pick her own breakfast—a cheese Danish from the plate of pastries Dominic had brought home yesterday. Making her a glass of chocolate milk and a mug of coffee for herself, she led her outside for an impromptu picnic.

Lillian joined them a short time later, carrying her own mug and a toy dog with hair as blond as Angie's.

"How's the neighborhood's favorite little princess?" she asked, handing the stuffed animal to Brynn's daughter. She then gave Brynn a knowing look. "I got a call from a mutual friend, who was concerned about you."

Brynn glanced toward Gideon's, but it was difficult to see anything from where they were sitting. "That was good of him. How did he sound to you?"

"Oh, you know Gideon, the original sleeping volcano. Not too happy with me, either, I might add."

Brynn didn't want too much said in front of Angie. Stroking her hair, she murmured, "Sweetheart, you stay put and show your new friend how you can eat all of your food. Mommy's going to show Mrs. Littlejohn how well the morning glories are doing."

She chose that location because it kept them out of sight of Gideon, unless he came out of his garage, and allowed them to see if Dominic returned sooner than expected. Admiring the blue, pink and white blossoming vines that nearly covered the south side of the garage, she said, "Dominic seems as upset with you as he is with me. Am I right?"

"I wouldn't be here checking on you otherwise. Do you think I'm looking forward to a run-in with him? I swear last night he really let me have it."

Brynn rubbed at her forehead, her lingering headache strengthening again. "Lillian, I know it's none of my business, but will you tell me what happened so I know what I'm dealing with?"

"I blew it." Lillian tried to sound flippant; even her shrug was carefree. But as she sipped her coffee, the eyes meeting Brynn's were shadowed with worry, too. "The evening started out quite wonderful, like last week. He can be such a charming man when he's being himself and not some strutting peacock out to impress me."

"He's intimidated by you," Brynn offered, realizing the truth herself. "Intimidated by your position, your stature in the community."

Lillian tossed her head. "You know what I call myself on a tough day? A schmoozer with a fancy title."

Brynn knew there was a bit more to it, but let that pass. "When did things change?"

"On the way home. The fireworks had been fun, the dinner romantic...I thought we'd reached a new plateau in our relationship—and, believe me, no one could have been more surprised. I wanted to be as honest with him as I thought he was being with me. So...I told him that I'd let Gideon know we would be away from the house for the evening."

"Oh, Lillian."

"What was wrong with that?" Despite her wide-eyed look, the sun exposed the deeper lines around her eyes and mouth, a result of her own sleepless night. "The next thing I know, he has me confessing that part of the reason I went out with him in the first place was to give you and Gideon more time together."

For a moment Brynn could only cover her mouth with her hand. "How could you think he would be okay with that?"

"I should never have let him order the wine. Red wine always goes to my head."

"No wonder he crept into the house like some cat burglar."

A flicker of the old Lillian returned. "Gideon admitted he was in your place, but I couldn't pull any details out of him."

"You won't from me, either."

"Drat. At least I'm glad you two did get to spend the evening together."

To Brynn it was like talking to a bulldozer, a well-meaning one, but a bulldozer all the same. "And the job? Was that part of the plan, too?"

"I plead the Fifth. Although you've seen for yourself, we were shorthanded and our computers need your talents."

Brynn decided to let that go and focus on the immediate problem. "You have to stop, Lillian. No more matchmaking. There's no future in it."

"I hear what you're saying, but then, why is Gideon so worried about you?"

"I didn't say he didn't like me."

"Oh, well. 'Like.' How nice." Lillian made a face. "You should see him when he's talking about you. The man is tormented."

Inevitably, the words moved through her like warm wine. They made her want to turn around, even though she knew he wasn't out there. Oddly enough, she felt him, whether she wanted to or not. Maybe he was thinking of her....

"And you're in similar shape yourself," Lillian drawled, pointing at her with her mug. "That face must get you in so much trouble."

Brynn blinked, realizing she'd missed something. "Pardon?"

"It's too open for your own good." Lillian reached out to squeeze her hand. "Look, no one would like to see Gideon forgive himself and have a real life more than me, dear. But I neglected to consider the price someone else might have to pay for that." She grimaced as she tasted her coffee, and tossed the remnants into the flower bed.

"Can't you tell me something that would help him? What do you mean about him not being able to forgive himself? I've sensed as much myself. And he's even referred to his guilt, said what a despicable person he is, but what *happened* specifically?"

"I only know a little, and I don't want to lose a good teacher by telling you that much. One thing you learn about Gideon Kane very quickly is that if you give your word, you'd better keep it. But I have a feeling that if he ever tells anyone everything—which I will bet my house he won't—

that person will walk around with more than the shadows I see under your eyes.''

Brynn's heart sank. "So you think it is that bad?"

"That's like asking is a black hole dangerous." Lillian considered the college seal on her mug. "I'll tell you this—he's paid a terrible price to become who he is, and that's the Gideon Kane I fight for and love as a brother.''

This Brynn understood. About to tell her, she glanced over at Angie and saw her getting increasingly curious about them. Perhaps there would be an opportunity to talk again, she thought, walking back toward her daughter.

Lillian put her arm around her. "He'll stay away from you now," she said, keeping her voice low.

"I know.''

"Not because it's easy for him to do, but because he feels it's the best way to protect you.''

Not trusting her voice at that moment, Brynn nodded. And as wise as she knew that decision was, she worried if he also intended to hide from Angie? No, no matter what, he wouldn't do that to her.

"About Dominic," she began, her voice a bit scratchy. "Don't take all the blame. It usually does take two to botch a relationship.''

"Oh, I believe it," the older woman replied, a wry expression curling the corner of her mouth. "But is this a good time to tell you that I'm a Gemini?''

It was the last thing she expected the dean of a college to say. Brynn chuckled, in spite of the sad events of the past twelve hours.

Brynn did try to follow Lillian's example in one respect, which was to keep a healthy sense of humor. For the rest of Sunday and into Monday and Tuesday, even though Dominic remained somewhat reserved if not outrightly cool toward her, she did her best to act as though nothing had happened. She sang as she always did to Angie while bathing her, and kept a smile on her face when anyone approached her, whether at the school or in town.

At the office she volunteered for any task, no matter how mundane. At home she put all of her energy into thinking up new activities for Angie, caught up with correspondence that had piled up the past weeks, and often anticipated a chore before Dominic could get to it. She avoided any mention of Lillian, and wasn't surprised when he didn't bring up Gideon again. As for the man who preoccupied her most secret inner thoughts, although Gideon didn't reinstate his old invisible man act, he did make a point not to be outside if she and Angie were, something that didn't please her daughter but satisfied Dominic. Brynn should have known Angie would make her feelings known sooner or later. Nevertheless, she wasn't prepared for how.

On Wednesday when she came to pick up her daughter, she was met by Vanessa Gordon, who politely but firmly forced her to detour into her office.

"Mrs. Delmarco, I want you to know first and foremost that I have loved having Angie at Good Beginnings. She is one of the sweetest children it's ever been my privilege to meet, a favorite with all the staff."

"That's very kind of you, Mrs. Gordon. Do I hear a 'but,' though?"

"I'm afraid so. You see, Angie has changed over the last few days, and I believe in quick action to keep things from mushrooming into something that could be disruptive to the whole operation of the school. Mrs. Delmarco, let me be frank—I'm concerned for Angie. You'll remember from our conversation when you first inspected the school that we don't have anyone else who is disabled."

Brynn stiffened at the term. "Angie isn't disabled, Mrs. Gordon. She's been severely traumatized and doesn't speak, that's all."

"But as a result of that, she's not making the progress a child her age should. The other children are passing her rapidly. It's understandable that she should be feeling more of an outsider than ever.''

Stunned, Brynn could only sit there and absorb this newest blow. "I had no idea she was. She hasn't given any evidence of that at home.''

"It's not something she would want you to find out about, is it? Especially if she was the cause?''

"Now, wait a minute, Mrs. Gordon—''

"The truth is, she's growing sullen,'' the woman continued. "I feel it's only a matter of time before she reacts violently to another child or one of the staff. That's why I feel it's important for us to work together to resolve the problem.''

Angie? Sullen? It simply wasn't her nature to be. "Um, naturally, I'll sit down with her as soon as we get home and find out what the problem is,'' she replied, hoping she didn't sound as shaken as she felt.

With a condescending smile, Vanessa Gordon reached for a card tucked into the left corner of her desk blotter. "Mrs. Delmarco, I hope you won't think me too forward, but I contacted the school's general practitioner, Dr. Mack, to ask for a recommendation.''

Brynn's spine went rigid. She knew what was coming. "My daughter has suffered at the hands of enough so-called experts, Mrs. Gordon.''

"It must have been a tedious and painful experience for both of you. Finding the right individual to click with a patient as—as sensitive as Angie would have to be a time-consuming and stressful process. At the same time, you can't give up. Tim Creighton has a renowned reputation with children.''

Brynn made no attempt to accept the card the woman held out to her. "I don't think you heard, Mrs. Gordon. I don't care if Dr. Creighton is the real Santa Claus, I promised Angie she wouldn't have to endure any more questioning until she was ready, and I intend to keep that promise.''

This time it was the administrator's turn to balk. "In that

case, Mrs. Delmarco, I'm afraid you leave me with no choice but to ask you to seek care for your daughter somewhere other than our school.''

By the time she got to the house, Brynn was steaming. ''Imagine!'' she said to Dominic. Under the circumstances, he'd beaten them home. ''She actually gave me an ultimatum. Do things her way, or get lost! Never mind what I know or think. Who cares if I feel a different approach might work better?

''And you, young lady,'' she added to her daughter. She stooped to search Angie's face. ''I think I know what you did, and I don't think you realize what a pickle you've put Mommy in.''

For his part, Dominic was anything but upset. ''The woman did you a favor. Our Angelina was happier at home than at that place. This is a sign that you should stay home and care for her yourself.''

That comment would have upset her if it wasn't for knowing who the real target of his ire was. ''You'd like to be the one to tell Lillian that I had to quit, wouldn't you?''

He rose from the dinette table. ''You want, I'll go knock on her door right now.''

''You'll do no such thing. Besides, she isn't home yet. And if she was, I'd remind you that this is my problem and I'll deal with it.''

''You'll let her fill your head with more crazy ideas.''

''I can't leave her shorthanded at the office.''

Of course, Dominic disagreed. ''Your family comes first.''

She knew meetings would keep Lillian away from her desk the rest of the afternoon and into the evening, so Brynn left a message on her answering machine at the house.

Early the next morning, Lillian phoned. Her solution was simple.

''Bring her with you,'' she said.

''Oh, that's asking too much.'' Brynn was touched by the gesture, but too conscientious to let herself accept the offer.

"I can't expect Reva and Elise to work around a four-year-old."

"We're talking about a little girl who would make a church mouse sound like the Mormon Tabernacle Choir!"

"You know she's uneasy around strangers."

"It's summer break! The campus is quieter than usual. You can set her up at one of the desks not being used and she can color or look at picture books to her heart's delight."

"And then what? I'd still have to interview to place her in a new school. That would mean more time off. No. I'll be in today and Friday, but you're going to have to accept my resignation and my apologies, Lillian."

The last thing Gideon expected to see when he stopped in at the administration building to pick up his mail on Thursday afternoon was Brynn's child under a desk, curled up on a throw and fast asleep. There was no sign of Brynn at the moment, but he saw the supply and equipment room door ajar and assumed she'd stepped back there for a moment.

Seeing that a stuffed toy dog had slipped out of her grasp and rolled a yard or so away, he rounded the counter and carefully tucked it back into her arms. He was just rising when he saw that Brynn had reappeared and was watching him.

He had, of course, seen her since that nightmare of a night last weekend, but this was the first time they'd been close enough to say anything to each other. That is, if one of them got around to speaking. She seemed to be having as much trouble as he was at initiating conversation. It didn't help that simply looking at her ate at his insides. Her lime green sheath showed off her graceful curves and elegant legs to the point of distraction. But it also bothered him that she seemed tired, and defeated.

"Thank you for doing that," she said at last, nodding at the toy. "I have enough on my conscience without seeing someone tripping and hurting themselves."

Gideon found it safer to focus on Angie. "Is she all right?"

"Nothing to trouble yourself over."

There was no trace of animosity in her voice; she was merely giving him a gentle reminder that putting some distance between them was as much her decision as his. But when she then told him about what had happened, he experienced a flood of contradictory feelings.

"I'm sorry. I had no idea. Maybe it's for the best." The words sounded lame to his ears. He wasn't surprised when she looked somewhat peeved.

"That sounds vaguely familiar."

Dominic. He should have known the one utterance that came out of his mouth would be what she least wanted to hear.

"I meant that this may give you a chance to catch up on your rest. You look exhausted, Brynn."

That didn't work, either, because her expression told him that he was the primary reason for her sleepless nights.

He sighed. "What will you do next?"

"I don't know."

"Are you sure, Brynn? What if that doctor could help her?"

She lifted her chin. Blue shards of ice flashed in her eyes. "People who aren't willing to take advice shouldn't give it."

He didn't blame her for disappearing back into the supply room. He had been out of line. Instead of comforting and reassuring her, all he'd done was question her judgment, the way everyone else was.

So great was his guilt over disappointing her that later that evening he couldn't focus on the exam he was supposed to be preparing. He'd already tried working in the garden, but that hadn't provided its usual relief, either.

He was considering a rare drink of Scotch when the front doorbell sounded. It was past nine, and the fact that he almost never had visitors had him warily approaching the door.

When he saw who it was, his fingers fumbled on the storm door lock like a self-conscious kid's.

"I know you'd rather see a magazine salesman than me, but...could I speak to you for a moment?"

He stepped back to let her enter. There was no car out front, and he wondered how she'd managed to evade her father-in-law.

"I told Dominic that I needed some air," she said, as though he'd voiced the thoughts out loud. "Angie's asleep. He's watching a miniseries."

She was dressed in jeans and some short-sleeved knit top in a buttery yellow that almost made his mouth water—not for the color, but for the way it caressed her breasts and hugged her waist. It also made him hate the idea of her being out in the dark, alone and vulnerable.

"Would you like to sit down?" The invitation was a joke. His home wasn't designed to receive guests; but if Brynn noticed that, she gave no sign.

"I can't stay. Besides, I know my being here makes you uncomfortable. Nevertheless I had to come."

"You're upset. Slow down. Tell me."

"What I said earlier, Gideon, it was rude and I'm so ashamed."

That was it? "What did you say that wasn't right?"

"I lashed out, wanting to hurt you."

He almost smiled. "You should know by now that my skin is thicker than most."

"I don't believe that. You just don't let anyone see when and where you're hurting. Oh, Gideon, I wanted to take back those words ten seconds after they came out of my mouth."

"Don't you think I know that?" As her gaze searched his, he struggled to share a portion of what was in his heart. "I didn't walk out because I was angry. I had to leave because you reminded me of too much that isn't going to be. You made me sorrier than ever that I'm not what you need, what you should have. I have enough to regret without taking that on."

She bowed her head. "It's egotistical, I know, but after the little you confided about yourself, I didn't consider that there'd been someone in your past, too."

He could almost shake her for insisting on being so blind. She didn't see anything. "Brynn. Look at me. I reacted to you the way I did last Saturday because it had been a long time since I'd touched a woman, a very long time. And I'd never touched anyone like you. Do you understand what I'm saying?"

"I'm not sure I even want to."

"Oh, yes, you do. You want to know, as much as I wish I could lie to you about myself. Almost as much as I wish I could make you promises."

"You don't have to do this. I didn't come—"

"The hell I don't," he growled, breaking yet another of the vows he'd made to himself. "Don't you get it? You're still here. I have to keep talking, keep trying to shock, frighten or disgust you, until you run as though the devil himself is after you. Do you know there are people who will tell you that's me? Correction, would tell you if they were still alive."

But he wasn't scaring her, he saw that clearly. All he was doing was making her look as though he was attacking her again and again with a razor.

Unable to continue, he closed his eyes. "Go home, Brynn. For the love of heaven, go home."

He heard her move, thought she was heading toward the door, only to feel her soft hand caress his cheek, his beard.

"You'll never make me hate or fear you," she whispered.

Then she was heading for the door.

You can do it. Hold on.

Despite the urgent words he spoke to himself, when he heard the door begin to open, something snapped inside him and he lurched forward and slammed it shut.

"Gideon!"

He wrapped his arms around her and drew her back against him as though she was the lost part of his own body.

"Gideon..."

"Kiss me." He slid one hand up her middle to the side of her face, keeping her from avoiding that. "Kiss me. You have to. Once more."

The sound that tore from her throat ripped at his heart, but it didn't stop him. There was no room for recrimination and regret. He wouldn't hear her despair. He only let himself focus on her mouth, that mouth that had left him completely sleepless for two nights, and reduced him to writhing in sweat-soaked sheets through the rest.

His will proved stronger than hers. He won.

He kissed her. Unable to get to her fast enough, deep enough, his wild assault moved all over her face, in the process absorbing as much of her as possible. He had to store up enough memories to live on until the end...and he had no hope that the gods would be kind and make that mercifully soon.

He kissed her and learned what he was already beginning to suspect—that in desire there could be violence. It forced him to hold tight to his control. He couldn't mark her. But something base in him wanted to, called on him to imprint himself on her like a brand. The cry shot through his blood...

Mine! Mine!

He kissed her—his sweet, soft woman. Never again Tony Delmarco's wife. Only his dream.

Wanting what was in her heart, he settled for what was in his.

And the kiss went on and on.

He turned her, lifted her so he could imprint her against his flesh for all time. The shifting joined her heartbeat to his, his need to her loneliness.

It was then that he knew his early, biggest fear had been realized.

He'd paid nothing on his debt.

Yet.

Sick at heart, he let her slide down his body, tried to drown himself in the bottomless pools of her eyes, and then at last focused on the moist, slightly swollen lips he would almost sell his soul to feel all over him. If he had one to sell.

He'd found his life. Everything precious was right here. Lost hope. Unexplored dreams. This was what had been waiting for him if things had been different.

And there it was again mocking him—that dreaded, hated word. *If.*

Before making himself let her go, he pressed a kiss to her feverish forehead, remembering her whispered prayer not so long ago. "Bless you," he rasped.

"Gideon. That sounds awfully like—"

"Go."

He spoke quietly and let his eyes say the rest.

She went.

The instant the door closed behind her, he slumped against it, then slid down, down, to the floor. Pressing his forehead against his knees, he wondered at hell being so cold, especially in July.

Chapter Nine

"You look like words I don't use."

Gideon stood resigned as Lillian brushed past him. It would take only one hand to count how many times she'd come over since he'd moved here. She preferred that he come to her house when she had something to discuss, because she didn't think much of his idea of interior decorating. Since he'd done little to improve things, he suspected this would be no more of a social call than the others had been.

He shut the door and stood with arms folded to await her explanation.

She did an about-face and matched his stance. "Aren't you going to invite me to sit down?" She glanced around the living room that was empty except for a leather couch, and rolled her eyes. "Forget it. I wouldn't turn down a drink, though."

"Last time we did this, people got hurt."

"Okay, make mine anything that doesn't require vodka."

"Lillian."

"This is an occasion that calls for a toast, and I know better than to ask if you have champagne."

"Scotch and water is the best I can do."

"Sold. Hold the water, be generous with the ice." As he headed for the kitchen, she followed. "And do please make one for yourself."

He was almost tempted, convinced that this had to be extra bad news, regardless of what she'd said. Besides, it was barely eleven o'clock and Saturday, which also meant it probably had nothing to do with school business. Consequently, Gideon took his time filling the tumbler with ice and pouring the potent amber liquid from the half-empty bottle he'd abused after Brynn's visit Thursday a week ago. Since then, he'd been functioning on a form of automatic pilot—so much so that even a few of his students had asked him if he was ill.

Maybe that was it. She was only here to congratulate him that no one had filed a complaint against him with her office this week.

When he turned, she was sitting at the pine butcher-block table. She looked as out of place in her white-and-pink golfing attire as he would be on a golf course. He handed her the drink, ignoring how she lifted her eyebrows at his other empty hand.

"It's a bit difficult to toast someone who doesn't have a glass."

He'd just come out of a shower not five minutes ago, and barely had had time to drag on jeans and a clean T-shirt thanks to her aggressive knocking. Before that, he'd been running, adding an extra two miles to his four in the hopes of burning up some of the tension coiling in him like a nasty rattler—made nastier thanks to a late start. He wanted a drink less than the day she'd made those killer Bloody Marys, but to pacify her, he reached into the refrigerator and grabbed a bottle of water.

"You're about as fun as my golfing partner this morning. For a lousy twenty-thousand-dollar-a-year endowment, I had to listen to every medical procedure he'd undergone since his sixtieth birthday. He's eighty-two. Ask me if I feel I know him as intimately as his doctor.''

"Why are you here, Lillian?"

"Good news, dear, only good news." She lifted her glass in a belated toast. "I have a project for you."

He almost choked on the first gulp. "No."

"You haven't heard what it is yet!"

"It has something to do with Brynn." No matter how brief the contact throughout the week, Lillian had always managed to bring up her name.

"That goes to show you what you know. It's about your plants. I want you to do that book we'd once discussed."

He frowned. The idea had come up some time back, and while it had been her suggestion, the timing had been wrong for several reasons, including insufficient funding. He'd never told her that he wasn't altogether unhappy about that.

"What's changed?"

She took another drink before answering. The ice clicking cheerfully in her glass matched the smile in her eyes. "The other pair of golfers with us were none other than C. C. Day and Floyd Crispin. The CEO and president of Lou-Day Paper Corporation? As it turns out, C.C. was looking for a way to improve his company's image, what with all the criticism about the amount of timbering going on throughout the south. He thinks it would be beneficial to be connected with something that shows the positive end results of what his company is all about."

Gideon had to be pleased for her, although he didn't know that he liked the affiliation with Lou-Day. "So you're going to get B.C. Press off the ground. Congratulations...provided you didn't sell your soul to achieve this."

"Thank you, Friar Worrywort. No, I did not. The school will retain full control. Lou-Day just gets to advertise the hell out of their role as benefactor, and that means free exposure for us, as well. It's a win-win deal." She raised her glass for a second toast. "Now, then, when can I have the book?"

"Whoa." Gideon put down the plastic bottle and crossed his arms over his chest. "I didn't say I'd do it."

"You have to. I already told C.C. about it, and he's wild for the idea that our first offering celebrates trees as an art form. Oh, the marketing ideas we tossed around…"

He definitely didn't like the sound of that. It was one thing to put his name on what amounted to a coffee-table book, although it would be a serious study. A few thousand copies would be sold, most falling into the hands of professional gardeners and students of bonsai who would care more about what he had to say than who he was. A few more copies would find their way to libraries, where after a few years of virtual neglect, many would be sold at book sales and they would end up in family homes—with people who wouldn't care who he was, either.

That was an acceptable scenario to him.

It was entirely something else to turn him into a product.

"Hello?" Lillian knocked on the table. "Could I get a little enthusiasm here?"

The water trickling down his back was no longer only dripping from his hair.

"You know I'm happy for you."

"Be happy for you, too! It goes without saying that we won't be pushing every title like this. It's a great opportunity."

"A firing squad would be easier," he muttered under his breath.

"What?"

"I, um, said there's a problem. Time. I can't just crank something like this out. I'd need the whole summer at least. But we're barely seven weeks away from the fall semester and you have me carrying a full load. I'd also need a terrific photographer, and—"

"What's with the excuses? We'll work through them."

"I don't see how." He smoothed his hand over his hair.

"Maybe you'd better consider letting someone else have the slot."

Lillian launched herself to her feet. "Have you lost your mind? I told you, C.C. has fallen in love with the idea. I can't go back to him and say, 'Stop the presses, we've had an even more brilliant idea. We're going to launch with another biography on Calvin Coolidge.'" She came around the table, her tone growing soothing. "We'll find someone to take your classes if necessary. The expense will be worth it. You know, what with the growing attention to Pacific Rim countries, the explosion of worldwide trade…there's an increased interest in Eastern gardening. You have the added knowledge of being able to show how the West can and is already embracing it, as well as adding their own influence to the art."

If Gideon was anyone else, he would be asking for a pen to sign on the dotted line. When Lillian turned on the master saleswoman charm, she could talk an alligator into leasing out his teeth. But he knew who he was, and not only did he not need any of the nasty surprises this idea could spawn, he owed Lillian too much to have her pet project blow up in her face.

"Do we have a deal?" she asked.

"I have reservations."

"About what?"

"The circus this could turn into."

"Ah-ha." She nodded, but looked relieved. "It's the lone wolf thing again. Maybe I did come on a bit strong, but only because I'm so excited that this is finally happening for us. You have my word, you get to veto anything you don't feel comfortable with."

He couldn't respond to that. It assured him of nothing.

It was Lillian who broke the silence, her laugh uncomfortable. "You know, you're beginning to worry me. After all these years, are you going to tell me that I shouldn't have taken your word for it and checked for your picture at the post office?"

She would be wasting her time, since that was the one place he didn't have to worry about showing up. But he didn't want to get into that with her if he could avoid it.

He tried a different tactic. "Regardless of what concerns me about the idea, I'm still a lousy typist. I'd have to find a researcher I was comfortable enough with to work here."

She smiled that smile that told Gideon she'd already anticipated him.

He lowered his head, leveling his eyes on her. "The answer is no."

"She can do it all—research and type."

"She'd never agree to do it. Brynn's too bright to waste her time on anything that mundane."

"Dear heart, I have a feeling the woman would iron your T-shirts if you whispered the right words in her ear."

"Lillian." He took a moment to check his temper. "I thought we'd discussed your meddling. For the last time."

"All right, then, I won't tell you that the other evening I heard her in the garage. Crying. It was probably the only place she thought she could do it without attracting unwanted attention."

God help him. He wished he could turn off his mind and not let that matter. But the questions came like bullets: Had Dominic done something to hurt her again? Had someone been unkind to Angie? Were her tears over him?

He closed his eyes and raked his hands through his hair.

"Gideon," Lillian continued, wholly sober now, "I believe there's something rare between you two. You have to sense it, too. Damn it, tell me!"

"Yes."

"Then why not reach for it? Grab it and hold it close before it gets away!"

"Because I have no right!"

"Who says? Why can't you let whatever is haunting you go? It's over!"

"It's never over." He went to the door and opened it. "But this conversation is."

Lillian flung back the remnants of her drink. Slamming the glass on the counter, she strode after him. "Fine. Get who you want. Just do the book."

"I'll consider it."

"Not this time," she replied, her gaze as tough as his. "I need it. You do it."

On the following Monday Brynn was waiting in her car in the faculty parking area. She'd managed to get the shady spot beside Gideon's sedan. Even so, she rolled down all the windows to take advantage of what little breeze there was. She didn't want to risk running the engine and the air conditioner because she didn't know how long she would have to wait.

Behind her, Angie sat flipping through pages of a magazine. As usual, the colorful pictures of animals and gardens in the glossy travel magazine kept her attention. Although she seemed content, Brynn eyed her in the rearview mirror, her heart tormented by the underlying silence that with every day seemed more permanent.

"You okay back there, sweetheart?"

Angie nodded and glanced out the window, expectation in her eyes. She knew where they were, and who they were waiting for. Brynn hoped that Gideon would be kind regardless of what else happened.

Thankfully, she didn't have to worry over that for long. The exodus of students eager for escape precluded staff departure. A few people recognized Brynn from her short term at the office and waved. The rest hurried to their cars and sped off. Not surprisingly, Gideon brought up the rear.

When he spotted her, he paused before rounding his own car to approach hers. His expression grew tender at the sight of Angie, and he leaned inside the back window to touch her cheek.

"Hello, angel. How pretty you look in that pink. Like Cinderella in her pumpkin carriage going for a ride."

It was the right thing to say. Angie smiled shyly, lifted

her dog to Gideon for a kiss, then, hugging it, gazed out the other side of the car.

Gideon shifted before the driver's window. His expression didn't grow any less tender, but an added sexual tension stirred in his eyes. "Everything all right?"

"That depends on you. I'd like to talk. Is this a bad time?"

He hesitated briefly, then asked, "Where would you like to go?"

"There's an abandoned farm with a pond a few miles from here." She gestured to the woven basket on the seat beside her. "I've packed a lunch as a bribe."

"You don't need bribes, Brynn." As someone else approached the parking lot, he straightened. "Lead the way. I'll be right behind you."

The farm had belonged to Marjorie Olsen's brother, who'd passed away recently. It was now on the market, and Brynn had driven Marjorie out there to check on the place during the week. She'd fallen in love with the slightly rolling terrain, and particularly the postage-stamp-size pond that Arne kept scenic by mowing with the tractor in the barn. He and Marjorie had graciously invited her to bring Angie out here whenever she wanted.

She explained all that as she unpacked the chicken-salad-filled croissants, cheese, wine, and lemonade for Angie, unable to bear the long silences that kept stretching between them.

How she swallowed a bite of anything she didn't know, and she was grateful when they got to the marshmallow brownies she'd made for dessert. As Angie took hers and her toy to inspect the edge of the pond, Brynn began packing away the empty containers and wrappings.

Gideon poured them each another measure of wine. "I now can understand the allure of picnics. Thank you," he said, swirling the amber liquid in his long-stemmed glass.

They'd been careful around Angie, almost formal except when talking to her, giving no hint of what was between them, except when their eyes met.

"I suppose this is a bit different than—what do you call them? K rations?"

He didn't reply.

"Personally, I love dining alfresco in any form. Give me the so-called atrium of a gutted building, or an intimate balcony, even a back porch, I don't care. Combining the ambience of nature with good food is sheer bliss."

"I can see that. You're radiant."

"And you're wary. More so than usual." Done with the fussing, Brynn reached for her glass. "Thinking about how you'd react, I almost lost my nerve to come. But then I decided that while you might be…disappointed in me, you wouldn't be angry."

"Never angry. Not with you." He took a sip of the wine, eyeing Angie's progress along the bank. "So Lillian told you about the book."

Brynn felt the corners of her mouth quirk. "Lillian's never going to change."

"No more than Dominic, eh?"

"Exactly. Are you pleased? I mean, about the project."

"I'm trying to be."

"That's what I thought." She felt the pull of his sharp gaze, but resisted. "I worried for you."

"I don't deserve that."

She moved her shoulders, letting him know that some things weren't as simple as a matter of choice. "You'll bring a great deal to the subject."

"I'll try—if I take it on."

Having had time to consider what the news would mean to him, she thought she understood his reluctance to share Lillian's enthusiasm. "You think Lillian's dismissing your concerns too easily. About the attention you might receive…?"

No, he clearly didn't like how much their mutual friend had told her.

"She talks too much."

"I also have eyes, Gideon. When I heard the news, that was the first thing I thought of."

"Not the fact that she wants you to work with me?"

"A close second," she replied, not afraid to be honest with him about that.

His sigh aged him. "Look, Brynn, if things were different I'd jump at the chance of having your help. But under the circumstances, it would be better all around if I didn't put either of us through that."

"Don't I get any input?"

"It's my book," he said gently.

Minnows jumped on the water's surface. A sparrow came closer to check on crumbs dropped from Angie's brownie. Brynn found a sweet grounding in the images around them, even though her heart was threatening a new crack.

"I'm not as weak as you think, Gideon."

He looked as though she'd sworn at him. "When did I say that? Yes, I think you're all things feminine and fine. But if I ever gave the impression—"

"Of course you have. You're worse about trying to protect me than Dominic is, and it drives me crazy. I've lived a privileged life in many ways, but you also know I've paid dearly for it. What more can you protect me from?"

"Me."

Because she was expecting that answer, Brynn was able to continue breathing normally. Almost normally. "And I'm telling you that you don't have to. I'm not going to insult the special bond between us by pretending it's easily controlled. But I do know and agree that it needs to be. I'm not…ready for a relationship yet, certainly not one this intense. And you've made it more than clear you'll never be."

"You think analyzing it is the solution?"

"Not at all. But being open and honest about it would allow us to work through the roughest moments."

He'd left his jacket in the car, and although they sat in the shade provided by a red maple tree's long graceful arms, he suddenly tugged brutally at two more buttons on his white linen shirt. The depth of his restraint was also evident in the strained muscles in his jaw; they grew so taut that she could see a nerve twitch again and again.

"How civilized," he said sarcastically. "Label it and tie a pastel ribbon around it, and you think you control the beast?"

His passion radiated from him like angry flames, and when his gaze blazed over her, she almost dropped her glass. Gray eyes shouldn't have been able to transmit such heat, and the only reason Brynn was able to bear the scorching was that she was hostage to the pain, the abject despair that lay behind it.

"Gideon…"

She reached toward him, only to be warned off by a sharp motion of his hand.

"Don't!"

She barely recognized his voice, thick, almost strangling; and she couldn't believe her eyes as she saw the moisture in his before he squeezed them tight and pinched the bridge of his nose with his fingers. Her own eyes filled as she realized what an injustice she'd committed.

In trying to inure herself from more hurt, as well as the forbidden temptation he represented, she'd been careless. She'd assumed. Insulting enough by any method of reckoning, to Gideon it was as denigrating, as wholly outrageous as it would be to take a chain saw to his garden.

"What have I done?" she whispered behind her clenched fingers. "Oh, Gideon…what have I done to you?"

He simply cleared his own throat and reached for one of the linen napkins, pressing it into her hand. "Angie's looking. Don't let her see your tears."

He was right, of course. Somehow she pulled herself together, actually managing a wave and smile—shaky though it was—when her daughter held up a daisy she'd picked.

"Don't berate yourself," he said, once Angie went back to her exploring. "You couldn't know. And don't the experts say that there's no equality in loving? Someone is always shortchanged. It can't be helped.

"Besides, I'm not worth your guilt," he continued, refocusing on the pond again. "Which is why it's time you know the truth about me. I won't have you shortchanging what you shared with your husband out of pity for—"

"Not pity, Gideon. Never pity."

He silenced her again with a brief motion of his hand. "Listen," he said urgently. "Please. This is going to be difficult enough without your generosity.

"I never knew my father," he began. "And if I'd had a choice, I'd have preferred not knowing my mother. It's never made sense to me why women like her bother claiming what they don't want. I've seen dogs treat their litters better than some women do their kids. But I suppose even they go through a few hours of maternal twinges. In my mother's case I think it more likely that she was just too embarrassed to put me up for adoption.

"Needless to say, I grew up on the streets. I was wild, and trouble was my first habit."

"Didn't the authorities try to put you in a foster home?" Brynn asked, hurting for him.

"What decent family wants an uncontrollable kid? The places they did send me were as bad as what I'd walked away from, and I left those, too.

"The last time I stood before a judge, he was ready to make an example out of me and gave me an option—the military or a visit to a full-fledged penitentiary. I was raw, but I wasn't stupid. I chose the military. But since I was still underage, I needed a parent's authorization. He located my mother himself to get her to sign the proper forms—the irony of which didn't escape any of us, since by then I hadn't seen her in two years."

"Oh, Gideon."

He continued as though she hadn't spoken. "In the service I came to the attention of people who had a use for someone with my particular skills, someone who was good at surviving, who didn't let little things like a conscience interfere with the job. Someone who had no ties anywhere, so that I wouldn't be missed if I suddenly disappeared. Most interesting to them was that I was dead accurate with a gun. Any gun. At any distance.''

"They put you in something like a special forces group?"

"Yeah, we were real special." He closed his eyes as though dreading the resurgence of those memories. "Did Tony ever have to take a life?"

"No. It preyed on his mind, though. Another officer later said that's why he died—because he always tried to find another way to resolve a problem.''

"Well, for a sniper there are no problems, there are only targets. And it's not like shooting a missile off a ship, or dropping a bomb from a multimillion-dollar jet to give you some distance. There's you, one bullet and a face in the crosshairs of your rifle. Those faces never go away.''

"But if it's a war—"

"War." He all but spat the word. "Historians aren't wrong in saying that the age of romantic warfare is over. The crap that goes on around the world these days—most of which isn't getting reported in the news—is about power. Ambitious men willing to wreak any havoc in order to control, and rich governments ready to deal with the winners. Don't try to rationalize what I did. I was as repugnant and indiscriminate as germ warfare, a mercenary never expected or *desired* by his government to survive.

"You know, they begin to worry about you after a while. In the last world war the number of known kills for an American sniper was over twenty and well past double that for the Soviets. When someone in so-called 'peacetime U.S.A.' starts to close in on the record books the people upstairs get nervous. Suppose I made it home? Suppose I opened my mouth in the wrong places?

"It got to the point where every time I went out, I lived with the constant feeling that someone I couldn't see was drawing a bead on me...or waiting for darkness to cut my throat.''

Brynn felt what little she'd managed to eat roll threateningly in her stomach.

''You're wondering how I got out,'' he said, once again picking up on her thoughts. ''Well, the expected finally happened. I'd gone too deep into the jungle, thanks to the logistics I'd been given. Apparently, some young lion in the U.S. Senate had gotten hold of top secret information about our group and the press was finally sniffing out our trail. The boys in the Pentagon wearing chestfuls of medals needed to do more than lose any paper trace so they could sit before a congressional committee hearing and deny we ever existed, let alone had any connection to them. They needed us dead.

''So halfway around the world, I found myself with God knows how many guerrillas converging on me. That's when I came across a woman holding what was left of her child. It had wandered into a booby trap. Not ours, but what difference did that make? Looking into her soulless eyes, I saw everyone I'd ever killed. In the space of three seconds I came to my edge and started falling. I had just enough of my mind left to realize that if the guys behind me got hold of the woman, she would be lucky if they only shot her.'' He swallowed hard. ''So I handed her my pistol. Maybe I was hoping she would put a bullet in me before using it on herself. It wouldn't have been anything less than what I deserved, and it might have made her think she'd gotten some revenge. It took me all these years, until meeting you, in fact, to understand she figured out a better way for me to pay.''

He needed a moment before he could speak again, and Brynn gladly gave him the silence. As it was, she didn't know what she would say when he did want her to speak.

''You think Dominic dislikes and distrusts me now with only his suspicions and imagination to goad him? Consider his reaction if he knew what I just told you. Not even Lillian has heard as much as you have. Can you begin to understand what I mean when I say that I haven't been with a woman in a long time? Heaven help me, I feel as though I need to wash my hands before I even allow myself anywhere near you.

"Your husband was a hero, Brynn. A man who died protecting all he held precious. You can call me a mercenary, but even that's too generous. At least they do what they do for money. I valued nothing!"

His shame and remorse came at her in waves like those from a blast furnace. Brynn couldn't begin to comprehend how it felt to be burdened with such self-loathing, let alone understood how he'd stepped back from that edge he'd mentioned.

"What did you do?" she whispered. "How did you escape?"

"The truth? I don't know. I must have run. Then I walked, and ran again."

"Where?"

"Everywhere. Nowhere. For months I wandered throughout the Far East. At a critical moment I came upon an abandoned Buddhist monastery. The lone inhabitant decided if I'd been meant to die, I wouldn't have made it to his doorstep, so he insisted I live."

That must have been the most unbearable challenge of all. "Is he the one who taught you about bonsai?"

"Well, he was the first to try."

Ah, Brynn thought. More penance for the artist too unworthy of even the smallest pride.

"It's worse than you expected."

"It's a terrible story. If I heard it from someone else, I might not believe it. But if you're asking me if I despise you...how can I? There's enough self-loathing in you to destroy three men. It's almost a punishment to watch you get through each day." She considered Angie, who was tossing blossom after blossom into the water. "Just tell me this...does whoever it was that you took orders from back then know you survived?"

Gideon nodded slowly. "Good for you, Brynn. It's the

only question that should matter to you. Is your child safe around me when her own father couldn't guarantee that in a perfectly normal neighborhood?" He, too, turned his attention to Angie. "The answer is—right now she is. I set off a few alarms when I first resurfaced back in the States. But after having me watched for a while, apparently they decided that ignoring me would be better than the attention killing me would garner. Hopefully, that policy will hold."

"Even though you criticize the government in your classes and cite lie after lie in textbooks?"

"Sometimes I almost convince myself that I'm getting back at somebody for taking a dumb kid and turning him into a monster, that what I stir up makes the bastards' jobs tougher in a small way when at least a few people learn to be better at disseminating information and keeping the system more honest. But that's a crock of bull. In the end Seneca was right when he said that all revenge is nothing more than a confession of pain. I'm a joke to Washington."

"But you still don't want to risk too much public attention by publishing a book."

His gaze locked with hers. "Not while you and Angie are anywhere nearby and you still look at me as though you want me to bare you to the sun and my mouth."

The heat flooding her body had nothing to do with the sun or the wine, and even though she wouldn't deny he was right, she had to make him understand what he didn't want to see.

"What about Lillian? You're old friends and she sounds as though she's gotten herself into a complicated corner."

"No less complicated than your life will be if Dominic finds out that you're working with me."

"It's not necessary that I tell him."

"Brynn, you're the most honest person I know. If you did manage to keep it a secret, don't you think the neighbors would figure something was up when you began coming and going from my house like the world's most inept cat burglar? They like and respect you. For Angie's sake, if not your own, don't sacrifice your reputation."

She understood everything he said, and couldn't deny that he was right, just as what he'd revealed about his past was shocking and heartbreaking. But there was one other motivator that drove her.

"Gideon, with every passing day that Angie doesn't speak, I'm facing the fact that she's going to have to learn to sign. Do you know what that means? A special school, and for the rest of her life dealing with the stigma of being different, somehow less than normal. I don't care that some people are recognizing that signing is a beautiful language, and that society can feel good about itself if they choose a deaf Miss America. This is my little girl who's already been rejected because she doesn't speak. I can't bear the thought of her having to endure that for the rest of her life.

"I keep thinking of how she responds to you. Maybe it's that you've both come through some awful darkness that only the two of you can fully understand. Whatever it is, I have this inexplicable *belief* that if she's allowed to keep that connection with you for a while longer, she'll experience a breakthrough."

Gideon hung his head. The strong planes of his face looked almost gaunt in the brutal sunlight, and she knew in that instant how deeply her child had been preying on his mind.

"Dear God, you're a worse dreamer than I thought."

"Please, Gideon."

"Don't do this—to either of us."

As he spoke, Angie returned to the blanket, her small hands cupping something. She stopped before Gideon and showed him a dead bream, its blue sides as bright as her eyes, its golden stomach not unlike her hair. One look at Angie's trembling lips and flooding eyes, and Brynn saw him transform. The mercenary turned to mush.

Rising to his knees, he said tenderly, "Well, you know who you found? It's my old friend Great-Great-Grandfather Bream. He's lived in this pond for...oh, nearly as long as the moon's been white. For years his job was giving tours to all the young bream who came to live here, so they would know how to find their way home after a long day of swimming.

"What a nice thing for him that you're here today, angel. Otherwise who would give him a special place here in the shade where he could watch his pond forever? Remember how the koi in my pond cluster under the shade of the dogwood tree?" As she began to nod, he reached into his pocket and pulled out a pocket knife. "You put Great-Great-Grandfather Bream right here, and go rinse your hands, and when you're done, I'll have him in his new home."

The next few minutes were quiet ones as Angie collected wildflowers in blue and yellow for the grave. As Angie stood gazing at the tiny mound, Brynn wondered if she was remembering that she'd missed her father's funeral, which the doctors had strongly suggested she be kept from. There was something working in her expression that almost had Brynn believing this had helped that somehow. When Angie took Gideon's hand and bravely smiled up at him, Brynn had to turn away to keep her emotions under control.

"Well done, angel," Gideon said softly. "Now I think we'd better head back toward town. Isn't your grampa due soon?"

Angie nodded and went to collect her toy dog.

Brynn knew Gideon was waiting for her, and she finally managed to face him. "You see?" was all she could say to him.

"Too much. And it doesn't change anything."

"You're right, it doesn't."

"Brynn, Brynn." He began to reach out, only to catch himself in the last moment. "Go home. Think about what you'd be doing. Tomorrow, if you still feel as you do now, come over when you can. I'll have one more question to ask you."

Chapter Ten

"Do you know anyone who's good with a camera?"

As Gideon asked the question, he knew it sealed his fate. But then, he believed it had been sealed from the moment Brynn Delmarco had moved across the alley.

As he'd directed, she'd shown up shortly after he'd returned from his morning at the college. Upon his arrival, he left the garage door open as a sign—not that he didn't think she'd been watching for him—and for easier access. She and Angie crossed over minutes later, Angie wanting to immediately dig in to the picnic basket her mother had once again brought. Although Brynn was pleased with her daughter's improved appetite, her pleasure had been subdued once she really had a chance to take in his home's stark interior.

The question about the photographer, though serious, was meant to make a point. Her visible relief relayed that she'd been expecting something far more complicated.

"That's all?" she asked. "I don't mean all, but I thought..."

"You didn't know what to think," he said from his seat across the small table. "Except that I might demand another promise out of you. Was the lunch to make me go gentle with you?"

The dark kitchen didn't hide her blush as she added a chicken leg to the small scoops of potato and carrot salad already on Angie's plate. "You're the second person lately to point out my transparency."

"I happen to like it, and your sincerity and good intentions. But—" he picked a breast and thigh for himself and held up his plate for her to portion more of the salad "—as much as I could get used to this, you'd better be careful. This is exactly the kind of thing I was talking about when I spoke of people noticing things. In the future, maybe I should bring the lunches."

"All right." She leaned forward slightly. "About the photographer, though, does the person have to have professional credentials?"

"Considering the time crunch I'm under, I'm not sure I can be that choosy. Why?"

"Because I don't have any. But when you asked me what you did…well, photography is something of a hobby of mine. My mother's older brother was actually the pro in the family, and I vaguely remember him carrying me on his back out on the roof of the house, and under the thickest bushes, always talking about angle shots, viewpoint and lighting. My mother, who never raised her voice, used to scream the entire duration of his visits. But after he was killed in Africa, they took my toy camera away from me and tried to discourage the interest."

Brynn shook her head, looking bemused. "It's amazing that I hadn't thought of that in so long."

What was left unsaid was that she'd had plenty of reasons not to. As interested as he was, Gideon wasn't overly hopeful about having his problem resolved so easily. "I thought Lillian said you were a computer whiz."

"Everyone who isn't thinks those who find them relatively

easy are. I did take some classes to go with my business degree and I'd do Ton— It's a utilitarian thing,'' she said with a shrug.

''Why the sudden hesitation to speak of him in front of me?''

She repositioned the carrot salad on her plate with her fork. ''It seems unkind to remind you, when you've had so little happiness yourself.''

''It pleases me to know you've known joy.''

She smiled. ''Sometimes when you say things like that, the phrasing is almost foreign. It's as though your old monk is speaking through you.''

''Everything I am is partly due to Tanka's patience with me.''

She repeated his name as though tasting it. ''Was he some kind of Zen master or something?''

''The label would mean nothing to him. But he did teach me how to abandon all conceptions, points of view and opinions.''

''What does that leave you with?''

''Clarity. Serenity. Truth.'' All foreign concepts to the burned-out soul who had stumbled into the old man's haven. But there would be time to get into philosophy with her later, as they worked on the text of the book, Gideon thought. In fact, it was inevitable. What he wanted to hear about was her passion—for when she'd spoken about her uncle and that toy camera, there'd been a special energy radiating within her. ''All those photo albums you took into the house from the garage. Were those your work?''

''For the most part. Tony gave me a 35 mm as a wedding present. It wasn't long before my closest female friend, Lark, gave me the nickname Cyclops. Would you like me to pick out some I think are my best work to show you?''

''Please.'' And not only for reasons related to the book. ''I also have another idea. It'll be several days before I can review my old notes on the project and those I've been collecting all along, also to rough a new outline about all that

I want to cover. In the meantime, why don't you start experimenting with shots of the specimens in my collection?
Remind me to give you a key to the back gate and the house
before you leave.''

Brynn stopped eating. "You trust me that much?"

"I've entrusted you with everything inside me. The house
is merely where I stay.''

She pressed her hand against her heart.

When she didn't speak or move for several seconds, and
he saw that Angie had noticed, he began speaking softly to
the child. He told her about the baby birds that had abandoned their nest in the corner of the porch and could be
frequently seen taking noisy baths in the *tsukubai.*

"Okay?" he asked, once Brynn returned to her meal.

She was quick to nod in the affirmative, but it was evident
that she'd experienced something profound she either wasn't
willing or able to talk about. Gideon had a hunch he knew
what it was, but there was nothing he could do to make it
easier for her—just as there was nothing he could do about
what was going on inside him.

Later, however, after they'd gone, he phoned Lillian's
home to leave a message on her machine: "You've got your
wish. All of it. But there's no way to insure the time we'll
need to accomplish this without certain assistance from your
end. Call me.''

During the abbreviated but intensified summer semester
Gideon taught every weekday, and for once Brynn was relieved. In fact, she could hardly contain her excitement.

Just thinking about the possibilities, she burned Dominic's
toast at breakfast. While estimating how much film she
should get to start, she ignored his fretting about tomato
worms in the garden. In the midst of a brainstorm that had
her rescheduling her plans to check what was available on
photography and gardening at the library, she failed to make
a suitable remark about the promise of rain in the forecast.

"The heat is tiring you," Dominic said as he kissed her goodbye. "You take it easy today."

It amazed her that he could be so blind, and saddened her, too.

As soon as he had the car out of the driveway, she spun around to a watchful Angie and clapped her hands. "Okay, angel, upstairs and brush those teeth, while I clean up the dishes. Then we're on our way!"

She'd explained things to the child as a bedtime story; how it would be necessary to keep Gideon's book and their visits to his house a secret until the project was completed. Angie had liked the idea of a surprise, and her studiousness and eagerness to please this morning was heartwarming.

Alone for a few minutes, Brynn let her thoughts drift again to Gideon—as they had constantly over the past two days. His childhood, she'd concluded, had been a tragedy, and she ached for the boy who'd had to begin his life with so many strikes against him. It could be argued that he'd been born to become little else than what he'd evolved into. Cities across the country were full of examples just like him. So were prisons. That he was alive to tell of it, let alone had transformed his life into something productive, spoke of some miracle, she was certain. How, then, could she harden her heart against him, as he clearly kept expecting her to? Especially after yesterday.

Oh, the generosity. He'd quite humbled her. Here was a man who should never be able to trust again, and he trusted her. Wanted her. Loved. Her.

How guilty she'd been in the beginning when he'd re-awakened her sexual desire. How strange that now, with the revelation of falling in love for only the second time in her life, there was no shame or regret at all. It resolved nothing—in fact, it complicated things all the more. But she cherished the knowledge blossoming inside her.

Angie reflected her own renewal. As they returned from town a short while later, she radiated a happiness that filled Brynn with new hope. Of course, the throwaway camera

Brynn had purchased for her helped. It was to be an experiment for her daughter, as well as a token of appreciation to the uncle whose sharing of his creativity had helped make today possible.

It took a bit of stealth to get from their driveway to Gideon's house. Brynn tried to be casual as she checked the yards of their nearest neighbors to make sure no one was out back, but as she and Angie let themselves into Gideon's yard, she had to admit he'd been right about her being a bad cat burglar.

Being in his yard without him seemed odd at first, too. She didn't exactly feel as though they were trespassing, but his persona was so strong that when he wasn't around, something of him lingered, prompting the feeling that if she turned around suddenly, she would find him standing there watching her.

He had left something. At the back door was a bud vase with a white rose in it. A card with the simple word, Welcome was left under the base.

Brynn found herself transfixed by his handwriting, realizing this was the first time she'd seen it. She liked the upright strokes of the letters, and although the black pen he'd used had a fine point, his stroke was strong. Just like the man.

Kind gesture aside, she still didn't go inside, but began experimenting, framing shots, then moving plants for maximum light effect and dramatic appeal. Sometimes Angie liked her subject, too, and took a picture of her own; more often than not, though, she moved around the yard by herself looking for birds, butterflies and beetles to snap.

When Gideon pulled in to the driveway, Brynn checked her watch to find it was, indeed, after noon. She unlocked the door to the house and they met him as he entered from the garage. In one arm he carried a large brown bag, and the scents emanating from it had her mouth watering.

"Mmm, Angie, what do you think it could be?" She placed the vase on the table against the wall and scooped up her daughter to give her a better view. Angie's response was to point to the chair she'd sat in yesterday, then to fold her hands perfecting a picture of ladylike patience.

"I suspected you wouldn't take things slowly and would be extra hungry," Gideon said, unpacking. "Chinese take-out. Are you game?"

"After you've gone through all this trouble? Of course. It really does smell delicious. Is it spicy?" She was concerned for Angie's sake.

"Some will be. But I had them marked to protect the little one's tender tummy." He drew out the last box and placed it before Angie. "Sweet-and-sour chicken for you, little Miss Chicken." Then he bent to kiss the top of Angie's head and said softly, "The bathroom is down the hall. Why don't you go rinse your hands before we eat."

Once she was heading that way, he faced Brynn. "You haven't been inside. Is something wrong?"

"No! And I love the flower and note. But, Gideon, I'm not going to easily forget that I've talked you into this, and I'm trying not to invade your privacy too much."

He exhaled with measured slowness. "Sweet fool. I want you so much, I let out my class fifteen minutes early and almost earned myself a ticket racing to get here. Let me worry about the coping."

Angie's return kept her from replying. But she thought it unfair to him that he assume all the responsibility for their unorthodox relationship.

He didn't give her time to brood, though. For the next half hour they were busy tasting and devouring the exotic selections he'd chosen for them. And when he let Angie open the last white box, Brynn chuckled at the three fortune cookies inside.

"I should have guessed! You pick first, sweetheart, and Mommy will read it for you."

Angie chose the one on top and snapped it as Brynn directed. At the first glimpse of paper, she sucked in her breath and held out both hands.

"Okay, let's see. It says, 'Chocolate is in your future!'"

"It does?" Gideon rose. "Well, we'd better make sure that comes true." He made a production of opening the refrigerator's freezer door and pretending to look all around the inside. Then with a satisfied "Ah!" he brought out the package of chocolate-dipped cones.

As Angie unwrapped hers, Brynn murmured to Gideon, "You really thought of everything."

"Are you sure you don't want one?"

"I'm full, thanks."

He returned the box to the freezer. "Then at least open your cookie. Angie is waiting to hear what the others say."

He was right, and Brynn pretended to be unsure which she should choose. Then, as Gideon had getting the ice cream, she made a show of opening it.

"'Yesterday can teach, but it cannot be relived,'" she finally read. Clearing her throat, she gave Gideon a wry look. "I think I got yours."

He pushed the box to her. "Then try again."

"Oh, no. That's yours."

The way he hesitated made her wonder if he was afraid of what it would say.

She put the cookie into his hand. "I saw on a news story that they always contain positive messages."

Looking less than convinced, he snapped the hard dough between his fingers and read the message quickly. Brynn could see he didn't care for what it said.

She reached over and eased it from his grasp. "'Love and a red nose can't be hidden.'"

The microwave clock switched to the next minute. Angie made lapping noises like a puppy.

"Well!" Brynn declared, not wanting the silence to continue for fear that Angie would sense something, "Speaking of red noses, we'd better put sunblock on our next shopping list, right, angel? And some hats. Otherwise we're going to have the red noses around here."

She thought it was a smooth save, and when Gideon

dampened a paper towel and saved Angie from dripping ice cream on her clothes, he did seem all right. But when they were cleaning up, he threw his cookie and fortune into the trash with considerable force, and the only small talk he initiated was with Angie.

Only after they had everything cleaned and put away did he finally seem to come back to himself. "Tell me how it went," he said. "Do you think you'll be able to get any good shots?"

Wishing he would tell her why he'd reacted the way he did, she replied, "You know I will. Your trees are superb specimens. But I'd like to experiment with staging more. I stopped at the library hoping to find something on the subject, but without much luck."

"I have a few books that you might want to look through before you continue. Come back to the office. You might as well see where you'll be spending a good deal of time."

The room was the most furnished in the house, containing a computer desk, a few filing cabinets and one bookcase. She could see into his bedroom across the hall, where there was a queen-size bed and nothing else, not even a headboard. It made her think that maybe he hadn't felt the calling to become a monk, but he certainly continued to live as sparely as one.

The bottom row of the bookcase was full of bonsai and garden books. When she inspected them more closely, Brynn could barely bring herself to touch them.

"They're so fine and old, like the trees themselves. Are you sure you want anyone handling them?"

"You're not anyone. Take them with you."

Whatever had disturbed him before, the warmth in his look told her that he was well over it. "In that case, you'd better lend me a bath towel, or something," she told him. "I'll wrap them to keep them safe, and get started on them tonight after everyone goes to bed." Not the text, of course, because it was in Japanese, but the photographs would tell her a good deal.

"Just don't let me see your light on too late."

She didn't think it wise to tell him that if she thought of him watching her window too much, she wouldn't get any sleep.

The rest of the week went much the same way. First thing in the morning Brynn would go to a one-hour photograph developing service, then she and Angie would spend the rest of the time at Gideon's. He would arrive from classes shortly after noon with lunch, and they would sit in his dark, cool kitchen to feast and talk.

She soon noticed Gideon allowed himself to be a different person with Angie. He let down barriers more readily, teased, although a bit awkwardly, and played with even more inexperience. His deep feelings for her daughter were unmistakable; just as it was impossible not to know he was trying hard not to expose what he felt for *her*.

But as soon as she began telling herself that she could be grateful if things could stay like this, they were thrown back into reality. On Friday Angie surprised Gideon by eating almost nothing and leaving the table to go outside, where she curled into a ball on the bench.

"What did I do?" He looked devastated.

"It's not you. Dominic wants me to enroll her in signing classes," she said, keeping her voice low. "Before, he agreed with me about sparing her that. But he's getting impatient because he can't communicate with her easily enough. He doesn't want to realize that if she learns to sign, he won't understand that, either."

Something of the old Gideon reappeared as his mouth tightened. "I see. And what did you say?"

"Not very much yet. I've been too busy trying to repair the damage. Angie overheard, of course. That's the way we are with children. If they're small or are quiet natured, we treat them like dolls, not human beings with working ears." Brynn shifted to keep her child in view. "Now all she wants to do is sleep. That's how she copes. She always sleeps when she's depressed or frightened about something. I can almost see her withdrawing into a cocoon, and it frightens me because it gets harder each time to coax her back out.''

She quickly dabbed at the corners of her eyes. ''This morning she wouldn't come down for breakfast until after Dominic left. I used the opportunity to explain to him, but he saw only the rebellion of a child. He told me I was spoiling her. He said she would never speak, because I was giving her permission—imagine, Gideon, *permission*—not to!''

He drew his chair closer to hers and offered her the comfort of his arms, his strong shoulder, despite her whisper, ''I'm all right. I'm not going to cry.''

''You're shaking.''

''I'm angry. This shouldn't be about what Dominic wants, it should be about what Angie needs!''

''What can I do? Do you want me to go talk to him?''

Brynn pressed her fingers to his mouth before she thought what she was doing. ''No! If he finds out now that we spend all this time with you— I've been trying to think of a way to tell him about working for you, but now there's no possibility of that until he gets over this.''

He took her hand within both his and kissed her fingers. ''There has to be something I can do.''

''Go out to her. Talk to her.''

''What can I say that you haven't?''

''Say what's in here.'' With her free hand she touched his heart. ''That will be more important to her. You two are on the same wavelength in that respect.''

He murmured her name and drew that hand, both arms, around his neck, then wrapped his around her, locking her against him. ''I wish I could make it stop for you. There's too much heartache. Too much.''

She could have stayed like that forever. His heat and strength replenished hers. The panic receded. Knowing how much Angie needed that, too, she stroked his cheek, kissed him and eased from his hold. ''Go,'' she whispered.

It was sweet to watch them. Gideon sat next to her at first, barely doing more than stroking her hair. Brynn couldn't hear what he was saying as he gazed out at his garden, but she saw her daughter's body slowly relax. After a while, Angie took his hand and drew it under her cheek like a pillow; and after another while, she climbed onto his lap.

He rocked her for the rest of their time together. Brynn busied herself by cleaning up their lunch things. Periodically she would go to the doorway, reassured by what she saw. As long as she protected that fine thread that bound those two, her child would find her way back out of the darkness.

His power to heal was proved later that evening when Angie didn't refuse to have supper at her grandfather's table. While she didn't look at him much, at least she didn't shrink away when he kissed her good-night.

To Brynn that was enough to work with.

"We interrupt this program to bring you this special bulletin…"

Brynn was in the kitchen Saturday afternoon preparing for the freezer the abundance of zucchini Domenic had harvested from the garden when she heard the interruption on the TV in the living room. As always, her heart started pounding, because it was never good news.

A part of her tried not to listen. She forced a chuckle at Angie, who was concentrating so intensely on sealing the filled plastic freezer bags correctly, her little face was scrunched into more of a growl than a grimace.

"Brynn! *Dio*—come quick!"

At the sound of Dominic's cry, she hurried to the living room, wiping her hands on her apron. He was sitting forward in his chair, pointing at the TV screen with one hand and punching up the volume on the remote control with the other.

As soon as she heard "hostage situation at Blanchette College," she bolted across to take the remote from him. "Dominic, Angie!"

That she managed that horrified whisper at all amazed her, because Gideon was at the school today. So was Lillian. The school was sponsoring a special lecture series, and Saturday's guest speaker was a controversial South American novelist whose lover was a high-ranking military official currently rumored to be taking kickbacks in return for allowing contraband headed for the U.S. to leave his country.

"We understand the man holding the hostages at gunpoint is an exchange student whose brother was killed by General Moroya's troops during a protest in the capital city last October." The anchorwoman looked straight into the TV camera, her expression grim as she held one hand to her earpiece and repeated the data she was being given. "We have no confirmation on the number of hostages at this time, or if there are any casualties. It is known, however, that the police have surrounded the auditorium where the event was taking place, and witnesses confirm several shots were fired in the initial moments."

As she continued with a plea that residents of the community not impede rescue vehicles and law-enforcement personnel on their way to the scene by driving there themselves, Dominic sprang to his feet.

"I'm going."

"Don't be ridiculous. Didn't you just hear what they said?"

"But there was shooting! Lillian may be hurt!"

And Gideon. Her own impulse was to race there herself, but she knew that would be counterproductive and exactly what Gideon wouldn't want. No, her concern at the moment had to be to keep Angie from finding out and getting upset.

"I'm taking the baby upstairs," she told him. "Please keep the sound down as you listen for news."

The next several hours were a nightmare. Somehow she managed to get Angie fed and into bed without catching on, despite the sound of sirens that could occasionally be heard even here at the house. The sirens did upset Angie, but Brynn told her it was only an old building across town that had caught fire.

"They need every fire truck they can get to keep the

flames from spreading, that's what all the excitement is about, angel. But you know what? You can sleep in Mommy's bed tonight. We'll turn on my CD player—you like going to sleep to the sound of the seashore and the seagulls talking, remember? I'll put those on and then you don't have to hear those loud sirens.''

The ruse worked, and Angie soon fell asleep.

Relieved, Brynn returned downstairs to find out what had happened since she'd last snuck down to get an update.

"It's over," Dominic said, slumped in his seat. He looked as exhausted as if he'd been through the ordeal himself. "They arrested the lunatic. Thank heaven no one was seriously injured. I'm going to bed."

"I thought you said you wanted to talk to Lillian when she came home?"

"She was right there." He gestured with both hands, framing the TV screen. "She's busy doing her work, talking to police, reporters. She won't be home for hours yet. We talk tomorrow. I gotta lie down."

It was just as well. With the house settled, she could concentrate on her own nerves. It never crossed her mind to go to bed herself.

In the darkness she kept silent vigil, waiting at the back door. When she saw Gideon's sedan pull in to his driveway, it was close to eleven o'clock.

Certain she could fly if she had to, she let herself out and ran to him.

When he heard her, he immediately shut off the garage light, but his aim was perfect as she rushed into the garage and into his arms.

"I was afraid you'd heard," he said against her hair.

"Everything. It was all they had on TV."

"Angie?"

"I managed to keep her from finding out. She's asleep. But what about you? Are you all right? I was so worried." The questions bubbled out of her, and she couldn't keep her hands still. It was as though they needed their own proof. She touched his hair, his face, the breadth of his strong back.

"I'm fine," he kept saying to her. But his hold was as fierce as hers.

"Was it terrible?"

"A little tense."

"I'll ask Lillian in the morning."

"She was magnificent."

"Dominic was a wreck. Today I saw how deeply he cares about her. I hope he remembers those feelings."

"I don't want to talk about him."

She understood. All he wanted was for the world to turn right side out again. It was the same for her.

"I worried you might offer your services," she whispered, unable to keep that from him.

"The situation could have been handled more quickly. You won't believe what stopped me, though."

"The thought of prison, I hope."

"No, of you. Of your disappointment in me if I botched things and that poor dumb kid got hurt."

"Or you!" She didn't want to even think about that. "When they were bringing him out, I thought I'd glimpsed you on TV."

"Not likely. I waited until Lillian had all the cameras on her and snuck away."

His heartbeat was strong and reassuring against hers; she would have been content to stay there like that for the rest of the night if she hadn't been concerned about him. "You must be exhausted. I should go and let you get some rest."

"Wait." His arms tightened. "Another minute. Holding you is more soothing than any warm shower or bed."

The truth was that she didn't want to leave him, either, and when he eased back against the Sheetrock wall, she let him take her with him, despite the effect the sudden intimate alignment of their bodies had on her senses.

She searched his face, difficult to do in the seductive darkness. But her body could register the heat and growing conflict in his.

"Gideon? Are you going to kiss me?"

"I told myself if I could just hold you, I would resist."

"Even though I want you to?"

"Brynn."

"I know. Undermining your noble intentions doesn't help. But I believed I could have lost you today, Gideon. It may not change any of our other hundred and one problems, but—"

He silenced her with his mouth. She knew he meant the contact to be brief from the hard, almost frustrated press of his lips. But the pleasure of being this close again, the celebration of being alive, obliterated his defenses as fast as her relief justified her intent.

A low, rough sound rose in his throat, then he was urging her to open for him, driving into her as if striving to capture something elusive, something forever just out of his reach. Brynn rose on tiptoe, wishing the soles of her sneakers were a fraction thicker to help him.

The kiss spoke honestly of what he wouldn't put into words, what he wanted to do to and with her. Images flashed behind her closed lids. She saw how it would be, both of them naked, their limbs entwined and gleaming from passion restrained and spent.

He broke the kiss and pressed her head against his chest. His heartbeat drummed into her ear.

"Don't let go."

"For the love of heaven, Brynn. I'm only human."

So was she. There were parts of her coming alive that she thought were dead forever. She couldn't be still; the ache was a fist in her womb, clenching and twisting.

"Please, Gideon."

"Don't you think I want to?" He pressed apologetic kisses across her damp forehead, a more anguished one against the side of her throat. "What little I sleep, I dream of being inside you. It never ends. The wanting, the need, the pleasure… Sometimes I think, this time. This time my heart will burst and there'll be relief from it at last.''

"Don't say that!" she gasped.

"It's the truth! Sometimes I wish I'd never met you. Dying would be easier."

She couldn't bear to hear him talk like that. "Then take me inside."

"No."

"I want you to."

"Damn it, no!"

But he was so tight she thought he would snap. It wasn't right that there should be so much pain from something so beautiful.

She rubbed her cheek against him. Brushed a kiss in the soft nest of hair exposed in the V of his shirt. "Gideon, help me." Kissing the spot where his pulse throbbed fiercely, she reached for his hand and drew it down to the front of her jeans. "Help me."

She rocked herself against him, almost coming apart at the slightest contraction of his hand. When he muttered what sounded like a prayer and began intensifying the caress, she thought she wouldn't be able to keep her legs from buckling. Only her need to share this with him kept her from losing control, and ever so slowly, she laced her fingers with his and pressed closer and closer until the back of her hand rubbed the front of his jeans.

"Brynn, we can't."

"We have to."

His breath sounded like someone suffocating. The hand gripping hers was tight enough to crush bones, but none of that outweighed the ecstasy that he was bringing to her, or the relief that she was about to give him.

But suddenly everything changed. He lifted and pressed her against the wall. "Hold me," he rasped against her mouth.

Even as she wrapped her legs around him, and drove her hands into his hair, he began rubbing and rocking against her. Around and around, just like his tongue dancing with and seducing hers. Long erotic strokes at first, then harder and faster in a rhythm that forced an end to the kiss and had them clutching each other and panting into each other's shoulder.

And then he was shuddering and she was sobbing, but from joy, and the night kept it all mercifully wrapped in its velvet cloak of secrecy.

When his heartbeat no longer felt like a sledgehammer trying to break out of his chest, and he let her slide slowly to her feet, she could feel his remorse bleed through, staining the beauty of what they'd shared.

"Don't regret this."

"How can I not? You forget—"

"Nothing." Saddened by his response, she eased around and away from him. "You're unlovable and I'm too good for anyone. Fine. But you can't deny that for a few moments we were perfect. I won't let you steal that from us."

As she ran out into the night, he called after her, but she ignored him. She couldn't afford to go back. She was afraid if she did, she would beg him to let her stay, and that was the last thing he wanted to hear from anyone, particularly *Mrs.* Brynn Delmarco.

Chapter Eleven

Sunday was brutal, and the rest of the week showed little more mercy. Oh, he saw her—Brynn proved to him she could be the consummate professional, stopping by to return books, to show him snapshots and sketches, to pick up the draft of the outline he'd finally pulled together. But that only got Gideon through Tuesday. He took care of Wednesday and Thursday by heaping a list of research questions on her. The look on her face as she'd walked out of his house had him grateful and ready when Lillian called him into her office on Friday afternoon.

She looked no worse for wear, considering the turmoil the school had been through. In fact, she was blossoming. Consequently, when she told him about her date with Dominic for the following day, and their intention to take Angie with them, he momentarily forgot that he'd come to tell her the book was a no-can-do project.

"You're what?" There was always the chance he'd heard incorrectly.

"I said, Dominic and I are taking Angie to New Orleans, and C.C. is lending us his corporate plane so we can avoid all that driving time. I have to make a special presentation, but that will only take an hour or so in the morning, and then I thought we would have lunch in the French Quarter, take a riverboat ride or whatever it is children like to do. Why are you looking at me like that? You told me that you needed my assistance with this project."

"To keep Dominic busy so he doesn't find out that Brynn is working on the book with me. But—"

"This is better. It's the real thing!"

He was afraid she was serious, and decided not to comment about that part. "I never said anything about Angie." He couldn't imagine Brynn would let her go.

There was more than a little amusement in Lillian's gaze. "If you're relying on one tiny girl as protection, you're in trouble, my friend."

"Lillian, I don't really need this right now."

"And I have another appointment in ten minutes, so relax, I'll stop teasing you. The reason I called you over was to tell you that I'm turning over a new leaf. The events of last week made me put my life under the sharpest of microscopes, and I've come to some startling revelations and decisions."

This was not starting well.

"As my oldest and dearest friend down here, and even though I know better than to get my hopes up about you surprising me with a bridal shower, I'm going to tell you anyway." She clasped her hands at her diaphragm like an opera singer. "I'm not going to fight it anymore. I'm going to let Dominic—as that delicious saying goes—court me."

"Thank you, Lillian. Thank you all to hell."

She looked more confused than offended. "What's wrong with you? And what's with the profanity?"

"You're not the only one into cultivating these days."

The rest of the sparkle went out of her eyes. "That had

better not mean what I think it does. I'm meeting with C. C. Day's publicity department the first of next week and, call me crazy, but I perform better when I'm not lying through my teeth.''

"If things get any worse, you'd better start practicing.''

That had her rising and circling the desk. "What's happened?''

What could he tell her? "The usual.''

"Don't try a garage sale version about 'the best-laid plans' with me. I may be as blind as a rhino when it comes to my own relationships, but Brynn is in love with you!''

She cared deeply for him, hurt for him and was intrigued with him. She was even "in lust" with him. But regardless of what had happened last Saturday night, Gideon couldn't allow himself to believe it was anything other than a momentary overload of adrenaline. Oh, he would always be grateful that it had been him she'd reached out to, but the result would be the same. When she awoke from the long sleep her soul had been in, he would not be the kind of man she would want to spend the rest of her days with.

"Brynn," he replied, "is a lovely and generous woman who's healing and about to move on to the rest of her life. Don't confuse her by making her believe that future has me in it.''

Lillian didn't counter with a smart-alecky remark as he expected, she merely crossed her arms over her chest. "You're serious. You're going to let the best thing that ever happened to you slip through your fingers?" She shook her head. "You're a fool, Gideon.''

He went to the door. "Don't make yourself late for your next appointment by waiting for me to deny it.''

He considered being gone on Saturday. He played with the idea of feigning some sudden emergency or forgotten commitment. But when Brynn finally arrived—later than he'd expected—she acted as she had all week, reserved and quiet, except for suggestions of how they should use this time.

He thought the idea of setting up computer files and transferring data from their joint notes to them was excellent. If only she hadn't come over looking like a buttercup in a sundress that brought out the sunshine in her hair and the cream in her skin. Everything he didn't need to be reminded of.

"Did Dominic and the, ah, girls get off all right?" he asked, leading the way to his office.

"Yes."

"I'm a bit surprised that you let Angie go with them." Realizing how that sounded, Gideon amended, "I meant to go at all. Did she want to?"

"Absolutely not. That's why when I told her she would get to fly again, ride a big old riverboat and get to eat every variety of junk food her grandfather was likely to find for her, and she threw a fit, I simply threw her favorite stuffed animal into the yard to get her out of the house."

He supposed he deserved that. She was an excellent mother who wouldn't have taken any risks with the child if she wasn't sure Angie could handle it. But he was taken aback by the fierce emotions with which she'd turned on him.

Excusing himself, he thought it wiser to make himself scarce.

It took him about forty minutes to figure out that she was still hurt, and that he was being a coward; also, that the only way to resolve this mess was to face it head-on.

Returning to his office, he drew up the other chair to face hers and took both of her hands within his. "Brynn, let me try to explain myself to you."

She tugged free and almost knocked her chair over as she backed away from him. "How dare you."

"What's wrong now?"

"How old are you, Gideon?"

"What does that—?" He saw her look of warning and sighed. "Forty-five."

"Well, I'm thirty. That doesn't quite give you the right to talk to me—no, at me!—as though you were my daddy."

Considering the life he'd lived, he felt like her great-grandfather. "I didn't think I was. I only meant to make you understand."

"I do understand. You!" she cried before spreading her arms wide. "But not the purpose for all this rehashing of the same old pain."

"Because it's earned. At least, mine is," he said with grim certainty. "I don't know what to tell you about yours except that innocent lambs have been sacrificed since the beginning of time."

She shook her head slowly. "You still don't get it, do you? I'm not innocent, and I'm definitely not perfect. But I do have needs and desires. I never thought I had to be ashamed of them, until I met you."

She'd gone away that night with that impression? "Never ashamed," he said, getting angry himself. "Don't you say that."

"Don't you tell me what I can and can't feel! The important moments in our lives can't be measured by a clock. They have to be taken and cherished for what they are." Brynn gestured toward the desk. "You trust me enough to help you with your book. Why can't you trust me enough to ease some of your loneliness? Why can't you let yourself help me forget some of mine?"

She fell silent as though suddenly realizing what she'd said. But accepting her own challenge, she stepped toward him.

"Do you want me? Really want me this time? Without clothes? Without the darkness? Nothing but you, me and what we can give each other?"

"Dumbest question of the century, Brynn," he replied softly.

"Then make love with me."

He didn't know about the "with" part; he would probably never convince himself that she could want him anywhere nearly as much as he wanted her. But he could show her what she meant to him with every ounce of his being.

He rose and gazed down at her.

How did that begin for a man and woman who had already shared all that they had?

With a kiss, he decided, doing so. Eyes open. Lips soft, inviting...a little dry, too, from nerves, and anticipation. Easily moistened by a suckling caress. His. Hers. Warmed then by mutual shimmering sighs.

Now hands. Gideon raised his to frame her face, his thumbs stroking, lifting her chin higher to give him complete access to that lovely bow that was her mouth.

Love in the afternoon. Bare. Bold. This was how honest she was. Anyone could champion the night, but the afternoon belonged to brave souls like Brynn, who held his steady gaze as determinedly as she refused to let him keep her enshrined or reduce her to some one-dimensional image.

Once again she'd surprised him. She was proving so much his equal in strength and determination, he stood awed.

Their next kiss was deeper, a reunion with heat and tastes that filled his senses and spread through his veins like steaming, honeyed wine. He wanted more and asked boldly, his mouth ravenous, eating at hers, drinking her sighs and moans as well as her sweetness. And all the while their eyes remained transfixed on each other, mesmerized by their sensual foreplay.

At last he could comb his fingers through the silk of her hair. Learning it was the only cool place on her, he wanted to rub it all over himself.

She indulged in her fascination with the precise line of his mustache and beard, and then with the effect her delicate touch had on his lips. When he decided she'd tormented him enough with her kitten play, he closed his hands over fistfuls of her hair and locked his mouth to hers, taking a bit of the edge off his hunger—and convincing the kitten he was ready for the lioness.

Her nails, though short, scored his back lightly before she

started tugging his T-shirt from his jeans. Excited, ready, he still wasn't prepared for his reaction when her flesh came in contact with his.

He sucked in a slow, long breath as she splayed her fingers and ran them from his waist to his shoulders.

"Do that again," he groaned. "Touch me."

"Don't you think you should take me to your bedroom first?"

He'd already lost track of everything but her, including where they were. Lifting her into his arms so fast it should have made her head spin, he brought her into that other spartan room, that was agreeably darker due to the drawn blinds. As soon as he set her on her feet beside the bed, she switched on the lamp on the table behind her.

There was a look of understanding in her eyes as she turned back to him. "Now it's less like a cloister or cell...or barren womb. I'm assuming that your whole inventory of T-shirts and jeans is hidden in the back of your closet?"

He wasn't in the mood for humor, even the gentle kind, and took hold of her waist, making circular strokes with his thumbs that slowly ventured upward, higher and higher. "Why don't you just tell me...what you want?"

A second before he reached the undersides of her breasts, she resumed trying to slide up his T-shirt. "This. Off."

Although reluctant to release her, he ripped it over his head and dropped it. His reward, or punishment, was to suffer the dreamy-eyed caress of her gaze, which all by itself had his nipples hardening and his stomach clenching.

"Touch me again," he rasped.

"Like this?"

Oh, she touched him, but not just with her hands. The instant the tip of her tongue came in contact with his nipple, he thought he would climax from the sheer pleasure of it.

Groaning again, he buried his hands in her hair and urged her closer.

As she wet him, and gently tested the sensitive nub with her teeth, her hands explored where she wanted to journey next. Watching, it was all he could do not to push her back onto the bed and take her right then and there.

Needing that mouth again, he drew her up. She opened to him eagerly, responded to everything he showed her he wanted, but even that wasn't enough now, and to satisfy the growing urgency rising within him, he ran his hands down the front of her body until he completely covered her breasts. He cupped and caressed, learning whatever bra she was wearing, it couldn't be much more than the barest of coverings. Wanting to see, more than he wanted his next breath, he tugged the tie at her waist and none too patiently unwrapped her to his gaze.

As he'd already learned through touch, she was beautiful, not really small, but delicate. Freeing her from that wisp of lace, his mind both provoked and punished: Had she been able to nurse Angie? How he wished he could have witnessed that. How he wished, how he wished. But nothing so precious would ever be for the likes of him, and the knowledge was a vise crushing his chest.

"Gideon."

He dragged his thoughts back to the present. To her.

Brynn's graceful movements were almost a dance as she brushed her dress and bra from her shoulders. "You're thinking too much again."

"Only of you. Of what I'm going to do to you."

"With me. Don't you want to lie down?"

Bloody hell, dressed in nothing but that bit of buttery lace between her legs, she could make him forget there was a bed. But as she slipped off her sandals and eased onto the ivory sheets, he followed like a compass chasing the North Star, tracing a line of kisses from her knee upward until he had her almost completely beneath him.

When she tried to pull him closer, he resisted, bracing himself on his forearms.

"I'm too heavy."

"I want your weight. And this—" she stroked his chest hair "—rubbing my breasts. And this—" she arched her hips

slightly to intensify the invasion of him between her thighs
"—feeling how much you want to be inside me."

It was a testament to his willpower, but he gave her what
she'd asked for, and added another delicious experience for
himself, by twisting around after several long moments to
wet her coral nipple, then suck her deep into his mouth.

Her erotic gasp of surprise and pleasure burned a few more
threads of his self-control. She almost annihilated the rest
when she wrapped her thighs around one of his and rubbed
herself against him in a restless search for relief.

"Not that way, my dream. Not this time."

Freeing himself, he slid down her body, his mouth open
and hot against her taut, flawless skin, growing more humid
as he came to elastic, then lace. The curls he glimpsed behind
the triangle were every bit as gold as her hair. What they
protected, he discovered upon drawing the confection down
her legs, was so perfect a rosebud, he couldn't resist pausing
to caress the dewy petals with his thumb.

Glancing up, he saw the growing need in her eyes. "I'd
want a night just to pleasure you with my mouth," he murmured, sweeping off her panties the rest of the way. But
unable to believe they would even be allowed to complete
this, he stroked her silken thighs to woo himself better access
and tried to bring her a lifetime of ecstasy with the most
intimate of kisses.

He reveled in the sounds she made, in her responsiveness
to his slightest ministrations. And he would have given anything to bring her to completion this way, first. But he'd
taught her not to trust him—at least, not about there being
more afterward.

Proving agility could outmaneuver size, she somehow
managed to scramble from beneath him and sat back on her
heels, a slightly flushed but delectable vision.

"Not twice without you inside me."

"It's your needs I care about. I don't care about me."

To prove otherwise, she inched closer, stroked the front

of his jeans, winning a shudder from him, as well as a rough oath.

The merciless streak of hunger that shot through his body was almost his undoing. "Ah, hell," he growled, grabbing her hand. He brought it to his lips for a quick kiss, wondering if it was possible to get the damned zipper down without losing control. It didn't help that Brynn had risen to her knees and was driving him to utter distraction, not only with her talented hands, but with her sleek body as she intentionally and unintentionally rubbed against him.

His muscles tighter than overstretched bindings, he succeeded in freeing himself and reached for her. Then he saw the flicker of doubt in her eyes as she looked down.

"Are you sure?"

"Yes." She reached between them. "But I want to touch you first."

He snatched her hand away and redirected her arm around his neck. "Only if you want to kill me."

When he felt himself probing her moist center, he figured he was finished regardless. "You do it. I don't want to hurt you."

"Then look at me. Don't close your eyes," she whispered, beginning to lower herself onto him. "Look at me. Let me see what it's like for you."

He wanted to watch her responses, too.

Mesmerized, he watched her pupils dilate, her skin grow more flushed and damp, the tension in her body build and build...until her fingers were butterfly wings on his shoulders, and she was pressing and rocking her forehead against his, whispering broken sentences and softer pleas.

They were part of each other.

It was too good. Impossible. The strain kept escalating inside and out. And at the very center of it all was her, so hot and tight gloving him, milking him.

The sensations wouldn't stop coming; they carried him on a relentless wave toward the very edge of reason. He wanted to throw back his head and roar like some wild animal, to roll her beneath him and pound himself into her until he was emptier than this room.

He wanted to weep.

The beauty of it was incredible, the blessing impossible to believe.

He took hold of her hips.

"Gideon, don't. I can't bear more."

"Only a little...and better."

"It's too much."

"Please," he crooned. "Please. Just stay with me, sweet. So sweet."

Like that...oh, like that.

The words echoed again and again in his head, but he didn't know whether he spoke them or she did. He did know her short nails bit into his arms and back again, hard enough this time to leave marks as he raced her closer and closer to the brink. Her breathing thinned, became a whimper, then a silent gasp, and he wanted badly to own it, too. And it was as he claimed her mouth with his that his body caught fire, and the convulsions overrode his control. All there was to do was clutch her fiercely to him and pray there would be something to salvage from the ashes.

A part of Brynn dreaded moving for fear of rousing him and triggering his withdrawal. Another part couldn't stop touching and stroking.

The contrasts between them enthralled her. The man himself made her ache all over again. She wanted to savor the subtle and not-so-subtle differences, to caress all those long-corded muscles, lick more of the droplets of perspiration from his body, to continue holding him, still throbbing, inside her forever.

Any head doctor would say that this had been a huge mistake. That they were risking a great deal by yielding to their physical appetites when their personal lives were such a mess. But she disagreed.

She doubted she and Gideon could ever be friends if they

couldn't be lovers. If Tony had not died and their paths had crossed, Gideon would have disappeared. The chemistry between them was simply too strong to believe otherwise. It would have gotten in the way of everything else.

That same chemistry now bound them irrevocably.

He was already worried about that, she could sense it. Soon he would insist this changed nothing. He would still see no future for them, and when her body stopped pulsating and her heart slowed to where she could think clearly, perhaps she would be able to see that as being for the best. He would never be an easy man to deal with long-term on any level. Damaged people never were. It did, however, make the unalterable fact that she'd fallen in love with him a poignant dilemma.

She welcomed his prolonged silence, for it insulated her own. Words weren't necessary right now, anyway. It was enough to stroke her cheek against his, to glide her thigh along his hip, to anticipate his every breath and the caress of that matted hair that made her sensitized flesh tingle as though his lips were moving over her.

Their languid writhing wasn't unlike two cats between sleep and wakefulness who were enjoying the sensual art and mysterious physics of touching.

She wasn't expecting it when he nudged her head up with his chin so he could get at her mouth again, and apparently he didn't anticipate that their gazes would meet. But they did—and held.

Suddenly, as if they hadn't dragged those last cries out of each other, he uttered a deep-throated groan and rolled her beneath him. It was another impaling, unapologetic and deep. Brynn hugged him to her, tempted to beg him to start all over again.

But it had to be his choice this time.

He shifted, and his gaze roamed her face. When it settled on her chin, he frowned. When he stroked the spot, she felt a slight burning sensation where his beard had rubbed her a little raw.

"I should be horsewhipped," he muttered.

She ran her fingertips over the spot. "How bad is it?"

"Maybe you can cover it with makeup, but that's not the point." He trapped her fingers with his and used the back of his hand to caress her. "This is too fine to be treated to crude groping and—"

"There was nothing crude about it."

"Not for lack of wanting there to be." He brushed away a strand of her hair stuck to her damp throat, then bent to kiss the sensitive spot. "In the end I felt something predatory taking over. It was too much a reminder of who I'd been, Brynn."

"I liked everything you did to me."

Her words had him stirring in the liquid depths of her body. But his expression was anything but sublime.

"I didn't even offer to take the proper precautions with you. Did you like that, too?"

She had wondered when they would get around to dealing with that. She sighed, and brushed back his hair off his brow. "Gideon, between your celibacy and mine, I think we're probably two of the surest bets on the planet for being safe."

"I wasn't talking about disease, I was talking about…"

He wouldn't say it. He'd let his gaze sweep down her body, and she'd seen the ghosts of dreams he wouldn't let himself have, along with the dread that he might, indeed, have put her at risk in that consequential way.

It broke her heart all over again, that having shared such intimacy, he couldn't be honest with her about his feelings now.

"You can relax," she told him. "I won't get pregnant, either. I'm still on the Pill…at least, until this prescription runs out in two more months."

"But you're Catholic."

"I know what I am, Gideon."

"I'm only trying to understand."

"It was stress. It had done such a number on my body, my doctor insisted I take them. Relieved?"

"I have to be."

The words might have come out reluctantly, but he managed all the same. "How complimentary. Do you think I'd force you to do something you didn't want?"

"Couldn't want," he corrected grimly.

"By your interpretation. Technically, there aren't any legalities standing in the way."

"Try your father-in-law. He would come after me with his gardening hoe in one hand and the kitchen cleaver in the other." His frown spoke of frustration at having to remind her of that.

In another moment he would be withdrawing completely, leaving the bed and her, and putting up those emotional walls again. Brynn touched his chest. "Forgive me. I shouldn't be saying those things."

"You have every right to." As he lifted his gaze to hers once again, that traitorous nerve in his cheek twitched. "Can I ask...? Were you intending Angie to be an only child?"

She shook her head, her smile all regret. "We wanted another baby once we moved. We discussed the situation with my doctor and she insisted that the Pill was the safest route for me. Of course, we never told Dominic. I don't know who would be more upset, him or our parish priest."

Gideon took some time to consider that. "Brynn," he said at last. "If things were different, I would have been honored to give you a child."

She knew what it had cost him to make that confession. It was his gift to her.

Touched, Brynn's eyes filled.

"No, don't." He kissed the fine trail of moisture that seeped down either side of her face. Then kissed her eyelids, her forehead, her lips. "Ah, Brynn. My sweet, sweet dream. I shouldn't have done that to you. It wasn't fair."

"I'm glad you did." She summoned a smile, watery though it was. "It makes this moment precious. For the rest of my life I'll always believe that second child I never had was ours, Gideon. Yours and mine."

"You can't say that. You're young. You'll meet someone."

"Is he going to look at me the way you do? Will he make my heart sing with the slightest caress? Will his kisses make me forget yours?"

He took her hand and pressed a fervent kiss into her palm. Then another. And another. But somehow that wasn't enough and her lips were then awarded the same attention.

These were different kisses—they spoke of desire, true, but also of something spiritually pure. They went on and on, stealing her breath, stealing her heart.

She realized what he was doing. As he framed her face with hands that worshiped, just as his gaze worshiped, he began moving inside her.

His tenderness enchanted her. His patient restraint awed her. Although his body soon grew hard and heavy with his need, he was making sure she understood what this loving should have meant for them.

Their beginning. Their child.

Oh, yes, he loved her. But his respect for her, his need to protect, as well as the rigid code he held for himself, would keep him from saying the words. But he loved her. It was a white-hot flame, pure beauty in his gray eyes, and in the meticulous care he took in reawakening every pore in her body, building a need only he could sate.

She gave herself up to it and him willingly, showed him a trust she hoped would speak to him long after she left him. Maybe it would be a seed to spawn something else—hopefully the strength to let go of the past.

He did love her.

As their bodies began vibrating with the magnificent tremors of their release, she held him ever tighter and relished the moment his seed shot deep into her body.

And she prayed.

For a miracle.

If only a miracle of time.

Chapter Twelve

"It's me. Am I calling at a bad time?"

He loved hearing her whisper. There was a velvety tone to her already soft voice that immediately aroused him. Only the anxiety beneath, and the knowledge that she would never call and risk exposure, had him frowning and gripping the phone.

"Of course not. But you don't sound like yourself."

"Wait until you hear why. How about we start with a question like—have you had chicken pox?"

He leaned back in his office chair and pinched the bridge of his nose. "Don't tell me...?"

"Apparently while she was in New Orleans with Lillian and Dominic, Angie got exposed to them."

"Poor baby." It had been a surprisingly positive excursion, from what Brynn had relayed to him. And she had sounded so upbeat and hopeful on Monday, convinced that Angie would experience that breakthrough. "How's she doing?"

"It's too early to say, but I can already tell it's not going to be a party for any of us."

"What can I do?"

An odd sound came across the line. "I'm telling you that your photographer-researcher-typist has suddenly announced a disappearing act for the next…two weeks, and you're asking what you can do for me?"

He didn't blame her for sounding as though she'd dialed the wrong number after all. Since Saturday's unforgettable but reprehensible tryst, he'd used every excuse he could think of to keep her busy and himself out of temptation's way. Now, after four days, the last thing he deserved being called was generous and sympathetic. Not when he'd worked them both like slaves so that Lillian—who was hounding him daily for a progress report on the book—would stay off his back. But what was really turning him into a prime candidate for a padded cell was that he missed her worse than she could imagine. He'd been thinking about her, wanting her so badly that his first hope when he'd recognized her voice was that she'd called to suggest phone sex.

Unfortunately, he knew he had to be cold-blooded if he was serious about protecting her, especially when she'd already proved too willing and wonderful to do and be anything for him.

"Would you be happier if I fired you?" he asked flatly.

Her surprise was palpable over the line. "It would be within your rights."

"The rights of a bastard." He leaned forward, resting his elbows on his knees, and rubbed at his forehead with his free hand. "Brynn. Stop doing this to yourself." It was all him. His fault for everything, especially not keeping his jeans zipped. He sighed. "We'll figure out something. By the way, where's Dominic?"

"Outside telling Lillian what the doctor said. He won't be long. It looks as though she was on her way out to some function."

"Is round forty-seven of the Littlejohn-Delmarco romance still on track?"

"They do plan to go out again on Friday."

The wistful note in her voice told him that, like him, she was too aware that they would miss a golden opportunity to spend a few hours together.

He had to rub his thigh hard to relieve the growing ache in his loins. "Give angel a kiss for me, will you?"

"As soon as she can really hear me. When she isn't in a delirious sleep she's getting her days and nights confused, and this afternoon she awoke not knowing where she was. The doctor says this isn't uncommon, but it is one of the worst cases he's seen in a while."

He could hear the undercurrents of anxiety in her voice and it tempted him to drop the phone to race over there to hold both mother and child.

She cleared her throat. "So anyway, I don't have to worry about you coming down with them?"

"What? Oh. No, forget about me. Are you getting any rest?"

"Enough."

Which left them with nothing more to say, Gideon thought, staring at the tile floor between his bare feet. At least, nothing that wouldn't finish turning him into a mental case.

"Um, I think I hear Dominic heading back inside. I'd better let you go."

He doubted that was the case at all, and that if he went to the back window he would see the old lion still out there salivating over Lillian. Brynn was just being Brynn and letting him off the hook. She had more selflessness and class in one strand of her glorious hair than...

"Ah, Brynn. I wish—"

"Don't go soft on me, Genghis Kane," she said, her gentle voice not quite steady.

The use of his students' nickname for him silenced him. Lillian...he thought darkly.

"We said no strings," she continued. "Or at least that's what we were both thinking the other day. I'm glad when you finally let yourself reach out, it was to me. I'm not sorry it happened."

No, but she would be eventually if she had to continue living behind the man who had sought oblivion again and again in her welcoming body, until the approaching night had forced her to go—and who now held her at arm's length.

It was several seconds before Gideon realized she'd hung up quietly.

"Brynn. Brynn."

Her name almost slurred together from the pent-up emotions clogging his lungs and veins. He hung up abruptly and pressed his palms against his eye sockets, willing the threatening moment to pass.

It didn't.

Certain that if he stayed in his asylum much longer, it would turn into a suffocating sweatbox, he got into his car and began driving.

He wasn't surprised when he ended up at the farm Brynn had taken him to...was it only two and a half weeks ago? In the amber of sunset, the August heat showed its most merciless effect on the pasture, and the pond was down several inches because the rain they were getting came in tenths and not inches these days. But as he came to the spot where Brynn had spread her blanket, where Angie had picked daisies and cried over a dead fish, the beauty of the place stung his eyes.

"Oh, God," he groaned. He let his head drop back, its weight almost too heavy to bear. "Help me or get me out of here!"

The birds and crickets fell silent at the harsh interjection, as though expecting an answer.

Gideon knew better. Just as he knew you couldn't force hope where there was none.

Brynn wrung out the handkerchief she'd dipped for the umpteenth time in the bowl of cold water, and, refolding it, carefully placed it over Angie's burning forehead. The child stirred in her fitful sleep, but didn't waken, and that was a minor relief to her.

After three days of watching Angie scratch and writhe, it was a blessing that exhaustion left the child beyond awareness. Brynn knew that it was just a matter of time before the fever broke and Angie started the healing cycle. But as it was when she'd gone through teething with her and all the rest, watching her baby suffer was one of the hardest things a mother could be asked to endure.

Rising from the edge of the bed, she massaged the tense muscles in her neck and shoulders and went to the window. As expected at three o'clock in the morning, all the neighboring houses were dark, including Gideon's, but she couldn't help wondering if he was even home. He came and went at such strange hours these days that if she didn't know better, she would have worried that he was seeing someone.

The thought was almost funny.

Not only didn't Gideon want another lover, he didn't want any lover. How they were going to get back to work on the book in a few days once Angie was feeling better, she didn't know. She had thought she could do this; to be a wholly modern, independent woman who could give and take, and walk away when necessary. But she was finding out what a fraud she was, and she didn't know how much more she could take—even for Angie's sake.

What fools people became when they tried to perform like a fence straddler and please everyone. No matter what decision she made now, someone would be hurt, someone else would feel betrayed. And she…oh, yes, she would lose somehow. It was just a matter of time to learn who or what.

On Tuesday Gideon limited his class to reviewing what they could expect on their final exam come Friday and released the students early. He was leaving the building when he nearly had a head-on collision with one of the young women who worked in the office. Her Rapunzel hair helped him remember her name was Reva.

"Mr. Kane, whew. Just in time, huh?"

She bent at the waist, resting her hands on her knees, struggling to catch her breath. As she did, her ponytail nearly brushed across the tops of her top-of-the-line athletic shoes.

"Dean Littlejohn...was afraid she would miss you...before you left campus," the girl said, panting. "She needs to speak with you—" The end of the sentence was reduced to a thumb hooked toward the administration building.

Gideon didn't like the sound of that summons. Lillian wasn't some power freak who sent others to do her bidding. If she needed to see him, there were any number of ways she could have done so.

"I'll go see her right now, Reva. But you'd better go inside and cool off before heading back. I'll let Dean Littlejohn know you'll be along directly."

The girl looked starstruck that he would remember her name. "Why, thanks, Mr. Kane. That's very thoughtful."

Machines were running, and student enrollees were lined up complaining at the front desk, no doubt making it difficult for Lillian to hear whoever she was on the phone with, since she'd left her office door open. She looked sharp, as usual, in a red blazer over a black shift, and anything but happy.

When she saw him approaching, she said something briefly to whoever was on the other end of the line and hung up, then motioned him inside.

His instincts already on red alert, he didn't need to hear her "Shut the door" when he entered her inner sanctum. He did it anyway.

She picked up a sheet of paper and walked to the window, reading it. Something about the way her eyes moved over the page told him that she was already familiar with its contents and liked it less after this run-through than before.

"What would be the gentlemanly phraseology for when

you find yourself standing in front of a wind tunnel fan with a bag of fresh cow chips?''

"'Mission Control, we have a problem.'''

"Mmm. Well, I won't be getting an Academy Award nomination for this attempt, but I do owe you an apology of that magnitude. It seems that in my enthusiasm to make record strides in advancing the breadth and scope of Blanchette College, I've contaminated its hallowed grounds with vermin."

"Save that speech for the regents, Lillian. What's up, and what does it have to do with me?"

"C. C. Day has given me a crash course in learning that guppies shouldn't get into ponds with great white sharks." She slid the page she'd been reading across her desk. "And it would appear that his idea of altruism, not to mention keeping his word, is nil where profit and useful press are concerned."

Feeling as though he was about to step before a firing squad, but not sure why, Gideon read the paper. It was a press release announcing Lou-Day's affiliation with B.C. What caught his eye, though, was his name and position at the school, followed by mention of the "still-untitled" book. He started reading carefully there.

"'What promises to be a real coup for Dean Lillian Littlejohn,''' he read out loud, "'is the guaranteed notoriety and bestseller status of this samurai gardener, whose insider knowledge of past covert U.S. military operations had, until now, kept him living in virtual seclusion in central Louisiana.'''

Gideon crushed the paper within his hands. "That belly-crawling piece of disease had me investigated," he muttered.

"Tell me it's not true, Gideon, and I'll haul in our attorneys and slap C.C. with an injunction before this can go to press."

He looked up. "You mean it hasn't?"

"He thinks he's living up to our agreement by faxing me a copy of the damned thing. I have it in our agreement that any and all explicit references to scheduled publications would be subject to approval by this office."

"So what's to stop him from letting one of his underlings leak it? All he has to say is 'Oops,' apologize in print, and you have no case, while I'm hanging out there like buzzard bait."

Lillian dropped into her chair. "Dear heaven. It is true."

"Like you didn't understand from what I told you that my past wasn't pretty?"

And it was about to get uglier, because the two people upstairs in D.C. that he knew were still alive and in control of his files were perfectly capable of embellishing and revising "official classified records" to make him look like anything they wanted, from a traitor to a psychopath. Not even a slick operator like C. C. Day would know that he was having his strings pulled, while thinking he was pulling strings.

"Good Lord, Gideon, are you telling me you were some kind of...of James Bond?"

He eyed Lillian from that deep inner place where nothing, especially not old affections, could touch him. "I don't like martinis, and a tux would be useless where I've been," he said flatly. "You'll have my resignation on your desk in the morning."

"What? You can't quit!"

"I'll finish this semester, of course."

"Damned straight."

"But I'll save you from having to fire me, and withdrawing the offer on the book. I would, however, appreciate it if you don't make a formal announcement to that effect until some later date."

"Damn it, that's not an answer!"

"I always warned you that it would be the only one you'd get."

"But what will you do? Where will you go?"

He didn't reply.

Her initial shock over, Lillian squared her shoulders. "Are

you going to treat Brynn like this when you tell her, or are you planning to simply disappear one night?''

"Brynn knows enough to expect the unexpected."

Lillian scoffed. "Please, Gideon. I don't care if she's a neurosurgeon or a fighter pilot. When a woman falls in love, what she's 'expecting' is at least twenty minutes in the happily-ever-after bubble, not a karate chop to the heart."

He tried to remain impassive, but Brynn's face kept appearing before him. Oh, yes, he knew what she would suffer, no matter what he'd tried to tell himself.

"What did I tell you about your matchmaking?" he growled. "You knew enough to suspect I wasn't on par with the Tony Delmarcos of the world, and I'm definitely not substitute father material."

Lillian refused to be intimidated. "This is supposed to be a democracy. More than one person gets to vote."

Gideon thought of what other headaches she was capable of causing all in the name of good intentions. Brynn didn't need that, either. He mentally realigned some of his plans.

"I'll speak to her."

"Lucky girl. Gideon, please. I'm sick about this. Okay, so I've helped to create a nasty mess, and I interfere worse than the queen of all mother-in-laws, but there has to be something I can do to make up for some of that?"

"Remember who you are," he said, heading for the door. "And go on as if nothing had happened—except perhaps to let useful sources in the media know that you're deeply disappointed with Lou-Day. That their attempt to manipulate Blanchette College is offensive, that the school refuses to be linked even briefly with what amounts to tabloid journalism."

"Exactly my sentiments. I assure you, when I get my hands on C.C.—"

Gideon glanced over his shoulder. "No, Lillian. Mr. Day is mine."

It was Gideon's long-held belief that when you wanted to get and not be gotten by a rattlesnake, you didn't stick your hand blindly or impetuously into his den. You waited until he focused on other things. As a result, he considered then passed on the opportunity to visit the pulpwood purveyor in his corporate headquarters, or in the family's gaudy replica of a French villa in Baton Rouge—where he wouldn't show up until the weekend, anyway.

He waited until the man left his secretary's apartment a few miles from the Lou-Day offices. And when C. C. Day drove out of the parking lot at 11:42 and onto the now-empty street that would take him to the corporation's condo, Gideon rose from the back floorboard and met the horrified gaze of the man staring into the car's rearview mirror.

"Good evening, Mr. Day."

"Oh, my God."

"No foolish attempts at bravery, please. I require only five minutes of your time, and then I'll say good-night."

"Don't hurt me. Is it money you want? Here's my—"

"Keep both hands on the wheel. Thank you." He pushed the butt of his flashlight into the back of the leather seat. "You do feel this? Excellent. I admire working with people who catch on quickly. Let me get straight to the matter with which my employer is concerned."

"Who's that?"

"Don't disappoint me, Mr. Day. You started off so well.

"It appears you've upset some influential people in positions of responsibility. These gentlemen don't like rodents like those you hired scurrying around in places where they don't belong. But my employer insists they're generous men. They're inviting you to spend the rest of your days enjoying the company of Thelma, Cory Calvin Jr. and Truvy Rachelle in good health."

"What kind of deal is that?"

He was edgy but ambitious. Day's nervous eyes kept darting to the mirror. Gideon knew all he saw was the silhouette of a man in black.

"You'd like to see the counteroffer. If you insist."

He picked up a leather-wrapped bundle from the floor. Tugging the rawhide tie loose with his teeth, he let the length of leather roll open, and held it up in the rearview mirror.

"Oh, my God. W-what's that?" C. C. Day cried.

"The only other option I was advised to extend."

"Wait a minute here. Th-that ain't right. I've got valuable information, and the guy's even hiding from your people!"

"That's our business."

"The public has a right to know he's not what he seems!"

"Just like they have a right to know how many environmental laws you break regularly at Lou-Day? Or how you only hire jobbers to haul your wood, who are paid on the number of runs they make a day, making them a driving hazard on public roads? Or let's not forget the young lady back at 14E who not long ago underwent some cosmetic surgery after receiving a sizable deposit in her bank account?

"You see? Information is very easy to come by. What people tend to overlook when they acquire it, as you have, is that it's not as free as it seems. And, Mr. Day, your tab is extremely high."

The older man pressed his chin into his chest, fighting the urge to challenge. He had a pugilist's face and the truculent personality to go with it. Gideon knew the best way to beat his combatant reflexes was with the silence of someone absolutely indifferent.

"Well, what reassurance do I have that this is over if I agree—to agree?" he said at last.

Gideon rolled up his pruning tools and retied the rawhide. "You'll know by never seeing me again. Pull over here."

As the businessman did as directed, he again looked nervously into the mirror. "This ain't a trick, is it?"

"Please, Mr. Day. I'm a professional. I would tell you if you needed to make other arrangements—unlike the man you thought you'd use to your advantage. Now, there's an unprincipled character. Do you know you could be sitting in your high-rise corner office thinking of what you'd like for lunch, while there he would be behind that billboard on

Broussard and Lacassine—you know the one I'm talking about—and do you know he would be slinging his rifle over his shoulder to climb down before you fell dead on your desk blotter?'' Gideon patted the man's shoulder. ''You're a fortunate man, Mr. Day.''

''Yeah. Yeah, uh, thank you!''

When Gideon returned home, he took a long shower that did as little for the tension in his mind and body as it did for the clock. It was late by anyone's standards but his, even though he'd been going strong since leaving Lillian's office. In fact, the last time he'd slept with any real sense of peace, it had been with Brynn in his arms.

It would be ludicrous to consider going to bed now. But he was tired. Too tired to continue making the decisions he had to make.

After walking through the dark house, he went out back with the intention of feeding the fish, but his gaze went immediately across the alley. The pull was strong, and the lonely part of him wanted her to come to the window; better yet, to run out of the house and race to him as she had that night of the hostage incident. He could see it so clearly that spasms had him flexing his fingers.

Did she know yet? He hoped not. If Lillian had contacted her, he supposed he could understand it, forgive. But the longer Brynn had to anticipate the inevitable, the worse it would be for her, as well as the child. Hopefully Lillian would figure out that much. Then again, knowing Lillian, he guessed she was thinking there was time to talk him out of things. Hadn't he said he would finish the semester?

He fed the fish and went inside to look through the phone book.

At the end of Wednesday's class, Lillian didn't risk sending for him—she came herself.

''I'll walk you to your car,'' she said. ''I'm on my way

out to lunch with our lawyers to rehash the possibilities for why C. C. Day decided not to make that press release this morning. You wouldn't know anything about that, would you?''

"Know anything about what?"

"Let's just say the steam seems to have gone out of his roller."

"Maybe he had one too many meatball po' boys at lunch."

"That's the point! He's a man with big appetites—power being among them. So what's happened to shut him down? From every impression I got from Pfeiffer, Lazenby and Razell last night, it wasn't due to anything they'd said." On cue she smiled at a pair of passing students, and waved at a group farther away. "I noticed you got in late."

"Concerned that I went to prune him with my bonsai tools?"

"You were pretty upset when you left my office."

"Guilty. For behavior unbecoming a staff member at B.C., I respectfully submit my resignation. Ah! But I already dropped that off at your office this morning, along with the letter confirming the cancellation of our book contract. Jeez, Dean—what's your point?"

She shot him an annoyed look. "You know damn well that's no longer necessary. I ripped it up and tossed it out as soon as I got the word about Day. Well, the resignation, anyway. I'm sorry about the book, but for the time being, I'm afraid our university press program is back on hold."

"You should have saved the other letter, as well."

"I'm telling you, the man was rattled. You can forget about him drawing all kinds of media attention down on your head. We have to explain his change of heart to the board of regents, of course, but we can leave that vague. The point is, you get to stay."

Gideon stopped beside his car. "A Realtor is supposed to meet me at the house in about twenty minutes."

She couldn't have looked more crushed if he'd pulled a weapon on her. "You're serious?"

"I'm holding you to your word about saying anything to Brynn."

Lillian recovered quickly. "Oh, I'm not worried about you going anywhere soon, old friend. That Realtor will take one look at your place and tell you she's seen mausoleums with more allure."

"She'll like the yard."

"Most of which goes when you do. What's left? Beach sand and enough pebbles to refilm *The Flintstones*." Wincing, Lillian grabbed his wrist. "That's sheer panic talking. You know I love your yard, and I'm crazy about you. You're my kid brother, my father confessor, my shrink. Who's going to listen to me fuss about Dominic if you go?"

Thinking of that, he opened his car door and tossed his briefcase onto the passenger seat. "Remind me to get a signed contract from you to keep Brynn out of it."

She was still standing there scolding him when he left her.

Gideon's mood didn't improve when the woman from the realty company arrived with signs on her car's doors announcing her affiliation. He was glad his neighbor across the street was out of town, others worked and those on either side of him were on vacation. Although he didn't socialize with them, Dominic occasionally did.

But what soon made the whole thing academic was when Brynn drove by as he was walking the woman back out to her car. He didn't see Angie, which told him that Dominic must have come home early and was watching her.

Of all the bad timing, he thought.

The look on her face was tougher to take than a blow.

Shocked as he knew she'd been, however, he was the one left wondering when he didn't hear from her that night. Especially when, obviously feeling stronger, Angie appeared at the window to wave good-night while he was in the yard.

Where was Brynn?

As in the beginning, she had set something in motion. This time he had his doubts about surviving it.

Brynn tried not to think about it. What could she make of things she didn't understand?

Exhaustion, that was her problem. She'd had too many stressful days worrying over and nursing Angie. It was perfectly logical for her eyes to be playing tricks on her.

That hadn't been a Realtor coming out of Gideon's house. He hadn't been standing right there beside the woman. It wasn't his street!

Would it scare you less if you thought he was having an affair with her?

The thoughts came like that, plentiful and mocking, and Brynn sat them out, spending the entire night in her room in the lovely rocker Dominic had given to her, her mind working harder than a coffee grinder. When she wasn't brooding about why he hadn't told her of his plans, she worried about what could be wrong.

By morning, the conclusion she came to was the one she'd begun with: he'd promised her nothing. He'd warned her that he would offer her nothing. It didn't matter.

Unfortunately, that didn't stop the ache in her heart from building.

She took Lillian arriving home in the midmorning as a sign. Hoping that Angie was content with her toys up in her room for a few minutes, she dashed outside to catch her before she disappeared inside.

From the instant she saw Lillian bite her lip, she knew. But she made herself go through the motions anyway.

"Lillian? Hi!"

"Brynn! How are you, dear? I understand Angie's coming along."

"The spots are almost all gone."

"Good. Good. You do need to catch up on your rest, dear."

"You're in a hurry?"

"Well, I am meeting some people…"

Brynn watched her neighbor's gaze do everything but rest on her. "Lillian, please. Why are you acting as though you're…embarrassed? What have I done?"

That had Lillian protesting. "Believe me, it's not you. It's…been a difficult week. At the school…everywhere."

Evasion. Brynn recognized it when she heard it. "It's Gideon. He's leaving."

"He told you?"

She shook her head. "I saw the Realtor's car in front of his house. I was trying to think of reasons to explain it—tax appraisal, insurance. Only one fits."

"There's still time for him to change his mind."

That told Brynn more than she wanted to know. "How long have you known?"

"Oh, dear. Well, you know he had to tell me, Brynn. After the book deal fell through…"

"*What?* Why?"

Lillian groaned and gestured helplessly. "He insisted I not say anything. But damn it, now that there's no threat of the media finding out—"

"They know?" The scenario was getting more terrible by the minute.

"No-no! Oh…Brynn, I really do have to go meet these people." Lillian gripped her hand. "Go to him later. Talk to him. I know he's in love with you. If anyone can get him to see reason, you can."

Yes, he loved her, Brynn thought as she watched Lillian hurry away. But just as love was sometimes not enough, once in a great, rare while it was too much.

The waiting was terrible. As much as she wanted to go to him the instant she saw him come home, she couldn't because of Angie. Dominic soon arrived, but he was feeling more talkative than usual, no doubt excited about his date with Lillian tomorrow night. She tried to be happy for him, but how could she when her heart was shriveling? Dying?

"You should turn in early, Brynn, *mia*," Dominic said, at last eyeing her with concern. "Angie is better. She'll sleep through the night, you'll see."

Angie had been sleeping through for three nights already, but Brynn was glad for the escape. Even though waiting for darkness took forever, and longer for the house to grow quiet.

Getting downstairs was the worst of it. She seemed to have forgotten which stairs betrayed and which were safe. Then there was the back door—swollen from the humidity, it didn't want to open. Not wanting to risk it sticking later, she merely pulled it until it hung and let herself out.

Then she ran.

She already knew he wasn't in the backyard, and she hoped she didn't stumble in the darkness and injure herself before she made her way to the front.

When she pressed his front doorbell, she was panting as though she'd run all the way to the college. Painfully aware that she didn't look the cool, calm woman she wanted to be, she waited...knowing it would be anticlimactic...knowing he would look through the security hole and be prepared when, if, he opened up.

The locks released and the door opened. Then she was looking into grim gray eyes.

"When were you going to tell me?" she whispered.

Chapter Thirteen

"As close to the end as possible."

The words barely moved Gideon's lips, but they slammed through Brynn like a commuter train.

"You'd better sit down before you drop." He stepped toward her, his hands coming up as though ready to catch her.

"No." She warded him off. "I...shouldn't have come."

Retreating, she would have fallen if not for his arm bracing her. Before she could do more than find her balance, he was muttering a soft oath and sweeping her into his arms. He carried her, as dazed as she was embarrassed, to the kitchen where he placed her on a chair.

"I'll get you a drink."

"I don't want anything."

"You can throw it in my face."

Taking several deep breaths to steady her stomach, she watched him move from one cabinet to another, first getting a glass, then a bottle of red wine. He was wearing only jeans, and seeing his muscles stretch and flex reminded her of when they'd made love and how wondrous it had been to be surrounded by him.

"The wine's warmer than you'd probably like," he said, pouring, "but it will feed your blood."

"Please. No more philosophizing." Funny how she could almost want to smile when her heart had just been pulverized by seven honest words. More remarkable was that she had any heart left to destroy.

Gideon squatted before her, filling her vision and demanding her attention. "Brynn, take a sip of this. Sweet heaven, you're exhausted. When did you last sleep?"

"I don't want to sleep. You're there."

He set the glass she'd refused on the table. "I know the feeling."

"Is that why you're selling?"

"It's a beginning."

"It won't work. I'll haunt you."

"I already know that, too."

She wanted to despise him, and instead he was saying things that made her want to cry. "You never made me do anything I didn't want."

"I'm not so sure about that. A part of me wanted you to want me from the moment I laid eyes on you. Maybe there's more to willpower than the science community wants to admit. Anyway, it's not just about doing, it's about who you are and what you feel."

What she felt, not what he did. He was still detaching himself, or worse yet, discounting himself.

"What about the book?" she asked, accepting she had nothing to lose.

"It's not going to happen. Not now, anyway."

"Why?" She saw that he didn't want to tell her and decided he needed some impetus. "I ran into Lillian."

He looked away. "Damn it, Brynn."

"Just tell me."

"The man who'd planned to underwrite the college's publishing venture got a little too ambitious for his own good," he began wearily. "He had me investigated and found out enough to put dollar signs in his eyes. He was planning a whole media circus to expose my whereabouts and whatever history he'd uncovered in the hopes that I'd gain enough notoriety to put the book on the big lists, and from there get him in front of national TV to play a hero for exposing one of the country's nastier secrets."

"Oh, Gideon."

"Do you think I care what they would do to me? No reporter legit or hack could do a better job profiling me than I've done on myself. But I knew what they would do to the school, and Lillian, and most of all you." He reached out and stroked her cheek. "You had a taste of the media feeding frenzy when Tony was gunned down, didn't you? Well, this would make you think that you'd been thrown into a tank of piranhas that hadn't eaten since spring. You wouldn't have survived, sweetheart." He dropped his hand. "So I had a brief visit with Mr. C. C. Day."

Brynn gasped. "No! Gideon, don't tell me you—"

"I didn't."

Weak with relief, she slumped back in the chair. "What did you do?"

"We had a chat, and he's seen the error of his ways."

Brynn searched his face, not sure she dared believe him, but not sure she could afford not to. "You're trying to frighten me again."

"No."

"How can you be sure he won't try something else?"

"Because he'll be too busy looking over his shoulder for the rest of his life." At Brynn's startled look, he shrugged. "People think playing the covert world's cat-and-mouse games are fun...until they find themselves face-to-face with an opponent who's better at it than they are. In the future,

C. C. Day is going to stick to his own speed, namely conning the EPA and chasing his secretary.''

"Then...you're safe? The men you'd mentioned in Washington don't know?''

"Oh, they do. Believe it. The clumsier the inquiries, the easier they are to track down. But you don't achieve what they have by succumbing to a twitchy trigger finger. No, the situation's resolved itself and everyone's receded back into the shadows for now.''

"For now, that's not fair,'' she whispered.

"*Fair* isn't a word that's used in the world I come from,'' he replied, his own voice as gruff as hers was shaky.

"Where will you go?''

"I've no idea.''

"And if you did, you wouldn't tell me.''

"What good would it do to remove myself from temptation and then give you the address?''

"Beautiful words, but you're still running.''

"I prefer to see it as protecting both you and Angie.'' His expression softened. "How're the polka dots coming along?''

Brynn couldn't answer right away. She was thinking about her angel, who didn't have a clue yet; the real innocent in all of this.

"Better. It's getting harder to play the join-the-dots game.''

His laugh was low and brief, like a stirring of the air at dawn.

Brynn touched his cheek before she could stop herself. "Gideon—you laughed. I was just thinking 'I'll never see him laugh,' and you did.''

With a groan, he buried his face in her lap. "You're killing me.''

She stroked his hair and his warm, bare back, wanting to memorize and absorb everything about him. As she felt his breath permeate the skirt of her favorite pink gauzy dress, she thought of the last time she'd worn it—that first time he let her and Angie into his garden.

"How am I going to tell Angie, Gideon? Her little heart will shatter. She's never going to recover now." She spoke without condemnation, merely to state the truth that was growing inside her like an approaching winter.

"Don't say that."

"Sometimes I wish I'd never moved us down here."

He straightened to look at her, the lines of strain etched deeply in his face. "Dominic needed you, and you needed him. He's your family. Angie's blood. My being here only threatens the harmony in that."

He was right that Dominic would always look at him as a usurper. And he would be consumed with jealousy if he knew how profound Angie's connection with Gideon really was. That, she knew, was as much behind this decision to leave as the rest, and the knowledge that she was helpless to change it, just as she was unable to do anything to ease his guilt about the past, had the room closing in on her with dreadful finality.

Knowing if she didn't get out of there she would lose control completely or get violently ill, she shot out of the chair, only to catch her foot in the wooden leg.

The hardwood floor rushed up at her, but Gideon's reflexes were once again impeccable. Powerful arms swept her high and hard against his strong body. When she dragged her hair from her eyes, she found herself trapped by his fierce gray gaze.

"Little fool," he whispered harshly. "Haven't you been hurt enough?"

"Let me go."

"Stop struggling and I will."

"I can't breathe."

"You're crying. You did hurt yourself!"

"No! I just can't. I can't."

His crude expletive shocked her—even knowing what she

now knew about him. But what upset Brynn most was that he dragged the chair back with his foot, sat down and set her across his lap.

She didn't want this, couldn't bear it.

"Stop now," he rasped. "Stop fighting me, Brynn. For the love of heaven...don't."

It was idiotic to think she could gain her freedom; his arms alone were unyielding manacles. He could overwhelm her in any and every way, but her dread of the tidal wave of hysteria fast descending on her had her trying nonetheless, until, unable to catch her breath, unable to fight another instant, she slumped against him, sobbing.

There could have been an earthquake and they would have missed it, she was shaking so hard. And her flood of tears soon had them both wet, although from the way he tucked her head against his chin and shoulder, she began to suspect some of the moisture on his face wasn't all hers.

They stayed like that. Captive and captor. All-too-brief lovers.

Eventually her tears stopped, primarily because she grew too tired to produce any more. A stillness filled the room, heavy but not unwelcome.

Gideon slowly rubbed his cheek against her hair, the gesture more reflex than voluntary. "Don't let it end with you hating me."

His words touched off a shiver inside her. She tightened the arms she'd kept wrapped around his neck. "How could I?"

"You'd have every right. I took advantage of your vulnerability to me."

Brynn didn't understand how he could see things that way. "We helped each other."

"You showed me not all dreams turn into nightmares."

He tightened his arms and she felt his lips move against her hair. But although she listened and hoped for the words she knew were there for her in his heart, they didn't come. Still, it was sheer bliss being this close to him.

And utter agony.

"I have to let you get back home," he murmured, shifting slightly.

Yes, he was feeling it, too. The change that was replacing the calm with awareness, and empathy with arousal. Not that she hadn't been conscious of his body's alertness to her from the moment he sat her on his lap. It was just getting less easy to pretend she wasn't.

He pressed another kiss against her hair. The next found skin, the highest point on her temple. A third found a home near her eye, and another against her cheek.

"Brynn, you have to help me."

No, she didn't. He wanted to obliterate everything they'd worked for these past months. He could strip her and rub her raw with sea salt and she wouldn't feel worse.

Intending to tell him so, she turned her head just a fraction and caused the gentlest collision of lips against lips.

His mouth. It could make her tremble and beg, and she would never stop wanting it. When he slanted it over hers, he made her feel like a baby bird searching for sustenance. Then slowly, slowly, belying the threat time presented to them, he pressed closer, delved his tongue into her mouth and seductively stroked. The kiss was a reminder of every one they'd shared, the touch of his hands a reminder of how well and quickly he'd learned the secrets of her body.

With a groan, he buried his face against her throat. "This has to stop here. Brynn, I won't do this to you."

But his body didn't want her to listen. And her heart was beyond saving itself.

"Do what?" Taking his hand, she brought it to her breast, letting him find out for himself how quickly she'd slipped back into her clothes to come here. "Make me feel like a woman one last time? Would that be so unforgivable?"

With gentle pressure she encouraged him to continue

touching and caressing. The hot kisses he slid down her throat, though, were his idea; it was also all him when he dragged down the elasticized empire bodice of her dress and covered her breast with his mouth. But she welcomed it all, and for a handful of precious moments she leaned back against the iron bar that was his arm and gave herself up to his hungry exploration.

But Gideon's conscience was like no one else's. When he abruptly covered her as quickly as he'd bared her, she knew what noble but dark side of him she would have to take on again. The unlovable one. The one who'd made too many unforgivable choices or mistakes despite having lived the past decade or more of his life proving himself better than most human beings even attempted to be.

Feeling overly warm and a little hopeless, Brynn eased free and crossed over to the sink. Turning on the cold water tap, she ripped a few sheets from the roll of paper towels and held them under the stream. Her hands weren't quite steady, but when she brought the cool, seeping mass to her chest, drew it along her throat and downward, unbuttoning her dress as she did, her previous calm and confidence returned.

Behind her Gideon was extraordinarily still. She knew he was watching, but she could only hope what he was thinking.

"Brynn," he began at last. "I didn't mean to embarrass you. I've treasured every moment we've shared. Just looking at you standing there now...that's how I'll always think of you."

She shut her eyes briefly. "I'm not embarrassed." Dropping the towels in the sink, she returned to him and sank to the floor between his legs. "Why should I be? I love you."

She knew he'd heard her, but he was also preoccupied, staring at the way her dress was almost slipping off her, except where the damp material clung to the fullest swell of her breasts.

Sliding her hands along his thighs, she smiled up at him. "I love you."

He sucked in a long, unsteady breath, and when he stopped her from reaching for the button at the waistband of his jeans, the hands that stopped her didn't wholly commit to the effort.

Brynn didn't persist, but nuzzled his chest, wet his nipples with her lips. "That may not mean enough to you. I may not be able to convince you to stay with me...." This time when she reached for the button she succeeded in opening it. "But I can make you do more than remember me."

His haunted eyes grew hunted. "Brynn, sweet, don't. I can't let it change anything, and you don't have to prove—"

She'd returned to kissing his chest, the caresses like a thirsty kitten finally finding the source of cream. But when she ventured beyond his opened jeans, caressed his rigid length and cupped him in her hands, his face took on that carved-out-of-granite rigidity, and his eyes could have been dug from the ashes of hell.

This wasn't what she'd expected. She watched with increasing dread as he seemed to drift away inside himself, becoming the terrible, agonized shell he'd been when he first walked out of the jungle.

"No," she moaned. She took his face in her hands. "Gideon, don't go there. Do you hear me? I won't let you!"

She wrapped her arms around him, spread kisses over his shoulders, his face and throat. "Oh, stay. Whatever I did, if I said too much..."

She climbed onto his lap, forcing him to meet her gaze—and almost lost her courage.

Her immediate thought was gratitude that she would never have to face him as an enemy. Instead of her brooding but tender Gideon, looking at her was a cold stranger, a man so void of emotion, so hard, she began to ease off him.

But as suddenly as he'd appeared he vanished, and Gideon narrowed his eyes. "Brynn?"

"Thank God." Weak with relief, she held tight. "What was that?"

He only clutched her tighter.

"What did I do?" she insisted.

"Loved me."

She leaned back to make sure she'd heard him correctly. "I don't understand. That didn't happen when we first made love."

"Brynn, no one has ever—" His sigh sounded almost embarrassed. "No one," he insisted. "Not like that. Not because she wanted to. Not without paying her to."

Her heart ached for the turmoil he was obviously in. "I think I understand. You don't have to go on. It's all right."

"No, damn it, it's not! You're going to leave here thinking it's you, and it's not! It's me—it's always me!" He gripped her shoulders. "I looked down, and it was…beautiful. *You* were so unbelievably beautiful, and it blew my mind. You couldn't be doing that. Not to Gideon Kane, A-1 lowlife, son of a—"

Brynn pressed her fingers to his lips. "I don't know him. The man I adore and want to make love to in every way is right here," she said, stroking the tension from his face.

Gideon whispered her name as if it were a prayer, and followed that with the longest, deepest kiss. But when she coaxed him to slide his hands under her flowing skirt, he shook his head and gently but grimly began buttoning her dress.

"Why?" she cried.

"Because if I don't let you go now, I won't. And Angie needs you, Brynn."

How could she argue with that? She had stayed a dangerously long time.

"You see? As much as you try to prove your heart is mine…it's not as free to give as you think. And while I know I have to deal with that down the road, I can't anymore tonight."

His sad tone made her ache for him anew, and yet as unhappy as he seemed, after they'd straightened their clothes he wouldn't hear of Brynn walking home by herself.

He led her out through the garden, and while he unlocked the gate, she looked around, reminiscing, unable to contemplate this belonging to someone else.

"Don't brood," he said, pulling open the gate. "There'll be plenty of time for that later."

"I'm not going to accept that. You won't leave me."

He didn't reply. In fact, they walked in silence until they got to the steps. Then, slipping his hand to her nape, he drew her close and looked deeply into her eyes. "It may kill me, but I'll leave you," he told her.

His kiss was devastating. Within seconds he had her clinging to him, ready to let him take her right there if he wanted.

When the storm door burst open, it was a little like déjà vu—a nightmarish one. Dominic stepped outside disheveled in his T-shirt and slacks. His hair was standing on end from sleep, proof that he hadn't had time yet to think of running his hands through it, and that added to his rather wild look as he stood on the landing and glared down at them.

"You do this to me again?" he roared. Then he burst into a stream of Italian that soon had dogs barking two streets over.

Brynn knew she looked exactly like what she'd been doing, and felt her blush staining all of her body, but she knew she needed to try to get him calmer and inside or lights would be coming on at every house in the neighborhood.

"Dominic, please. It's late and—"

"I know how late it is," he snapped, tapping his chest. "Do you? I'm the one who goes from room to room calling for you, thinking heaven forbid what because the child cries for her mama."

"Angie!" Brynn started for the stairs.

Dominic stuck out his hand to stop her, his long face implacable. "So, now you are a mother again?"

Gideon stepped forward. "Be careful, Delmarco."

"You don't give me orders on my property."

Dominic's face grew feral as he glared down at him, and Brynn tried to calm him down.

"Pop," she said gently, "what's wrong with Angie?"

He didn't take his eyes off Gideon, but Dominic's mouth twisted with distaste. "You come from his house, you call me that?"

This wasn't threatening to become a nightmare, Brynn thought, humiliated by that last remark. It was in full horrific swing. "Let's go inside and talk like reasonable adults. Angie had been sleeping peacefully. You were here, and I needed to talk to Gideon about what Lillian had told me."

"You leave her out of this."

"That would be lovely," Lillian said from behind them. She was dressed in a silk dressing gown that gleamed like moonlight, and her haughty look was all for Dominic. "The problem is some big gorilla is making it impossible for me to sleep."

He was immediately apologetic. "Lillian, *mia*—"

"Don't start cooing at me," she snapped back at him. "I've been listening to you. The woman is over twenty-one and this isn't fourteenth-century Italy. How dare you treat her as though it was!"

"Go get him, tiger," Gideon muttered.

Stopping just below Brynn, Lillian shot him a quelling look, too. "Oh, don't think I don't have a few choice words for you."

"If you would all excuse me," Brynn interjected, "all I want is to see about my daughter."

Before she could get up another step, though, the storm door inched open and Angie's little face peered out. Her eyes were the size of saucers and her small bow mouth was puckering.

"Oh, sweetheart." Brynn caught her as she rushed the rest of the way outside and launched herself at her. Fortunately,

Gideon had anticipated the jump and had moved behind her to keep her from stumbling backward. Shooting him a quick, grateful look, she hugged Angie tight. "What happened, angel? Bad dream, huh? Mommy's here. It's all over." Over her shoulder she said to Dominic, "Please. I don't want to fight, not with you, and definitely not in front of the little one."

"This is my house." He pointed between his slippered feet. "I say what does and doesn't happen here."

"Oh, brother," Lillian drawled.

Brynn touched her arm, signaling her not to make the situation more incendiary. "Dominic," she said softly, "I've told you before, there's nothing wrong with Angie's hearing. Now, before we say anything—"

"She's a Delmarco. She should hear the truth, not the fairy tales you'll make up."

That one was a blow Brynn couldn't accept. "What's that supposed to mean? You act as though there's been some betrayal, when there hasn't. Please, Dominic. Don't ruin the affection we have for each other—"

"Then you begin acting like my son's wife!"

"He's gone!" she whispered, covering Angie's exposed ear. "We can't change that, and we can't go into his grave with him!"

"But you should behave like *mia figlia,* not a—a—"

"Dominic!" Lillian snapped.

"That's it." His teeth clenched, Gideon drew Brynn back from the steps. "I've listened to enough. You're not staying with him another night."

"Will you two guys listen to yourselves," Lillian snapped. Shaking her head, she took Brynn and Angie into her arms. "You're tearing her apart. I'll tell you where she and this child are going, it's to my house where they don't have to feel like half-time entertainment at the Roman Colosseum. I've never seen a worse display of male sense in my entire life.

"You!" she said to Dominic. "You're lucky she's toler-
ated your autocratic, male-porky attitude for as long as she
has. If that isn't an indication of how much she cares for
you, you don't deserve her as a daughter-in-law." Then she
turned her censuring tone on Gideon. "And you! You
wouldn't recognize a gift if it dropped on your head straight
from the Pearly Gates! You're right that you don't deserve
her. No woman in love should have to live with a man whose
chief goal in life is to see how deep he can whip himself
into the ground."

Brynn winced and saw the muscles in Gideon's cheeks
flex. But when he turned to her, his gaze was tender.

"She's right about one thing. You'll be better off over at
her house." He kissed Angie's forehead. "Forgive me for
my part in upsetting you, angel. Try to have sweet dreams."

When Angie caught his finger and held fast, Brynn bit her
lip to keep from weeping at the complete adoration and
yearning in Gideon's eyes. Gently extricating himself, he
spun around and strode away.

"Good riddance," Dominic muttered after him. "All I can
say is I'm glad to hear he's leaving. Maybe I get a good
neighbor next time."

Hearing him, Angie stiffened in Brynn's arms.

Brynn groaned. "Dominic. Must you...?"

"Lillian told me that he's moving." When Lillian rolled
her eyes, he lifted his shoulders questioningly. "What did I
say wrong? It's true, no? He walks out on his job, he's selling his house..."

Angie had twisted around to listen to her grandfather, and
now twisted back to touch Brynn's cheek and shake her head
vehemently.

Brynn couldn't bear the panic in her child's eyes. When
tears flooded them, it was all she could do not to start weeping herself.

"Oh, baby. I know that's not what you want to hear, but
there's nothing we can do. Mommy tried."

With a strangled whimper, Angie began wriggling and squirming like a little wild animal. Brynn could no more keep hold of her than she could a wildcat cub bent on gaining its freedom.

Once on the ground, Angie started running.

"Angie!"

Ignoring her call and Dominic's bellow, she raced across the lawn following Gideon.

"Angie! Come back!"

The child's sobs tore at her heart, and she took off after her. Then she heard a sound she hadn't heard in over a year.

"Gid-e-on!"

Chapter Fourteen

"*G*ideon!"

Angie's cry as she reached the iron gate of Gideon's yard was the sweetest and yet most heartrending sound Brynn could imagine, and her progress was immediately impeded by a flood of tears blinding her. She did, however, see well enough to watch Gideon jerking open the gate he'd been about to lock and scooping her daughter into his arms.

"My God—Angie. You spoke. You did it!"

"Gideon." Angie clutched him around his neck and buried her face in his shoulder. "D-don't go!"

Brynn grabbed the fence to help her stop and met Gideon's dazed gaze over Angie's blond head.

"Did you hear?" he whispered.

"Yes." Brynn laughed and cried all at once. "Oh, yes!"

He extended an arm to her, and she went eagerly. The three of them stood that way until Lillian and Dominic reached them.

"Is she all right?" Lillian asked, her hand against her

chest. She looked unsure whether she should be jubilant or concerned.

"She spoke, did you hear it?" Brynn replied.

Gideon kissed the child's forehead. "She's also shaking." He shot Brynn a concerned look. "What happened?"

"She, um, she overheard the news about your plans. It really jarred her."

"I think we should get her to the hospital so they can check her out. Come on, I'll drive you."

Lillian gripped a dazed Dominic's arm and drew him toward his house. "We'll lock up and follow you."

Inside his house Gideon passed Angie to Brynn to finish getting dressed. When he returned, he led Brynn and Angie to the garage. Angie protested.

"No go."

Brynn shot Gideon a distressed look. Angie had never gotten over her aversion to hospitals.

"Hey, angel," he said, opening the passenger door for them. "This is the good kind of visit. And Mommy and I will be with you all the time."

Angie still whimpered, but it wasn't the panic-filled outburst it could have been.

Brynn held her in her arms for the short drive. Because they weren't wearing their seat belts, Gideon drove with extra care and double-checked every intersection. There was virtually no traffic on the road, and they made good time anyway.

For the entire drive, Brynn couldn't take her eyes off her child. She knew she must have whispered "I don't believe it" a dozen times.

After parking outside Emergency, Gideon insisted on carrying Angie for her, which appeared to please her daughter as much as reassure her. Angie wrapped her arms around his neck and kept patting his back as though he was the one in need of encouragement.

Once inside, Brynn got the impression the staff concurred.

"From the looks on our faces, I don't think anyone's sure which of us needs the doctor," she mused as they were shown into a cubicle.

"Tell you what," Gideon replied, "at first I could have used a few pulls on an oxygen mask."

There was a bad moment when the doctor arrived, but Gideon showed remarkable instincts by climbing up on the examination table and setting Angie on his lap. "Okay, Doc," he said, winking at the younger man, who looked as though he'd been on duty for over twenty-four hours. "We're kind of a team here, but you don't mind doing two examinations for the price of one, do you?"

The doctor caught on right away and whispered conspiratorially to Angie, "And if there needs to be a shot, we'll give him both, deal?"

Angie just leaned back against Gideon's chest and sighed contentedly.

It was only about thirty minutes later that they were exiting the building. Dominic and Lillian were just arriving.

"What did they say?" Dominic asked.

He appeared no less anxious than anyone else had been, but now more subdued, almost meek. Brynn wondered how much of a role Lillian had played in that, and while she was glad he'd come, the hurt she'd experienced from his earlier words lingered.

"She's fine."

"They suggested she have a complete physical in a few days," Gideon added, as though recognizing her inner conflict. "It's too early to tell about the, ah, psychological aspects or her, ah, recall. But physically things look good."

Brynn caught Lillian's look and knew she'd been concerned about how they would speak in front of Angie regarding what she might remember of the past trauma, as well as worrying how Angie's long silence could have affected the development of her throat muscles, not to mention her linguistic skills.

''Gideon's right,'' she said to her with a relieved but tired smile. There would undoubtedly be some things that needed attention down the road, but healthwise, everything seemed wonderfully normal.

''Thank heaven. Thank heaven.''

Dominic reached for Angie, but she shied away and clung harder to Gideon.

''Angel...what's this? You don't give your grampa a hug?''

She shook her head, her expression sad. ''You were bad to Gid-e-on. Go to your room.''

Lillian cleared her throat. ''Oh, my, my, my. What say you good people if we adjourn for the evening and start fresh tomorrow after we've all had a chance to collect ourselves?''

Gideon cleared his throat. ''With one slight alteration, Lillian. As much as I appreciate your willingness to have Brynn and Angie over for the evening, I seem to have given my word to Angie that we wouldn't be separated.''

Brynn raised her eyebrows.

''When you went to fill out forms,'' he told her.

Dominic wasn't as accepting as Brynn or as pleased as Angie. ''I don't think—'' he began.

''That that's a bad idea at all,'' Lillian interjected, linking her arm through his. ''Because it just so happens that we have other plans, too. Good night, children. Gideon, try not to forget you have finals.''

As she led a gaping Dominic away, Brynn asked quietly, ''What are you doing?''

''Can the answer wait until we get Angie tucked in?''

''I suppose. But...tucked in where?''

The ride to his house wasn't exactly awkward—how could it be when Angie's breakthrough continued to be like a ray of sunshine in the dark car, even though the child seemed ready to go back to sleep. At the same time, Brynn couldn't help wondering why Gideon was prolonging the inevitable.

Either he was taking his kindness to Angie to a new level, or he was turning into an incredible masochist.

When they reached his house, Gideon unlocked the door and then once again relieved Brynn of a drowsing Angie. She followed him down the hallway to his bedroom.

Within a few minutes they had Angie tucked in, and the bathroom light on in case she awoke and forgot where she was. Adding his own kiss to the impressively calm child, Gideon then took Brynn's hand and led her back down the hallway.

"I can't get over how she's taking this all in stride," he told Brynn.

"Unlike her mother, who would like to know where she's supposed to sleep." That had him leading her to the only piece of furniture in the living room. He sat down in the middle of the black leather couch and once again extended his hand to her.

"Not that I'm expecting to get much sleep," he said. "We do have a great deal to discuss."

His serious tone had her doubting she really wanted to, even though he looked so appealing in the faint light bleeding through from the kitchen. That's why she continued to stand there contemplating him as soberly as he watched her.

"You don't believe me," he murmured.

"Believe what? You haven't said anything yet."

"I thought maybe it showed somehow. I certainly feel different."

"Gideon, if you're trying to say that you've had a change of heart about everything you said to me not two hours ago, I won't buy it. People don't change that much in a matter of hours. Not people like you."

"You mean what happened with Angie wasn't impactful enough?"

"What happened to Angie is a blessing, and I will always be grateful for the role you played in her recovery. But you're still who you are, and that includes all those worries about your past.''

"So why does the thought of letting you two walk away from me, of continuing this rootless existence and turning my back on the first real sense of home I've ever had suddenly make me feel as though somebody has slipped me an emulsion cocktail? The way you made love to me in that kitchen, then hearing your child speak for the first time, *my* name, and then that painful but accurate dressing-down from Lillian... I realized I've finally found something, someone—make that two someones—worth fighting harder for.''

"Oh, Gideon." Brynn wrapped her arms around her waist to keep from reaching for him.

"I know that's only a start and that it doesn't erase all that I've said, nor will it miraculously make the wall I keep around me disappear. I can't guarantee you that I will ever fully forgive myself for who I was and what I did, or that Dominic and I will become friends, let alone best pals. But I love you. I've been holding back those words from you for a long time. Too long. They're yours now and always. I love you.''

Brynn clutched her hand to her throat and escaped to the kitchen, where she stopped by the sink and clutched the edge of the counter for several long seconds. She heard Gideon come up behind her, felt the heat of his body before his arms came around her waist.

"It's customary when a man who's been a particularly huge coward and idiot admits those things, to reward him somehow.''

She did give him a tender kiss on the underside of his chin. But she also murmured, "I already know you love me, Gideon. The words are wonderful to hear, and I did want them. But they're that—just words.''

He was frowning as he turned her around to face him. "Go on.''

"I don't know what they mean to you. You loved me and

were willing to leave me. You said it yourself seconds before Dominic came bursting out of the house. Now you say you don't want to uproot yourself or lose us. All that says to me is that everything remains as it is, except that our relationship is out in the open, which wouldn't work. Not when I have a small child and a father-in-law to worry about.''

"You think...?'' He threw back his head and exhaled heavily. "Of course you do.'' Groaning, he enfolded her in his arms and held her close. "I'm sorry. I'm so sorry for doing it again.

"No, I don't want the status quo,'' he continued, his gaze moving possessively over her face. "If you told me you did, I'd be stunned, not to mention disappointed. You're too good a mother to allow Angie to see you going from your bed to mine. What I want is for you to marry me, Brynn. I want you as my wife, the three of us to be a family. But I know there's a great deal more that goes along with that. Complications. That's what I was leaving for you to decide for us. You have the experience where I don't when it comes to loving and relationships, what'll work and what may be asking for trouble. You have Angie to help verbalize her terrible experience. If she can describe anyone, you'll have decisions to make about taking her back to Chicago. Lord, I don't even want to think about what you two might be facing. Then there's Dominic and all he represents. And you have me.''

He cleared his throat. "If I give you too much time to think about it, you'll be able to talk yourself out of any reason for saying yes to me. I'm never going to want an extremely public life. I won't promise that I'll ever smile and laugh as much as you'd probably like. I think I can safely guess that we'll be left alone by the people from my past, but I can't give you a guarantee that there's not another C. C. Day out there. That still bothers me big-time. You and Angie deserve guarantees.''

"That's what Tony thought, too.''

"Yeah. That's what I kept coming back to while I wondered if I had the right, let alone the guts, to make this speech." He framed her face with his hands. "So what it really comes down to is you and what you think you're capable of handling."

"Anything. As long as you're with me."

He kissed her then, and Brynn thought it was the best one yet because there was nothing to hide and everything to look forward to.

"Dear God, I love you," he rasped when they broke to catch their breaths. "You're the gift I never expected, the one I still can't believe I deserve, but I want you. And I'll take on anyone I have to now to make you mine."

Brynn smiled. "Already getting that bossy macho attitude, are we?"

"It's always been there, sweet. There just wasn't a reason to expose my two angels to that side of me. But you're my responsibility now. You'll have to suffer my strong protective streak."

Brynn knew they could work around that. "You have to trust me to handle Dominic, though," she told him.

He didn't look happy about that. "No one should ever talk to you the way he did. Don't ask me to stand by and tolerate that, Brynn."

"I'm not condoning anything he's done or said, but he's from another generation as well as another country, Gideon. And, too, I don't think he's come to terms with losing Tony yet, so it made perfect sense for him not to consider that I would fall in love again. Look how long he mourned his wife. The fact that you're the one to win my heart makes it a double insult to him. You, who rejected his gestures of friendship and remained so self-contained for so long. For a competitive man who needs to control, you were a threat in every way imaginable and it pushed all his wrong buttons."

"There you go being too generous again." Stroking her hair, Gideon sighed. "I don't know, sweet. This one will be hard for me."

"Then I'll talk to him first thing in the morning while you're at school. This way your mind will be on other things."

"My mind will be on *you*, where it's been all along."

Her talk with Dominic wasn't without some tension. She was right about him feeling that she still belonged to Tony. On the other hand, he wasn't about to jeopardize having regular contact with Angie.

"So when are you going to marry him?" he asked.

They were sitting at his kitchen table, sharing a cup of coffee. Angie was playing up in her room.

"Actually, we haven't discussed dates," Brynn replied gently. "But it will be soon. We want Angie to feel settled before she starts day school again."

"Lillian said you would. I'm sorry, I can't say it pleases me."

"I understand…and that you won't want to come to the ceremony. But I hope you'll give him a chance, Pop. He's had a difficult life, and he's worked very hard to make something positive out of a great many negatives. At least give Angie's instincts the benefit of the doubt. She wouldn't be talking if it wasn't for her special connection with him."

He frowned, but she no longer sensed his fierce anger.

"Just promise me you won't let him have her calling him 'Daddy' too soon."

"She does need a strong male influence in her life, but I'm never going to let her forget what a wonderful man her father was. And it will be up to her what she calls Gideon."

"He'll adjust," Lillian assured her when they spoke a short time later. "I'll help."

The twinkle in her eye had Brynn guessing that her relationship with Dominic had, indeed, taken a crucial turn. She wouldn't ask, though, unless and until Lillian wanted to talk. Instead, she focused on Gideon.

"He really doesn't want to leave Blanchette."

"I know. I ripped up his resignation. Where else would he find a boss as supportive as me?"

"You're too much, Lillian."

"And you're going to be very good for him. A man in search of a purpose for living can be a frightening thing to watch. Thank you for saving my friend."

Gideon married Brynn two weeks and a day later, at the end of the brief break between semesters. Lillian was disappointed that they didn't have a formal ceremony, or at least let her host a little reception at her home, but what with Gideon's aversion to parties and Brynn's respect for Dominic, she understood why they politely declined.

The service was performed by a justice of the peace in the next parish, in the living room of his gingerbread-style house that Angie thought was magic, especially when the J.P. and his wife looked so much like leprechauns.

Afterward they picked up Chinese takeout because that's what they'd all decided on beforehand in memory of their second "date." Then they returned to their new home…or, more accurately, future home.

For much of the past two weeks they'd been getting the old farmhouse habitable. They had almost simultaneously suggested buying the small farm from the Olsens, his reason being that Angie would find his house depressing, while Brynn felt that with a bit of distance Dominic might adjust more easily.

His Brynn had been growing more radiant with every day they made some improvement. Now as he stood by the pond, while Angie put a flower from her mother's bouquet on the bream's grave, he could see how the rolling acreage would look by this time next year. He was already eyeing a spot for a Japanese garden, and he could see the slope by the water where Brynn planned to put the daylilies that Lillian had promised her.

It was a good place. Its aura pure like Brynn and Angie. With any luck he wouldn't change that—not if loving like crazy and soul-deep gratitude had any pull for him upstairs.

He felt a tug on his pants leg and looked down. Angie was watching him with eyes that were as gentle and sometimes as wise as her mother's. She crooked her finger and he crouched beside her.

"Okay here?" she asked, patting his heart.

It had become a shorthand for them when they caught each other getting a little too melancholy.

"Very okay here." He gently touched hers. "Okay there?"

She sighed. "D'you think Great-Great-Grampa Fish will share the flower with Daddy?"

"I think he already is, angel." He lifted her into his arms and, giving her a nuzzling kiss as an excuse to draw her sweet smell into his lungs, he headed back to the house and the other half of his heart.

Once Angie was tucked into bed and Brynn blew out the candles on the kitchen table they'd decided to keep from Gideon's belongings, he saw her secret smile as she pushed in the chairs.

"Nice memories?"

She looked ethereal in her gauzy ivory dress, and as always he experienced an instant of fear that this was a dream and that at any moment she would vanish.

"Very nice. The wedding reception was memorable, too."

He brushed her hair back over her shoulder to expose her throat, which he kissed, tasted and kissed again. "Too bad we don't have it on video."

She laughed and turned to him, surprised. "Gideon—another joke."

His third in two weeks. She had taken up counting. "Well, who would have guessed the same three fortunes in the fortune cookies? One more time and I'm going to complain to the Board of Health that they're recycling them.''

She slipped her arms around his neck. ''I have a better idea. Why don't you let humble wife share ancient custom of hundred and one ways to please honorable husband?''

He thought that occasionally sassy mouth almost as tantalizing as her honesty and eagerness when they made love—which hadn't been for a frustrating ten days, thanks to their schedules, and concern that Angie feel very much a part of their new lives.

Growling playfully, he lifted her into his arms and carried her to their bedroom. After kissing him, she freed herself to light candles scattered around the room.

After he quietly shut the door, he leaned back against the wall to watch the play of light in her hair and on her skin. ''Dear heaven, you're lovely.''

She smiled that smile that always stirred embers deep in his loins, and turned down the bedsheets that were the same color as her skin.

''Aren't you going to get undressed?''

''Uh-uh. Remember, lesson one is enjoying the stimulus of watching the wife disrobe first.'' Ever since that evening in his kitchen at the other house, he'd been fantasizing about a repeat performance.

Pushing away from the wall, he went to his briefcase beside the antique armoire that had been delivered yesterday. ''Actually, I have something for you.''

He drew out the business-size envelope and handed it to her.

''What's this?''

''It's in place of the honeymoon you didn't want.''

''A wedding present!''

Her expression had him deciding he would inundate her with gifts from now on just to see that velvety look in her eyes. ''Call it a brainstorm…and an apology.'' He ran his hand over his hair, suddenly not as confident as he had been that it was the right thing to do.

Brynn gave him a perplexed frown. "Apology? For what?"

Any other woman would have had the envelope in shreds by now. "Sweet, open it and put me out of my misery, please. I'm deciding this gift business is harder on the nervous system than it's worth."

She bit her lip. "That reminds me—I forgot the champagne."

As she headed for the door he caught her and tugged her onto the bed, following to keep her there with the lower half of his body.

"Now hear this, Mrs. Kane. Forget the champagne. Open the blankety-blank envelope."

There was another Brynn-ism. She'd cured his renewed predisposition to swearing by getting him to use that ridiculous term. He'd used it in front of Lillian the other day and she'd almost swallowed both olive and toothpick in her martini.

With a loving smile, Brynn opened the envelope. Then she stared at the registration sheet. "Photography classes."

"You're good, my love. I hope you won't be embarrassed, but I showed some of your work to the guy who teaches at the school and he says you're a natural with shadow play and metaphor."

"Yes, but—"

"I know you keep telling me that all you want is to be a wife and mother, and believe me, nothing would make me happier." Nothing. "But..." Until he convinced himself he really could be what she wanted, what was the harm of a little insurance in the happiness department? "I thought just in case I need a great photographer for a book someday..."

"Oh, Gideon!"

She'd covered her face with her hands and that damned paper, and he couldn't tell if she was going to cry or what.

"Brynn?"

She let her hands fall beside her head and smiled up at him. "This is so funny."

He had thought she might think it a number of things—touching and generous came to mind—but funny wasn't on the list. "Why?"

Instead of answering, she pushed him onto his back and kissed him. "I have a gift for you, too."

She went to the dresser with the antique mirror that had been in the house and opened the top drawer. Bringing out a small tissue-wrapped package, she offered it to him.

It was light...really light...round and flat. As he fingered the foil ribbon, he didn't have a clue.

"Have you ever read *The Gift of the Magi,* Gideon?" she asked, still smiling.

"O. Henry, right?" When she nodded, her smile growing more secretive, he shook his head. "Not recently."

"Open it."

He did. And he still didn't have a clue. If he had to use his imagination, the round plastic thing with all the empty holes made him think of a crashed-and-burned UFO.

"I threw out the rest of my Pills."

"Your Pills." *Pills.*

He was beginning to feel like smiling, too. "You wouldn't mind not...?" He wiggled the empty container meaningfully.

She shook her head and did the same with the registration sheet. "You wouldn't mind not...?"

He drew her over him and gave her his reply as a kiss.

When he let her breathe again, her eyes were filled with dreams and candlelight.

"I'm going to make you very happy, Genghis Kane."

"I believe it, love. I really believe it."

* * * * *

Turn the Page

for a

Sneak Preview

of

COME SUNDOWN

by

HELEN R. MYERS

Coming from Mira Books

May 1998

Come Sundown

It was only midmorning but Ben Rader could feel sweat soaking through his shirt. In another few minutes—thanks to the steamy air whipping through the open windows of his Chevy Blazer—the cotton would be clinging to him like an aroused woman. Such erotic thoughts should have been an agreeable diversion; after all, there were less pleasant ways to kill time than fantasizing about how it felt to be lying naked in bed with a cold beer and a willing female. Today, though, diversions of any kind were unwelcome.

With downtown Parish in his rearview mirror, he turned onto the farm-to-market road leading to the Maitland estate.

Hell, but it was hot. By noon the heat index would be edging into triple-digit territory, and the radio station out of Greenville would be issuing an advisory to the residents northwest of the Mississippi to use extreme caution when engaging in any form of physical activity.

But no one needed much of an excuse, let alone a recommendation to take things slow in these parts. Why, even as he'd exited the police station moments ago, the early birds had begun to collect in their customary array of cliques. Ben well remembered how it worked. With each newcomer's arrival, the topic of conversation would return to the current heat wave, how if June was this hot, what would the rest of the summer bring? That would spawn a few moments of silence as everyone contemplated the possibilities. But move on they would because gossip was, irrefutably, the chief recreational activity in this community. At least until sundown. Ben believed that just as he knew *he* would be the second most discussed topic in town today.

No, some things never changed. It had been eight years since he left Parish for what he'd thought was the last time. And although there were indications of some improvements—for one thing, he hadn't seen the all-powerful Maitland name on every other store sign, and Hughes Hardware and Lumber had practically doubled in size, although God only knew why—it would take much longer, probably generations, to alter something as ingrained as human behavioral patterns. Besides, folks here were almost as fond of their eccentricities as they were their little local scandals. No doubt that was the real reason Ben was here.

Ben yielded to a heavy sigh. He should have done it. Two weeks ago, when Fred Varnell had called, he should have followed his first instinct and hung up on His Honor the Mayor. Even as he listened to the old fool plead, heard the surprisingly decent salary being offered, he couldn't imagine anyone intentionally choosing to move here. Short of facing a sentence at Parchman Penitentiary, what native would voluntarily come back?

But damned if the son of a—hadn't broadsided him with a good one. "Lem Cobb is dead, Ben," Fred had said. "You've gotta come."

Fred explained that he'd drowned over at Moss Lake, but even before hearing anything else, Ben had rejected the news, because Lem, the youngest brother of his childhood best friend, could swim better than a starving bass chasing down a fat polliwog.

Dead. That he had to accept, but drowned...? Only if someone had put a bullet in Lem's head first....

After driving another half mile, he passed a sporty white convertible parked on the shoulder of the road. Not far beyond it, he spotted someone walking. He didn't need any ID to tell him that she must be the driver.

A petite blonde packaged as compactly as her car walked with an exaggerated sway of rounded hips in a skirt the color of cotton candy.

Instinct urged him to keep driving. He was in no mood to tangle with jailbait. Unfortunately, twenty minutes ago he'd taken his oath as town sheriff, so he had no choice but to stop.

"Problems?"

"Not anymore."

She gave him a smile that made her powder blue eyes sparkle with mischief. As she tilted her head, her pale blond hair caressed her collarbone. The fringed style framed a heart-shaped face still childlike, despite an excessive amount of black mascara and equally overdone eyeliner. Ben wouldn't have recognized her as easily if it hadn't been for the cleft in her chin, a family trademark confirming her pedigree. The last time he'd seen her, she'd been a ten-year-old hellion.

Ben ignored the invitation in her eyes. "What's wrong with your car?"

"Well, I'm no mechanic, but I think it's out of gas."

"All right, come on," he told her. "I'll drive you home."

She was inside before he could remove the folders and pads he'd collected from the station. He jerked the things from under her bottom, hoping she would get the message, but she merely giggled and squirmed this way and that in a dubious attempt to assist him.

"There now, that's better," she purred, when she finally settled down.

"Uh-uh...and fasten your seat belt."

"Oh, that's okay. My place is only a little ways down the road."

"I know. Do it anyway."

Instead of obeying, she eyed him with the shrewdness of someone twice her age. "What do you mean you know? We have never met. Believe me," she added, her smile aging her more than the cosmetics ever could, "I would have remembered."

"It's been years. I only just moved back."

As she traced the shoulder seam of his shirt with frosted-pink fingernails, Ben took hold of her wrist and redirected her hand back onto her own lap.

"What I am, Miss Maitland, is too old to be used as an outlet for your boredom." He shifted so she could spot the badge on his left shirt pocket. "And since I'm sure you wouldn't indulge in behavior that might be misconstrued as a proposition, I know you'll want to refrain from saying or doing anything else that'll give me the wrong impression of you."

He watched Gabrielle Maitland's eyes grow wide, then narrow with renewed interest.

"Ben Rader. I should've recognized you."

"You were barely out of training pants when I left."

"When I heard old man Varnell was going to ask you back, I thought for sure you'd tell him to go to hell."

"And I thought your daddy would have packed you off to a convent years ago."

The mask slipped momentarily exposing a sad young woman. "He threatened to until the very end, but I guess he never found one he thought could keep me."

"So what are you doing with yourself these days besides pouring money into the gas tank of that hot rod back there, and driving up and down Main Street tormenting the local boys?"

"Whatever it takes to get through the day. And night," she told him, with a sidelong look.

"Ever consider getting a job?"

She laughed. "Doing what? And where? Daddy put all kinds of restrictions on my trust fund. I have to live in this godforsaken place until I'm twenty-one, and even then I'll either have to have a college degree or a marriage license to touch it. Shoot, I'll probably end up the same way poor Lem did—planted before my time." She parted her sweater, inviting what breeze there was to caress her perspiration-free skin. "Weren't you friends with his older brother Luther?"

Ben managed to ignore the view she was offering by thinking of the scar near his hairline and how he'd earned it years ago. The six stitches had been a result of siding with Lucas Cobb after three local boys claimed Luther's catfish had come off their trotline—the first of several occasions when Ben found himself in deep trouble for siding with the wrong people. The scar also reminded him again that there had been no sign of Luther at his swearing in.

"We hung around together," he said, telling himself he was a fool for letting Luther's absence matter.

"Rumor has it that's why you took this job. People say you don't think the coroner's report was right about Lem's death being an accident."

Ben had already ascertained that the coroner, a general practitioner that Parish shared with a handful of equally small communities, was a half-blind senile fossil who would impress everyone if he could successfully differentiate a hemmorrhoid from a heart attack.

"This town couldn't survive without its rumors. Now be

a good girl and fasten that seat belt.'' He slipped on his
sunglasses and started the engine.

"Sure thing, Chief. And, listen, if there's ever anything
else I can do for you...well, I hope you know you only have
to ask.''

Ben kept his eyes on the road. "Kid, the only thing you
can do for me is to remember that I don't waste energy
telling people to do things twice....''

Coming this December 1997 from

Silhouette®SPECIAL EDITION®

AND BABY MAKES THREE: THE NEXT GENERATION:

The Adams women of Texas all find love—and motherhood—in the most unexpected ways!

The Adams family of Texas returns!
Bestselling author **Sherryl Woods** continues
the saga in these irresistible new books.
Don't miss the first three titles in the series:

In December 1997: **THE LITTLEST ANGEL** (SE #1142)
When Angela Adams told Clint Brady she was pregnant, she
was decidedly displeased with the rancher's reaction. Could
Clint convince Angela he wanted them to be a family?

In February 1998: **NATURAL BORN TROUBLE** (SE #1156)
Dani Adams resisted when single dad Duke Jenkins claimed
she'd be the perfect mother for his sons. But Dani was
captivated by the boys—and their sexy father!

In May 1998: **UNEXPECTED MOMMY** (SE #1171)
To claim his share of the White Pines ranch, Chance Adams
tried to seduce his uncle's lovely stepdaughter. But then he
fell in love with Jenny Adams for real....

Available at your favorite retail outlet.

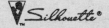

ALICIA SCOTT

**Continues the
twelve-book series—
36 Hours—in March 1998
with Book Nine**

PARTNERS IN CRIME

The storm was over, and Detective Jack Stryker finally had a
prime suspect in Grand Springs' high-profile murder case. But
beautiful Josie Reynolds wasn't about to admit to the crime—
nor did Jack want her to. He believed in her innocence, and he
teamed up with the alluring suspect to prove it. But was he
playing it by the book—or merely blinded by love?

For Jack and Josie and *all* the residents of Grand Springs,
Colorado, the storm-induced blackout was just the beginning of
36 Hours that changed *everything!* You won't want to miss a
single book.

Available at your favorite retail outlet.

BESTSELLING AUTHORS
IN THE SPOTLIGHT

.WE'RE SHINING THE SPOTLIGHT ON SIX OF OUR STARS!

Harlequin and Silhouette have selected stories from several of their bestselling authors to give you six sensational reads. These star-powered romances are bound to please!

THERE'S A PRICE TO PAY FOR STARDOM... AND IT'S LOW

$1.99 U.S.
$2.50 CAN.
Special Offer

As a special offer, these six outstanding books are available from Harlequin and Silhouette for only $1.99 in the U.S. and $2.50 in Canada. Watch for these titles:

At the Midnight Hour—Alicia Scott
Joshua and the Cowgirl—Sherryl Woods
Another Whirlwind Courtship—Barbara Boswell
Madeleine's Cowboy—Kristine Rolofson
Her Sister's Baby—Janice Kay Johnson
One and One Makes Three—Muriel Jensen

Available in March 1998
at your favorite retail outlet.

PBAIS

RETURN TO WHITEHORN

Silhouette's beloved **MONTANA MAVERICKS** returns with brand-new stories from your favorite authors! Welcome back to Whitehorn, Montana—a place where rich tales of passion and adventure are unfolding under the Big Sky. The new generation of Mavericks will leave you breathless!

Coming from Silhouette Special Edition®:

February 98: LETTER TO A LONESOME COWBOY by Jackie Merritt

March 98: WIFE MOST WANTED by Joan Elliott Pickart

May 98: A FATHER'S VOW by Myrna Temte

June 98: A HERO'S HOMECOMING by Laurie Paige

And don't miss these two very special additions to the Montana Mavericks saga:

MONTANA MAVERICKS WEDDINGS
by Diana Palmer, Ann Major and Susan Mallery
Short story collection available April 98

WILD WEST WIFE by Susan Mallery
Harlequin Historicals available July 98

Round up these great new stories
at your favorite retail outlet.

Silhouette®   Look us up on-line at: http://www.romance.net

SSEMMF-J

Return to the Towers!

In March
New York Times bestselling author

NORA ROBERTS

brings us to the Calhouns' fabulous
Maine coast mansion and reveals the
tragic secrets hidden there for generations.

For all his degrees, Professor Max Quartermain has a
lot to learn about love—and luscious Lilah Calhoun is
just the woman to teach him. Ex-cop Holt Bradford is
as prickly as a thornbush—until Suzanna Calhoun's
special touch makes love blossom in his heart.
And all of them are caught in the race to solve
the generations-old mystery of a priceless
lost necklace…and a timeless love.

Lilah and Suzanna
THE
Calhoun Women

**A special 2-in-1 edition containing
FOR THE LOVE OF LILAH and
SUZANNA'S SURRENDER**

Available at your favorite retail outlet.

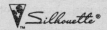